Monster

"Unsettling and thrilling . . . Right from the start of *Monster*, Jonathan Kellerman does everything right."

—*The Baltimore Sun*

Dr. Death

"Intriguing . . . Stylish . . . A brazenly clever denouement."

—*The New York Times*

Flesh and Blood

"Razor-sharp . . . A skillful piece of work."
—*The Washington Post Book World*

The Murder Book

"Dense plotting keeps the pages flying. . . . The outcome is one of perfect justice, which, like revenge, turns out to be a dish most delectable when served cold."

—*People* (Page-turner of the Week)

BLOOD TEST

JONATHAN KELLERMAN

BALLANTINE BOOKS • NEW YORK

A Ballantine Book
Published by The Random House Publishing Group
Copyright © 1986 by Jonathan Kellerman

This edition published by arrangement with Bantam Books, a division of Random House, Inc.

www.ballantinebooks.com

ISBN 0-345-46661-6

Manufactured in the United States of America

First Ballantine Books Edition: November 2003

OPM 10 9 8 7 6 5 4 3

*As always, for Faye, Jesse, and Rachel,
and welcoming Ilana*

BLOOD
TEST

1

I sat in the courtroom and watched Richard Moody get the bad news from the judge.

Moody'd come dressed for the occasion in a chocolate polyester suit, canary yellow shirt, string tie, and lizard skin boots. He grimaced and bit his lip and tried to lock eyes with the judge, but she outstared him and he ended up looking at his hands. The bailiff at the rear of the room held his gaze on Moody. As a result of my warning he'd been careful to keep the Moodys apart all afternoon and had gone so far as to frisk Richard.

The judge was Diane Severe, girlish for fifty, with ash blond hair and a strong, kind face; soft-spoken, and all business. I'd never been in her court but knew her reputation. She'd been a social worker before going to law school and after a decade in juvenile court and six years on the family bench was one of the few judges who really understood children.

"Mr. Moody," she said, "I want you to listen very carefully to what I'm going to say."

Moody started to assume an aggressive body posture, hunching his shoulders and narrowing his eyes like a bar fighter, but his attorney nudged him and he loosened up and forced a smile.

"I've heard testimony from Dr. Daschoff and Dr. Delaware, both eminently qualified as experts in this court. I've spoken to your children in my chambers. I've watched your behavior this afternoon and I've heard your allegations against Mrs. Moody. I've learned of your instructions to your children to run away from their mother so that you could rescue them."

She paused and leaned forward.

"You've got serious emotional problems, sir."

The smirk on Moody's face vanished as quickly as it appeared, but she caught it.

"I'm sorry you think this is funny, Mr. Moody, because it's tragic."

"Your Honor," Moody's lawyer interjected.

She cut him off with the flick of a gold pen.

"Not now, Mr. Durkin. I've heard quite enough wordplay today. This is the bottom line and I want your client to pay attention."

Turning back to Moody:

"Your problems may be treatable. I sincerely hope they are. There's no doubt in my mind that psychotherapy is essential—a good deal of it. Medication may be called for as well. For your sake and the sake of your children I hope you get whatever treatment you need. My order is that you have no further contact with your children until I see psychiatric evidence that you are no longer a threat to yourself or to others—when the death threats and talk of suicide cease, and you have accepted the reality of this divorce and are able to support Mrs. Moody in the raising of the children.

"Should you get to that point—and your word won't be sufficient to convince me, Mr. Moody—the court will call upon Dr. Delaware to set up a schedule of limited and monitored visitation."

Moody took it in, then made a sudden move forward. The bailiff was out of his chair and at his side in a flash. Moody saw him, gave a sick grin, and let his body go slack. The tears flowed down his cheeks. Durkin pulled out a handkerchief, gave it to him, and raised an objection concerning the judge's encroachment upon his client's privacy.

"You're free to appeal, Mr. Durkin," she said evenly.

"Judge."

It was Moody talking now, the bass voice dry and strained.

"What is it, Mr. Moody?"

"You don't unnerstand." He wrung his hands. "Those kids, they're my life."

For a moment I thought she was going to tongue-lash him. Instead she regarded him with compassion.

"I do understand, sir. I understand that you love your children. That your life is in shambles. But what *you* need to understand—the whole point of the psychiatric testimony—is that children can't be responsible for anyone's life. That's too big a burden for any child to bear. They can't raise *you*, Mr. Moody. You need to be able to raise them. And right now you can't. You need help."

Moody started to say something but choked it back. He shook his head in defeat, gave the handkerchief back to Durkin, and tried to salvage a few shards of dignity.

The next quarter hour was spent on property settlement. I had no need to listen to the distribution of the meager estate of Darlene and Richard Moody and would have left, but Mal Worthy had said he wanted to talk to me afterward.

When the legal mumbling was over, Judge Severe took off her glasses and ended the hearing. She looked my way and smiled.

"I'd like to see you in chambers for a moment if you've got the time, Dr. Delaware."

I smiled back and nodded. She swept out of the courtroom.

Durkin ushered Moody out under the watchful eye of the bailiff.

At the next table Mal was pep-talking Darlene, patting her plump shoulder as he scooped up handfuls of documents and stashed them in one of the two suitcases he'd brought. Mal was compulsive and while other lawyers made do with an attaché case, he carted around boxes of documents on a chromium luggage rack.

The former Mrs. Richard Moody looked up at him, bewildered, cheeks feverishly rosy, bobbing her head in assent. She'd stuffed her milkmaid's body into a light blue summer dress as frothy as high tide. The dress was ten years too young for her and I wondered if she'd confused new-found freedom with innocence.

Mal was decked out in classic Beverly Hills attorney mufti: Italian suit, silk shirt and tie, calf-skin loafers with tassels. His hair was styled fashionably long and curly, his beard cut close to the skin. He had glossy nails and perfect teeth and a Malibu tan. When he saw me he winked and waved and gave Darlene one last pat. Then he held her hand in both of his and saw her to the door.

"Thanks for your help, Alex," he said when he came back. Piles of papers remained on the table and he busied himself with packing them.

"It wasn't fun," I said.

"No. The ugly ones aren't." He meant it but there was a lilt in his voice.

"But you won."

He stopped shuffling papers for a moment. "Yeah. Well, you know, that's the business I'm in. Jousting." He flipped his wrist and looked at a wafer-thin disc of gold. "I won't say it pains me to dispose of a turkey like Mr. M."

"You think he'll take it? Just like that?"

He shrugged.

"Who knows? If he doesn't we'll just keep bringing in the heavy artillery."

At two hundred dollars an hour.

He lashed the suitcases to the rack.

"Hey listen, Alex, this wasn't a stinker. For those I don't call you—I've got hired guns up the wazoo. This was righteous, no?"

"We were on the right side."

"Precissimoso. And I thank you again. Regards to the lady judge."

"What do you think she wants?" I asked.

He grinned and slapped me on the back.

"Maybe she likes your style. Not a bad looking gal, heh? She's single, you know?"

"Spinster?"

"Hell, no. Divorced. I handled her case."

Her chambers were done in mahogany and rose, and permeated with the scent of flowers. She sat behind a glass-topped, carved wood desk upon which stood a cut-crystal vase filled with stalks of gladiolus. On the wall behind the desk were several photographs of two hulking blond teenage boys—in football jerseys, wetsuits, and evening wear.

"My gruesome twosome," she said, following my eyes. "One's at Stanford, the other's selling firewood up at Arrowhead. No telling, eh, Doctor?"

"No telling."

"Please have a seat." She motioned me to a velvet

sofa. When I'd settled she said, "Sorry if I was a little rough on you in there."

"No problem."

"I wanted to know if the fact that Mr. Moody wears women's underwear was relevant to his mental status, and you refused to be pinned down."

"I didn't think his choice of lingerie had much to do with custody."

She laughed. "I get two types of psych experts. The puffed-up, self-proclaimed authorities, so taken with themselves they think their opinions on any topic are sacrosanct, and the cautious ones, like you, who won't give an opinion unless it's backed up by a double-blind, conrolled study."

I shrugged. "At least you won't get a Twinkie Defense out of me."

"Touché. How about some wine?" She unlatched the doors of a credenza carved to match the desk and took out a bottle and two long-stemmed glasses.

"My pleasure, Your Honor."

"In here, Diane. Is it Alexander?"

"Alex is fine."

She poured red wine into the glasses. "This is a very fine cabernet that I save for the termination of particularly obnoxious cases. Positive reinforcement, if you will."

I took the glass she offered.

"To justice," she said, and we sipped. It was good wine and I told her so. It seemed to please her.

We drank in silence. She finished before I did and set down her glass.

"I want to talk to you about the Moodys. They're off my docket but I can't help thinking about the kids. I read your report and you have good insights on the family."

"It took a while but they opened up."

"Alex, are those children going to be all right?"

"I've asked myself the same thing. I wish I could tell you yes. It depends on whether or not the parents get their act together."

She clicked her nails against the rim of the wineglass.

"Do you think he'll kill her?"

The question startled me.

"Don't tell me it didn't cross your mind—the warning to the bailiff and all that."

"That was meant to prevent an ugly scene," I said, "but yes, I do think he could do it. The man's unstable and profoundly depressed. When he gets low, he gets nasty and he's never been lower than right now."

"And he wears ladies' panties."

I laughed. "That, too."

"Refill?"

"Sure."

She put the bottle aside and laced her fingers around the stem of her wineglass, an angular, attractive older woman, not afraid to let a few wrinkles show.

"A real loser, our Mr. Richard Moody. And maybe a killer."

"If he gets in a killing mood, she'd be the obvious target. And the boyfriend—Conley."

"Well," she said, running the tip of her tongue over her lips, "one must be philosophical about such things. If he kills her it's because she fucked the wrong guy. Just as long as he doesn't kill someone innocent, like you or me."

It was hard to tell if she were serious or not.

"It's something I think about," she said, "some warped loser coming back and taking out his troubles on me. The losers never want to take responsibility for their crappy little lives. You ever worry about it?"

"Not really. When I was clinically active most of

my patients were nice kids from nice families—not much potential for mayhem there. I've been pretty much retired for the last couple of years."

"I know. I saw the gap in your resumé. All that academic stuff, then blank space. Was that before the Casa de Los Ninos thing or after?"

I wasn't surprised she knew about it. Though it had been over a year, the headlines had been bold and people remembered. I had my own personal reminder—a reconstructed jaw that ached when the weather got clammy.

"A half year before. Afterwards I didn't exactly feel like jumping back in."

"No fun being a hero?"

"I don't even know what the word means."

"I'll bet." She gazed levelly at me and adjusted the hem of her robe. "And now you're doing forensic work."

"On a limited basis. I accept consultations from attorneys I trust which narrows the field substantially and I get some directly from judges."

"Which ones?"

"George Landre, Ralph Siegel."

"Both good guys. I went to school with George. You want more work?"

"I'm not hustling. If the referrals come, okay. If not, I can always find things to do."

"Rich kid, huh?"

"Far from it, but I made a few good investments that are still paying off. If I don't get sucked into a Rodeo Drive mentality I'm okay."

She smiled.

"If you want more cases, I'll spread the word. The members of the psych panel are booked up for four months and we're always looking for guys who can think straight and put it into language simple enough for a judge to understand. Your report *was* really good."

"Thanks. If you send me cases I won't turn you down."

She finished the second glass. "Very mellow, isn't it? Comes from a tiny little vineyard up in Napa. Three years old and still operating at a loss, but the place is turning out limited bottlings of very fine reds."

She got up and walked around the room. From the pocket of her robe she removed a pack of Virginia Slims and a lighter. For the next few moments she stared at a wall decorated with diplomas and certificates and dragged deeply on the cigarette.

"People really manage to fuck up their lives, don't they? Like Miss Bright Eyes Moody. Nice country girl, moves to L.A. for a taste of excitement, gets a job as a checker at Safeway and falls in love with the macho man in lace undies—I forget, what is he, a construction worker?"

"Carpenter. For Aurora Studios."

"Right. I remember. Builds sets. The guy's an obvious loser but it takes her twelve years to figure it out. Now she's extricating herself and who does she hook up with? The loser's clone."

"Conley's a lot more mentally intact."

"Maybe so. But take a look at them side by side. Twins. She's being pulled to the same type. Who knows, maybe Moody was a charmer, too, in the beginning. Give this Conley a few years, he'll turn. Bunch of losers."

She turned and faced me. Her nostrils flared and the hand holding the cigarette trembled almost imperceptibly: alcohol, emotion, or both.

"I hooked up with an asshole and it took me a while to get out of it, Alex, but I didn't turn around and do the same damn thing first chance I got. Makes you wonder if women will ever get smart."

"I wouldn't bet on Mal Worthy having to give up his Bentley," I said.

"Nor I. Mal's a smart boy. Did *my* divorce, did you know?"

I feigned ignorance.

"Probably conflict of interest, my hearing this case, but who cares, it was open and shut. Moody's crazy, he's screwing up his kids, and my order was the best shot at getting him straightened out. Any chance he'll follow through on therapy?"

"I doubt it. He doesn't think anything's wrong with him."

"Of course not. The craziest ones never do. Baloney afraid of the slicer. Assuming he doesn't kill her, you know what's going to happen, don't you?"

"More days in court."

"Absolutely. That idiot Durkin'll be in here every other week with some ploy to reverse the order. In the meantime Moody will harass Bright Eyes and if it keeps up long enough the kids will be permanently screwed up." She walked back to her desk with a long graceful stride, took a compact out of her purse and powdered her nose.

"On and on. He'll drag her through the system, she'll bleat and weep, but she'll have no choice." Her expression hardened. "But I don't give a damn. In two weeks I'm out of it. Retirement with pension. I've got some investments of my own. And one big money-loser. A tiny little vineyard up in Napa." She grinned. "This time next year I'll be in my cellar sampling the vintage until I reel. If you travel that way, be sure to drop in."

"I'll make it a point to do that."

She looked away from me, talked to her diplomas.

"Do you have a lady friend, Alex?"

"Yes. She's in Japan now."

"Miss her?"

"Very much."

"Figures," she said good-naturedly. "The good ones get snapped up." She rose to indicate the audience was concluded. "Good to meet you, Alex."

"My pleasure, Diane. Good luck with the vines. What I tasted was great."

"It's gonna get better and better. I can feel it."

Her handshake was firm and dry.

My Seville had cooked in the open parking lot and I pulled my hand away from the heat of the door handle. Midway through the motion I sensed his presence and turned to face him.

"S'cuse me, Doc." He was looking into the sun and squinting. His forehead was sweat-glossed and the canary-colored shirt had darkened to mustard under the arms.

"I can't talk now, Mr. Moody."

"Just a sec, Doc. Just lemme connect with ya. Lemme zero in on some main points. *Communicate*, you know." His words came out in a rush. As he spoke, the half-closed eyes darted back and forth, and he rocked on his boot heels. In rapid succession he smiled, grimaced, bobbed his head, scratched his Adam's apple, and tweaked his nose. A discordant symphony of tics and twitches. I'd never seen him this way but I'd read Larry Daschoff's report and had a good idea what was happening.

"I'm sorry. Not now." I looked around the lot but we were alone. The rear of the court building faced a quiet side street in a run-down neighborhood. The sole sign of life was a scrawny mutt muzzling a patch of overgrown grass on the other side of the road.

"Aw, c'mon, Doc. Just lemme make a few main points, lemme break on through, lemme zero in on the main facts, like the shysters say." His speech picked up velocity.

I turned away from him and his hard brown hand closed on my wrist.

"Please let go, Mr. Moody," I said with forced patience.

He smiled.

"Hey, Doc, I jus wanna talk. State my case."

"There's no case. I can't do anything for you. Let go of my arm."

He tightened his grip but no tension registered on his face. It was a long face, sun-cured and leathery, with a broken pug nose at center, a thin-lipped mouth, and an oversized jaw—the kind of mandibular development you get from chewing tobacco or gritting your teeth.

I put my car keys in my pocket and reached around to pry his fingers loose but his strength was phenomenal. That, too, made sense, if what I suspected was true. It felt like his hand had become heat-welded to my arm and it was starting to hurt.

I found myself assessing my chances in a fight: we were the same height and probably just about the same weight. Years of hauling lumber had given him an edge in the physical strength department, but I'd been sufficiently diligent about karate practice to have a few good moves. I could stomp down hard on his instep, hit him when he was off-balance, and drive away as he writhed on the cement . . . I interrupted that train of thought, ashamed, telling myself that fighting him would be absurd. The guy was disturbed and if anyone should be able to defuse him, I should.

I dropped my free arm and let it fall idly to my side.

"Okay. I'll listen to you. But first let go so I can concentrate on what you have to say."

He thought about it for a second, then grinned broadly. His teeth were bad and I wondered why I hadn't noticed it during the evaluation, but he'd been different then—morose and defeated, barely able to open his mouth to speak.

He released my wrist. The piece of sleeve where he'd held me was grimy and warm.

"I'm listening."

"Okay, okay, okay." His head continued to bob. "Just gotta connect with you, Doc, show you I got plans, tell you how she twisted you roun' her little finger jus' like she did me. There's bad stuff in that house, my boys tell me how he's makin' the kids do things his way, and she lets it happen, she says okay, okay. Fine and dandy with her, they be cleanin' up after a scumbag like that, who knows what kind of dirt he's leavin' around, the guy's not normal, you know? Him wantin' to be man of the house and all that, all I gotta say is har, har, you know.

"Know why I'm laughin', doc, huh? To keep from cryin', that's why, keep from cryin'. For my babies. The boy and the girl. My boy tol' me the two of them be sleeping together, him wantin' to be the daddy, to be the big shot in the house that I built with these two hands here."

He held out ten large-knuckled, bruised fingers. There was an oversized turquoise and Indian silver ring on each ring finger, one in the shape of a scorpion, the other a coiled snake.

"You unnerstan', Doc, you grab what I'm tossin' at you? Those kids are my life, I carry the burden, not nobody else, that's what I tol' the lady judge, the bitch in black. I carry it. From me, from here." He grabbed his crotch. "My body into hers when she was still decent—she could be decent again, you unnerstan', I get hold of her, speak some sense, straighten her out, right? But not with that Conley there, no way, no fuckin' way. My kids, my life."

He paused for breath and I took advantage of it.

"You'll always be their father," I said, trying to be reassuring without patronizing him. "No one can take that away from you."

"Right. Hunnerd procent right. Now you go in there and tell that to the bitch in black, straighten her out. Tell her I got to have those kids."

"I can't do that."

He pouted like a child denied dessert.

"You *do* it. Right *now*."

"I can't. You're under a lot of stress. You're not ready to take care of them. You're going through a full-fledged manic episode, Mr. Moody. You're a manic-depressive and you need help badly. . . ."

"I can handle it, I got plans. Get a trailer, get a boat, take 'em outta the dirty city, outta the smog-clouds, take 'em to the country,—fish for trout, hunt for meat, teach 'em the way to survive. Like Hank Junior says, country boy will *survive*. Teach 'em to shovel shit and eat good breakfasts, get away from scumbags like him and her until she gets straightened out, who knows when it'll come she keep up with him, humpin' him in front of them, a disgrace."

"Try to calm down."

"Here, watch me calm down." He inhaled deeply and let the air out in a noisy whoosh. I smelled the stench of his breath. He cracked his knuckles and the silver rings sparkled in the sun. "I'm relaxed, I'm clean, I'm ready for action, I'm the father, go in and tell her."

"It doesn't work that way."

"Why not?" he growled and grabbed the front of my jacket.

"Let go. We can't talk if you keep doing that, Mr. Moody."

Slowly his fingers parted. I tried to edge away from him but my back touched the car. We were close enough to slow-dance.

"Tell her! You fucked me up, you fix it, Head-shrinker!"

His voice had taken a decidedly menacing tone. Manics could do damage when they got worked up. As bad as paranoid schizes. It was obvious that the power of persuasion wasn't going to do the trick.

"Mr. Moody—Richard—you need help. I won't do anything for you until you get it."

He sputtered, sprayed me with saliva, and jacked upward viciously with his knee, a classic street brawl-er's move. It was one of the gambits I'd figured him for and I swiveled so that all he made contact with was gabardine.

The miss threw him off-balance and he stumbled. Consciously sad, I caught his elbow and threw him off my hip. He landed on his back, stayed down for a quarter second, and was at me again, arms chopping like a thresher gone mad. I waited until he was almost on me, ducked low, and hit him in the belly just hard enough to knock some wind out. Moving out of the way I let him double over in privacy.

"Please, Richard, calm down and pull it all to-gether."

His response was a growl and a snivel and a grab for my legs. He managed to get hold of one cuff and I felt myself going down. It would have been a good time to jump in the car and tool out of there, but he was between me and the driver's door.

I contemplated a move for the passenger door, but

that would mean turning my back on him and he was strong and crazy-fast.

As I contemplated, he bounded up and charged toward me shouting gibberish. My pity for him had made me too careless and he was able to connect with a punch to the shoulder that made my body rattle. Still stunned, I cleared my eyes soon enough to see the follow-through: a left hook aimed squarely at my manmade jaw. Self-preservation won out over pity and I slid away, took hold of his arm, and threw him fullforce against the car. Before he could have second thoughts I jerked him up, yanked the arm behind him, and pulled up to the point where it was just short of snapping. It had to be agonizing but he evinced no sign of suffering. Manics could get like that, on a perpetual speed trip, impervious to minor details like pain.

I kicked him in the butt as hard as I could and he went flying. Grabbing for my keys, I jumped in the Seville and spun out.

I caught a glimpse of him in the rear-view mirror just before turning onto the street. He was sitting on the asphalt, head in hands, rocking back and forth and, I was pretty sure, weeping.

2

The big black and gold koi was the first to surface, but the other fish soon followed his lead and within seconds all fourteen of them were sticking whiskered snouts out of the water and gobbling down food pellets as fast as I tossed them in. I knelt by a large smooth rock fringed with creeping juniper and lavender azaleas and held three pellets in my fingers just beneath the surface of the water. The big one caught the scent and hesitated, but gluttony got the better of him and his glistening muscular body snaked its way over. He stopped inches from my hand and looked up at me. I tried to appear trustworthy.

The sun was on its way down but enough light lingered over the foothills to catch the metallic glint of the gold scales, dramatizing the contrast with the velvety black patches on his back. A truly magnificent kin-ki-utsuri.

Suddenly the big carp darted and the pellets were gone from my hand. I replaced them. A red and white kohaku joined in, then a platinum ohgon in a moonlight-colored blur. Soon all the fish were nibbling at my fingers, their mouths soft as baby kisses.

The pond and surrounding garden refuge had

been a gift from Robin during the painful months of recuperation from the shattered jaw and all the unwanted publicity. She'd suggested it, sensing the value of something to calm me down during the period of enforced inactivity, and knowing of my fondness for things oriental.

At first I'd thought it unfeasible. My home is one of those creations peculiar to southern California, tucked into a hillside at an improbable angle. It's an architectural gem with spectacular views from three sides but there's very little usable flat land and I couldn't envision room for a pond.

But Robin had done some research, sounding out the idea with several of her craftsmen friends, and had been put in touch with an inarticulate lad from Oxnard—a young man so outwardly stuporous his nickname was Hazy Clifton. He had arrived with cement mixers, wooden forms, and a ton or two of crushed rock, and had created an elegant, meandering, naturalistic pond, complete with waterfall and rock border, that weaved its way in and around the sloping terrain.

An elderly Asian gnome materialized after Hazy Clifton's departure and proceeded to embroider the young man's artistry with bonsai, zen grass, juniper, Japanese maple, long-necked lilies, azalea, and bamboo. Strategically placed boulders established meditative spots and patches of snowy gravel suggested serenity. Within a week the garden looked centuries old.

I could stand on the deck that bisected the two levels of the house and look down on the pond, letting my eyes trace patterns etched in the gravel by the wind, watching the koi, jewellike and languid in their movement. Or I could descend to the floor of the garden and sit by the water's edge feeding the fish, the surface breaking gently in concentric waves.

It became a ritual: each day before sunset I tossed pellets to the koi and reflected on how good life could be. I learned how to banish unwanted images—of death and falsehood and betrayal—from my mind with Pavlovian efficiency.

Now I listened to the gurgling of the waterfall and put aside the memory of Richard Moody's debasement.

The sky darkened and the peacock-colored fish grayed and finally melted into the blackness of the water. I sat in the dark, content, tension a vanquished enemy.

The first time the phone rang I was in the middle of dinner and I ignored it. Twenty minutes later it rang again and I picked it up.

"Dr. Delaware? This is Kathy from your service. I had an emergency call for you a few minutes ago but nobody answered."

"What's the message, Kathy?"

"It's from a Mr. Moody. He said it was urgent."

"Shit."

"Dr. D?"

"Nothing, Kathy. Please give me the number."

She did and I asked her if Moody had sounded strange.

"He *was* kind of upset. Talking real fast—I had to ask him to slow down to get the message."

"Okay. Thanks for calling."

"I've got another one, came in this afternoon. Do you want to take it?"

"Just one? Sure."

"This one's from a doctor—let me get the pronunciation right—Melendrez—no Melen*dez*-Lynch. With a hyphen."

Now that was a blast from the past . . .

"He gave me this number." She recited an exchange I recognized as Melendez-Lynch's office at Western Peds. "Said he'd be there until eleven tonight."

That figured. Raoul was a notable workaholic in a profession famous for them. I recalled seeing his Volvo in the doctors' lot no matter how early I arrived at the hospital or how late I left.

"That's it?"

"That's it, Dr. D. Have a nice one and thanks for the cookies. Me and the other girls finished 'em off in one hour."

"Glad you enjoyed them." That was a five-pound box she was talking about. "Munchies?"

"What can I say?" she giggled.

A switchboard staffed by potheads and they never fouled up a message. Someone should be researching it.

I drank a Coors before addressing the question of whether or not to return Moody's call. The last thing I wanted was to be on the receiving end of a manic tirade. On the other hand, he might be calmer and more receptive to suggestions for treatment. Unlikely, but there's enough of the therapist left in me to be optimistic past the point of realism. Recalling that afternoon's scuffle on the parking lot made me feel like a jerk, though I was damned if I knew how it could have been avoided.

I thought it over and then called, because I owed it to the Moody kids to give it my best shot.

The number he'd left had a Sun Valley exchange—a rough neighborhood—and the voice on the other end belonged to the night clerk at the Bedabye Motel. Moody'd found the perfect living quarters if he wanted to feed his depression.

"Mr. Moody, please."

"Second."

A series of buzzes and clicks and Moody said, "Yeah."

"Mr. Moody, it's Dr. Delaware."

"'lo, Doc. Don't know what got into me, jus' wanted to say sorry, hope I dint shake you up too badly."

"I'm fine. How are you?"

"Oh fine, jus' fine. Got plans, gotta get myself together. I can see that. What everyone's saying, gotta have some sense to it."

"Good. I'm glad you understand."

"Oh, yeah, oh yeah. I'm catchin' on, jus' takes me a while. Like the firs' time I used a circular saw, supervisor tol' me, Richard—this was back when I was a kid, jus learning the trade—gotta take your time, take it slow, concentrate, 'thwise this thing chew you up. And he'd hold up his left hand with a stump where the thumb shoulda been, said, Richard, don' learn the hard way."

He laughed hoarsely and cleared his throat.

"Guess sometimes I learn the hard way, huh? Like with Darlene. Mighta listened to her before she got involved with that scumbag."

The pitch of his voice rose when he talked about Conley so I tried to ease him away from the subject.

"The important thing is that you're learning now. You're a young man, Richard. You've got a lot ahead of you."

"Yeah. Well . . . old as you feel, y'know, and I'm feeling ninety."

"This is the roughest time, before the final decree. It can get better."

"They say that—the lawyer tol' me, too—but I don feel it. I feel shit on, y'know, shit on first class."

He paused and I didn't fill it in.

"Anyways, thanks for listenin', and now you can talk to the judge and tell her I can see the kids, take 'em with me fishin' for a week."

So much for optimism.

"Richard, I'm glad you're getting in touch with the situation but you're not ready to care for your children."

"*Whythefucknot?*"

"You need help to stabilize your moods. There are medications that are effective. And get someone to talk to, like you're talking to me."

"Yeah?" he sneered, "If they're assholes like you, goddamn money-chasing fuckers, talkin' to them ain't gonna do me no good. I'm telling you I'm gonna take care of the problems now don't give me any shit, who the fuckareyou to tell me when I can see my kids."

"This conversation isn't going anywhere—"

"Hunnerd procent right, Headshrinker. You listen and you listen good, they'll be hell to pay'f I'm not set up in my rightful place as daddy . . ."

He emptied a bucket of verbal swill and after listening for several minutes I hung up to avoid being sullied.

In the silence of the kitchen I became aware of the pounding of my heart and the sick feeling at the pit of my stomach. Maybe I'd lost the touch—the therapist's ability to put distance between himself and the ones who suffered so as to avoid being battered by a psychological hailstorm.

I looked down at the message pad. Raoul Melendez-Lynch. He probably wanted me to give a seminar to the residents on the psychological aspects of chronic disease or behavioral approaches to pain control. Something nice and academic that would let me hide behind slides and videotape and play professor again.

At that moment it seemed an especially attractive prospect and I dialed his number.

A young woman answered the phone, breathless.

"Carcinogenesis lab."

"Dr. Melendez-Lynch, please."

"He's not here."

"This is Dr. Delaware returning his call."

"I think he's over at the hospital," she said, sounding preoccupied.

"Could you connect me to the page operator, please."

"I'm not sure how to do that—I'm not his secretary, Dr. Delray. I'm in the middle of an experiment and I really have to run. Okay?"

"Okay."

I broke the connection, dialed the message desk at Western Peds, and had him paged. Five minutes later the operator came and told me he hadn't answered. I left my name and number and hung up, thinking how little had changed over the years. Working with Raoul had been stimulating and challenging, but fraught with frustration. Trying to pin him down could be like sculpting with shaving cream.

I went into the library and settled in my soft leather chair with a paperback thriller. Just when I'd decided the plot was forced and the dialogue too cute, the phone rang.

"Hello."

"Hello, Alex!" His accent turned it into *Ahleex*. "So good of you to return my call." As usual, he talked at a breakneck pace.

"I tried to reach you at the lab but the girl who answered wasn't too helpful."

"Girl? Ah yes, that would be Helen. My new postdoc. Brilliant young lady from Yale. She and I are collaborating on an N.I.H. study aimed at clarifying the metastatic process. She worked with Brewer at New Haven—construction of synthetic cell walls—and we've been examining the relative invasiveness of varying tumor forms on specific models."

"Sounds fascinating."

"It is." He paused. "Anyway, how have you been, my friend?"

"Fine. And you?"

He chuckled.

"It's—nine forty-three and I haven't yet finished charting. That tells you how I've been."

"Oh come on, Raoul, you love it."

"Ha! Yes I do. What did you call me years ago—the quintessential type A personality?"

"A *plus.*"

"I will die of a myocardial infarct but my paperwork will be completed."

It was only a partial jest. His father, dean of a medical school in pre-Castro Havana, had keeled over on the tennis court and died at forty-eight. Raoul was five years from that age and he'd inherited his sire's lifestyle as well as some bad genes. I'd once thought him changeable but had long ago given up trying to slow him down. If four failed marriages hadn't done the trick, nothing would.

"You'll win the Nobel Prize," I said.

"And it will all go for alimony!" He thought that tremendously funny. When his laughter died down he said:

"I need a favor, Alex. There's a family that's giving us some trouble—noncompliance problems—and I wondered if you could talk to them."

"I'm flattered but what about the regular staff?"

"The regular staff made a mess of it," he said, peeved. "Alex, you know the high regard I have for you—why you abandoned a brilliant career I'll never know, but that's another issue. The people Social Services are sending me are *amateurs*, my friend. Rank amateurs. Starry-eyed caseworkers who see themselves as patient advocates—provocateurs. The psych people will have nothing to do with us because Boorstin has a death phobia and is terrified of the word cancer."

"Progress, huh?"

"Alex, nothing's changed in the last five years. If anything it's gotten worse. I've even started opening my ears to other offers. Last week I was given the chance to run an entire hospital in Miami. Chief of Staff. More money and a full professorship."

"Considering it?"

"No. The research facilities were Mickey Mouse and I suspect they want me more for my Spanish than my medical brilliance. Anyway, what do you say about lending the department a hand—you're still officially listed as our consultant, you know."

"To be honest, Raoul, I'm not taking on any therapy cases."

"Yes, yes, I'm aware of that," he said impatiently, "but this is not therapy. Short term liaison consultation. I don't want to sound melodramatic, but the life of a very sick little boy is at stake."

"Exactly what kind of noncompliance are you talking about?"

"It's too complicated to explain over the phone, Alex. I hate to be rude, but I must get over to the lab and see how Helen is doing. We're pacing an in vitro hepatoblastoma as it approaches pulmonary tissue. It's painstaking work and it requires constant vigilance. Let's talk about it tomorrow—nine, my office? I'll have breakfast sent up, and voucher forms. We're prepared to pay for your time."

"All right, Raoul. I'll be there."

"Excellent." He hung up.

Being released from a conversation with Melendez-Lynch was a jarring experience, a sudden shift into low gear. I put down the receiver, regained my bearings, and reflected on the complexity of the manic syndrome.

3

Western Pediatric Medical Center occupies a square block of mid-Hollywood real estate in a neighborhood that was once grand but is now the turf of junkies, hookers, drag queens, and fancy dancers of every stripe. The working girls were up early this morning, halter-topped and hot-panted, and as I cruised eastward on Sunset they stepped out from alleys and shadowed doorways sashaying and hooting. The whores were as much a fixture of Hollywood as the brass stars inlaid in the sidewalks, and I could swear I recognized some of the same painted faces I'd seen there three years ago. The streetwalkers seemed to fall into two categories: doughy-faced runaways from Bakersfield, Fresno, and the surrounding farmlands, and lean, leggy, shopworn black girls from South Central L.A. All of them raring to go at eight forty-five in the morning. If the whole country ever got that industrious the Japanese wouldn't stand a chance.

The hospital loomed large, a compound of aged dark stone buildings and one newer column of concrete and glass. I pulled the Seville into the doctors' lot and walked to Prinzley Pavilion, the contemporary structure.

The Department of Oncology was situated on the fifth floor. The doctors' offices were cubicles arranged in a U around the secretarial pool. As head of the department, Raoul got four times as much space as any of the other oncologists, as well as privacy. His office was at the far end of the corridor and cordoned off by double glass doors. I went through them and walked into the reception area. Seeing no receptionist, I kept going and entered his office through a door marked PRIVATE.

He could have had an executive suite but had chosen to use almost all the space for his lab, ending up with an office only ten by twelve. The room was as I remembered it, the desk piled high with correspondence, journals, and unanswered messages, all ordered and precisely stacked. There were too many books for the floor-to-ceiling bookcase and the overflow was similarly heaped on the floor. One shelf was filled with bottles of Maalox. Perpendicular to the desk, faded beige curtains concealed the office's sole window as well as a view of the hills beyond.

I knew that view well, having spent a significant proportion of my time at Western Peds staring out at the crumbling letters of the HOLLYWOOD sign while waiting for Raoul to show up for meetings he had scheduled but inevitably forgot about, or cooling my heals during his interminable long-distance phone chats.

I searched for signs of habitation and found a Styrofoam cup half-filled with cold coffee and a cream-colored silk jacket draped neatly over the desk chair. Knocking on the door leading to the lab brought no response and the door was locked. I opened the curtains, waited a while, paged him and got no callback. My watch said ten after nine. Old feelings of impatience and resentment began to surface.

Fifteen minutes more, I told myself, and then I'll leave. Enough is enough.

Ninety seconds before the deadline he blew in.

"Alex, Alex!" He shook my hand vigorously. "Thank you for coming!"

He'd aged. The paunch had grown sizably ovoid and it strained his shirt buttons. The last few strands of hair on his crown had vanished and the dark curls around the sides bordered a skull that was high, knobby, and shiny. The thick mustache, once ebony, was a variegated thatch of gray, black, and white. Only the coffee bean eyes, ever moving, ever alert, seemed agelessly charged and hinted at the fire within. He was a short man given to pudginess and though he dressed expensively, his wardrobe wasn't selected with an eye toward camouflage. This morning he wore a pale pink shirt, a black tie with pink clocks, and cream-colored slacks that matched the jacket over the chair. His shoes were mirror-polished, sharp-toed tan loafers of perforated leather. His long white coat was starched and immaculate but a size too large. A stethoscope was draped around his neck, and pens and documents stuffed the pockets of the coat, causing them to sag.

"Good morning, Raoul."

"Have you had breakfast yet?" He turned his back to me and moved his thick fingers rapidly over the piles on the desk like a blind man speed-reading Braille.

"No, you said you'd—"

"How about we go to the doctors' dining room and the department will buy you some?"

"That would be fine," I sighed.

"Great, great." He patted his pockets, searched in them, and muttered a profanity in Spanish. "Just let me make a couple of calls and we'll be off—"

"Raoul, I'm under some time pressure. I'd appreciate it if we could get going now."

He turned and looked at me with great surprise. "What? Oh, of course. Right now. Certainly."

A last glance at the desk, a grab for the current copy of *Blood*, and we were off.

Though his legs were shorter than mine by a good four inches, I had to trot to keep up with him as we hurried across the glassed-in bridge that connected Prinzley with the main building. And since he talked as he walked, keeping up was essential.

"The family's name is Swope." He spelled it. "The boy is Heywood—Woody for short. Five years old. Non-Hodgkin's lymphoma, localized. The initial site was in the G.I. tract with one regional node. The metastatic scan was beautiful—very clean. The histology is nonlymphoblastic, which is excellent, because the treatment protocol for nonlymphoblastics is well-established."

We reached the elevator. He seemed out of breath, tugging at his shirt collar and loosening his tie. The doors slid open and we rode down in silence to the ground floor. Silence—but not serenity, because he couldn't stand still: he tapped his fingers on the elevator wall, played with strands of his mustache, and clicked a ball-point pen open and shut repeatedly.

The ground floor corridor was a tunnel of noise, glutted with doctors, nurses, techs, and patients. He continued talking until I tapped his shoulder and shouted that I couldn't hear him. His head gave a curt little nod and he picked up his pace. We zipped through the cafeteria and passed into the dimly lit elegance of the doctors' dining room.

A group of surgeons and surgical residents sat eating and smoking around a circular table, dressed in greens, their caps hanging across their chests like bibs; otherwise the room was unoccupied.

Raoul ushered me to a corner table, motioned for service, and spread a linen napkin over his lap. He picked up a packet of artificial sweetener and turned it on its side, causing the powder within to shift with a dry whisper, like sand through an hourglass. He repeated the gesture half a dozen times and started talking again, stopping only when the waitress came and took our order.

"Do you remember the COMP protocol, Alex?"

"Vaguely. Cyclophosphamide, um—methotrexate and prednisone, right? I forget what the O stands for."

"Very good. Oncovin. We're refined it for non-Hodgkin's. It's working wonders when we combine it with intrathecal methotrexate and radiation. Eighty-one percent of patients are achieving three-year, relapse-free survival. That's a national statistic—the figures on my patients are even better—over ninety percent. I'm following a growing number of kids who are five, seven years and looking great. Think of that, Alex. A disease that killed virtually every child it got hold of a decade ago is potentially curable."

The light behind his eyes picked up extra wattage.

"Fantastic," I said.

"Perfect word—fantastic. The key is *multimodal chemotherapy.* More and better drugs in the right combinations."

The food came. He put two rolls on his plate, cut them into tiny chunks, and systematically popped each piece in his mouth, finishing all of it before I'd downed half my bagel. The waitress poured coffee, which was inspected, creamed, stirred, and quickly swallowed. He dabbed his lips and picked imaginary crumbs out of his mustache.

"Notice that I used the word curable. No timid

talk of extended remission. We've beaten Wilm's Tumor, we've beaten Hodgkin's disease. Non-Hodgkin's lymphoma is next. Mark my words, it will be cured in the near future."

A third roll was dissected and dispatched. He waved the waitress over for more coffee.

When she'd gone he said, "This isn't really coffee, my friend. It is a hot drink. My mother knew how to make coffee. Back in Cuba we had the pick of the coffee crop. One of the servants, an old black man named José, would grind the beans by hand with great finesse—the grind is essential—and we would have *coffee*!" He drank some more and pushed his cup away, taking a glass of water as a replacement and emptying it. "Come to my home and I'll make you real coffee."

It occurred to me that though I'd worked with the man for three years and had known him twice that long, I'd never seen his living quarters.

"I may take you up on that one day. Where do you live?"

"Not far from here. Condo on Los Feliz. One bedroom—small but sufficient for my needs. When one lives alone it is best to keep things simple, don't you agree?"

"I suppose so."

"You do live alone, don't you?"

"I used to. I'm living with a wonderful woman."

"Good, good." The dark eyes seemed to cloud. "Women. They have enriched my life. And torn it apart. My last wife, Paula, has the big house in Flintridge. Another's in Miami, and two others, God knows where. Jorgé—my second oldest, Nina's boy—tells me his mother is in Paris, but she never stayed in one place very long."

His face drooped and he drummed on the table

with his spoon. Then he thought of something that made him suddenly brighten.

"Jorgé's going to medical school next year at Hopkins."

"Congratulations."

"Thank you. Brilliant boy, always was. Summers he would visit me and work in the lab. I'm proud to have inspired him. The others are not so on the ball, who knows what they will do, but their mothers were not like Nina—she was a concert cellist."

"I didn't know that."

He picked up another roll and hefted it.

"Drinking your water?" he asked.

"It's all yours."

He drank it.

"Tell me about the Swopes. What kind of non-compliance problems are you having?"

"The worst kind, Alex. They're refusing treatment. They want to take the boy home and subject him to God knows what."

"Do you think they're holistic types?"

He shrugged. "It's possible. They're rural people, come from La Vista, some little town near the Mexican border."

"I know the area. Agricultural."

"Yes, I believe so. But more important, close to Laetrile country. The father is some kind of farmer or grower. Crass man, always trying to impress. I gather he'd had some scientific training at one time or another—likes to throw around biological terms. Big heavyset fellow, in his early fifties."

"Old to have a five year old."

"Yes. The mother's in her late forties—makes you wonder if the boy was an accident. Maybe it's guilt that's making them crazy. You know—blaming themselves for the cancer and all that."

"That wouldn't be unusual," I said. Few nightmares compare to finding out one's child has cancer. And part of the nightmare is the guilt parents inflict upon themselves, searching for an answer to the unanswerable question: *why me?* It's not a rational process. It occurs in doctors and biochemists and other people who should know better—the mental floggings, the I should haves and I could haves. Most parents get over it. The ones who don't can be crippled. . . .

"Of course in this case," Raoul was hypothesizing, "there would be more of a basis for it, wouldn't there? Aged ovaries, etc. Well, enough conjecture, let me go on. Where was I—ah, Mrs. Swope. Emma. A mouse. Obsequious even. The father's the boss. One sibling, a sister, around nineteen or so."

"How long's the boy been diagnosed?"

"Officially just a couple of days. A local G.P. picked up the distended abdomen on exam. There'd been pain for a couple of weeks and fevers for the last five days. The G. P. had sneaking suspicions—not bad for a country doc—didn't like the local facilities and sent them up here. We had to do an extensive eval— repeat physical, bloodwork, BUN, uric acid, bone marrows from two sites, immunodiagnostic markers—the non-Hodgkin's protocol demands it. It wasn't until a couple of days ago that we had it staged. Localized disease, no disseminated mets.

"I had a diagnostic conference with the parents, told them the prognosis was good because the tumors hadn't spread, they filled out informed consents, and we were ready to go. The boy has a recent history of multiple infections and there was pneumocystis swimming around in his blood so we put him in Laminar Flow, planned to keep him there for the first course of chemo, and then check how the immune system was working. It looked open and shut and then I got a call from Augie Valcroix, my clinical Fellow—I'll get to him in a minute—and he told me the parents were having cold feet."

"No indication of problems when you first spoke to them?"

"Not really, Alex. The father does all the talking in this family. She sat there and wept, I did my best to comfort her. He asked lots of picky questions—like I said, he was trying to impress—but it was all very friendly. They seemed like intelligent people, not flaky."

He shook his head in frustration.

"After Valcroix's call I went right over, talked to them, thinking it was momentary anxiety—you know sometimes parents hear about treatment and get the idea we're out to torture their child. They start looking for something simple, like apricot pits. If the doctor takes the time to explain the value of chemo, they usually return to the fold. But not the Swopes. They had their minds made up.

"I used a chalkboard. Drew out the survival graphs—that eighty-one percent stat I gave you was for localized disease. Once the tumors spread the figure drops to forty-six. It didn't impress them. I told them speed was of the essence. I laid on the charm, cajoled, pleaded, shouted. They didn't argue. Simply refused. They want to take him home."

He tore a roll to shreds and arranged the fragments in a semicircle on his plate.

"I'm going to have eggs," he announced.

He beckoned the waitress back. She took the order and gave me a look behind his back that said *I'm used to this*.

"Any theory as to what caused the turnaround?" I asked.

"I have two. One, Augie Valcroix mucked it up.

Two, those damned Touchers poisoned the parents' minds."

"Who?"

"*Touchers*. That's what I call them. Members of some damned sect that has its headquarters near where the family lives. They worship this guru named Noble Matthias—that's what the social worker told me—and call themselves the Touch." Raoul's voice filled with contempt. "*Madre de Dios*, Alex, California has become a sanctuary for the psychic refuse of the world!"

"Are *they* holistic types?"

"The social worker says yes—big surprise, no? *Ass*holistic is more like it. Cure disease with carrots and bran and foul-smelling herbs thrown over the shoulder at midnight. The culmination of centuries of scientific progress—*voluntary* cultural regression!"

"What did these Touch people do, exactly?"

"Nothing I can prove. But all I know is things were going smoothly, the consents were signed, then two of them—a man and a woman—visited the parents and *disaster*!"

A plate heaped with scrambled eggs arrived along with a dish of yellow sauce. I remembered his affection for hollandaise. He poured the sauce on the eggs and used his fork to divide the mound into three sections. The middle segment was consumed first, followed by the one on his right, and finally the left third disappeared. More dabbing, more imaginary crumb disposal.

"What does your Fellow have to do with it?"

"Valcroix? Probably plenty. Let me tell you about this character. On paper he looked great—M.D. from McGill—he's a French-Canadian—internship and residency at Mayo, a year of research at Michigan. He's close to forty, older than most applicants, so I thought he'd be mature. Ha! When I interviewed him I talked to a well-groomed, intelligent man. What showed up six months later was an aging flower child.

"The man is bright but he's unprofessional. He talks and dresses like an adolescent, tries to get down to the patients' level. The parents can't relate to him and eventually the kids see through it, too. There are other problems, as well. He's slept with at least one mother of a patient that I know about and I suspect there've been several others. I chewed him out and he looked at me as if I were crazy to be worried about it."

"A little loose in the ethics department?"

"He has no ethics. Sometimes I'm convinced he's drunk or on something, but I can't trip him up on rounds. He's prepared, always has the right answer. But he's still no doctor, just a hippie with a lot of education."

"How'd he get along with the Swopes?" I asked.

"Maybe too well. He was very chummy with the mother and seemed to relate to the father as well as anyone could." He looked into his empty coffee cup. "I wouldn't be surprised if he wanted to sleep with the sister—she's a looker. But that's not what's bothering me right now."

He narrowed his eyes.

"I think Dr. August Valcroix has a soft spot in his heart for quacks. He's spoken up at staff meetings about how we should be more tolerant of what he calls *alternative health care approaches*. He spent some time on an Indian reservation and was impressed with the medicine men. The rest of us are discussing the *New England Journal* and he's going on about shamans and snake powders. Unbelievable."

He grimaced in disgust.

"When he told me they were pulling the boy out of treatment I couldn't help but feel he was gloating."

"Do you think he actually sabotaged you?"

"The enemy from within?" He considered it. "No, not overtly. I just don't think he supported the treatment plan the way he should have. Dammit, Alex, this isn't some abstract philosophy seminar. There's a sick boy with a nasty disease that I can treat and cure and they want to prevent that treatment. It's—*murder!*"

"You could," I suggested, "go to court on it."

He nodded sadly.

"I've already broached the subject with the hospital attorney and he thinks we'd win. But it would be a Pyrrhic victory. You remember the Chad Green case— the child had leukemia, the parents pulled him out of Boston Children's and ran away to Mexico for Laetrile. It turned into a media circus. The parents became heroes, the doctors and the hospital, big bad wolves. In the end, with all the court orders, the boy never got treated and died."

He placed an index finger against each temple and pressed. A pulse quivered under each fingertip. He winced.

"Migraine?"

"Just started. I can handle it." He sucked in his breath. The paunch rippled.

"I may have to take them to court. But I want to avoid it. Which is why I called you, my friend."

He leaned forward and placed his hand over mine. His skin was unusually warm and just a bit moist.

"Talk to them, Alex. Use any tricks you've got up your sleeve. Empathy, sympathy, whatever. Try to get them to see the consequences of what they're doing."

"It's a tall order."

He withdrew his hand and smiled.

"The only kind we have around here."

4

The walls of the ward were covered with sunny yellow paper patterned with dancing teddy bears and grinning rag dolls. But the hospital smells that I'd grown used to when I worked there—disinfectant, body odor, wilting flowers—assaulted my nostrils and reminded me I was a stranger. Though I'd walked this same corridor a thousand times, I was gripped with the chilling uneasiness that hospitals inevitably evoke.

The Laminar Airflow Unit was at the east end of the ward behind a windowless gray door. As we approached, the door swung open and a young woman stepped into the hallway. She lit up a cigarette and began to walk away, but Raoul hailed her and she stopped, turned, bent a knee and froze the pose, one hand on the cigarette, the other on her hip.

"The sister," he whispered.

He'd called her a looker but it was an understatement.

The girl was stunning.

She was tall, five eight or nine, with a body that managed to be both womanly and boyish. Her legs were long, coltish, and firm, her breasts high and small. She had a swan's neck and delicate, slender hands ending in crimson lacquered nails. She wore a white dress made of T-shirt material and had cinched it with a silver cord that showed off a tiny waist and flat belly. The soft fabric molded to every angle and curve and ended midthigh.

Her face was oval with a strong cleft chin. She had prominent cheekbones and a clean jawline leading to lobeless ears. Each ear was pierced with two thread-like hoops of hammered gold. Her lips were straight and full, her mouth a generous red slash.

But it was her coloring that was most striking.

Her hair was long, lustrous, combed straight back from her high smooth forehead, and coppery red. But unlike most redheads she had no freckles and lacked the buttermilk complexion. Her skin was blemishless and burnished a deep California tan. Her eyes were wide-set, thick-lashed, and inky black. She'd used a bit too much makeup but had left her eyebrows alone. They were full and dark, with a natural arch that gave her a skeptical look. She was a girl anyone would notice, with a strange combination of simplicity and flash, almost overwhelmingly physical without trying to be.

"Hello," said Raoul.

She shifted her weight and looked both of us over.

"Hi." She spoke sullenly and regarded us with boredom. As if to underscore her apathy, she gazed past us and sucked on her cigarette.

"Nona, this is Dr. Delaware."

She nodded, unimpressed.

"He's a psychologist, an expert in the care of children with cancer. He used to work here, in Laminar Flow."

"Hello," she said, dutifully. Her voice was soft, almost whispery, the inflection flat. "If you want him to talk to my parents, they're not here."

"Uh, yes, that is what I wanted. When will they be back?"

The girl shrugged and flicked ashes onto the floor.

"They didn't tell me. They slept here so they probably went back to the motel to clean up. Maybe tonight, maybe tomorrow."

"I see. And how have you been doing?"

"Fine." She looked up at the ceiling and tapped her foot.

Raoul raised his hand to offer the classic physician's pat on the back, but the look in her eyes stopped him and he immediately lowered it.

Tough kid, I thought, but then, this was no day at the beach for her.

"How's Woody?" he asked.

The question infuriated her. Her lean body tensed, she dropped the cigarette and ground it under her heel. Tears collected in the inner corners of the midnight eyes.

"You're the damned doctor! Why don't you tell *me*!" She tightened her face, turned, and ran away.

Raoul avoided eye contact. He picked up the crushed butt and deposited it in an ashtray. Covering his forehead with one hand he took a deep breath and gave a migraine grimace. The pain must have been excruciating.

"Come on," he said. "Let's go in."

A hand-scrawled sign in the nurses' office said "Welcome to Space Age Medasin."

The bulletin board was tacked with layers of paper—shift schedules, cartoons cut out of magazines, chemotherapy dosage charts, and an autographed picture of a famous Dodger with a young bald boy in a wheelchair. The child held a bat with both hands and gazed up at the baseball player, who looked slightly ill at ease among the I.V. lines.

Raoul picked a medical chart out of a bin and flipped through it. He grunted and pushed a button on a panel above the desk. Seconds later a heavyset woman dressed in white stuck her head in.

"Yes—oh, hi, Doctor Melendez." She saw me and gave a nod with a question mark stuck to the end of it.

Raoul introduced me to the nurse, whose name was Ellen Beckwith.

"Good," she said, "we could use you around here."

"Dr. Delaware used to coordinate psychosocial care on this unit. He's an international expert on the psychological effects of reverse isolation."

"Oh. Great. Pleased to meet you."

I took the proferred fleshy hand.

"Ellen," said Raoul, "when are Mr. and Mrs. Swope due back on the unit?"

"Gee, I dunno, Doctor. They were here all last night and then they left. They usually come in every day, so they should be around sometime."

He clenched his teeth.

"That's very helpful, Ellen," he said sharply.

The nurse grew flustered and her meaty face took on the look of an animal corralled in an unfamiliar pen. "I'm sorry, Doctor, it's just that they're not required to tell us—"

"Never mind. Is there anything new with the boy that hasn't been charted?"

"No sir, we're just waiting for—" she saw the look on his face and stopped herself. "Uh, I was just going to change the linens in unit three, Doctor, so if you have nothing more—"

"Go. But first get Beverly Lucas over here."

She glanced at a chalkboard across the room.

"She's signed out to page, sir."

Raoul looked up and stroked his mustache. The

only evidence of his agony was the slight tremble beneath the bristly hairs.

"Then *page* her, for God's sake."

She hurried off.

"And they want to be professionals," he said. "Working hand in hand with the doctor as equal partners. Ludicrous."

"Do you use anything for the pain?" I asked.

The question threw him.

"What—oh, it's not so bad," he lied, and forced a smile. "Once in a while I take something."

"Ever tried biofeedback or hypnosis?"

He shook his head.

"You should. It works. You can learn to vasodilate and constrict at will."

"No time to learn."

"It doesn't take long if the patient's motivated."

"Yes, well—" He was interrupted by the phone. He answered it, barked orders into the receiver, and hung up.

"That was Beverly Lucas, the social worker. She'll be here shortly to fill you in."

"I know Bev. She was a student here when I was an intern."

He held out his hand palm down and moved it side to side. "Soso, eh?"

"I always thought she was pretty sharp."

"If you say so." He looked doubtful. "She wasn't much use with this family."

"That may be true of me as well, Raoul."

"You're different, Alex. You think like a scientist but can relate to patients like a humanist. It's a rare combination. That's why I chose you, my friend."

He'd never chosen me but I didn't argue. Maybe he'd forgotten the way it really started.

Several years back, he was awarded a government

grant to study the medical value of isolating children with cancer in germ-free environments. The "environments" came from NASA—plastic modules used to prevent returned astronauts from infecting the rest of us with cosmic pathogens. The modules were filtered continuously and flooded with air blown out rapidly and smoothly in laminar flow. Such smooth flow was important because it prevented pockets of turbulence where germs collected and bred.

The value of an effective way to protect cancer patients from microbes was obvious if you understood a little about chemotherapy. Many of the drugs used to kill tumors also knock out the body's immune system. It was as common for patients to die of infection brought about by treatment as to perish from the disease itself.

Raoul's reputation as a researcher was impeccable and the government sent him four modules and lots of money to play with. He constructed a randomized study, dividing the children into experimental and control groups, the latter treated in regular hospital rooms using conventional isolation procedures such as masks and gowns. He hired microbiologists to monitor the germ count. He gained access to a computer at Cal Tech to analyze the data. He was ready to go.

Then someone raised the issue of psychological damage.

Raoul pooh-poohed the risk, but others weren't convinced. After all, they reasoned, the plans were to subject children as young as two to what could only be termed sensory deprivation—months in a plastic room, no skin to skin contact with other human beings, segregation from normal life activities. A protective environment, to be sure, but one that could be harmful. It needed to be looked into.

At the time I was a junior level psychologist and

was offered the job because none of the other therapists wanted anything to do with cancer. And none of them wanted to work with Raoul Melendez-Lynch.

I saw it as an opportunity to do some fascinating research and prevent emotional catastrophe. The first time I met Raoul and tried to tell him about my ideas, he gave me a cursory glance, returned his attention to the *New England Journal*, and nodded absently.

When I finished my pitch he looked up and said, "I suppose you'll be needing an office."

It wasn't an auspicious beginning, but gradually his eyes were opened to the value of psychological consultation. I badgered him into building the unit so that each module had access to a window and a clock. I nagged him until he obtained funds for a full-time play therapist and a social worker for the families. I cadged a healthy chunk of computer time for psychological data. In the end it paid off. Other hospitals were having to release patients from isolation because of psychological problems but our children adjusted well. I collected mountains of data and published several articles and a monograph with Raoul as co-author. The psychological findings received more scientific attention than the medical articles, and by the end of three years he was an enthusiastic supporter of psychosocial care and somewhat humanized.

We grew friendly, though on a relatively superficial level. Sometimes he talked about his childhood. His family, originally Argentinian, had escaped from Havana in a fishing boat after Castro nationalized their plantation and most of their wealth. He was proud of a family tradition of physician-businessmen. All of his uncles and most of his cousins, he explained, were doctors, many of them professors of medicine. (All were fine gentlemen except Cousin Ernesto, who was a scum-sucking Communist pig. Ernesto had been a doctor, too, but he'd abandoned his family and his profession for the life of a radical murderer. No matter that thousands of fools worshipped him as Ché Guevara. To Raoul he'd always be despicable Cousin Ernesto, the black sheep of the family.)

As successful as he was in medicine, his personal life was a disaster. Women were fascinated by him but ultimately repelled by his obsessive character. Four of them endured marriage with him and he sired eleven children, most of whom he never saw.

A complex and difficult man.

Now he sat in a plastic chair in a drab little office and tried to be macho about the buzz saw ripping through his skull.

"I'd like to meet the boy," I said.

"Of course. I can introduce you now, if you'd like."

Beverly Lucas came in just as he was about to get up.

"Good morning, gentlemen," she said. "Alex—how nice to see you."

"Hi, Bev."

I rose and we embraced briefly.

She looked good, though considerably thinner than I remembered. Years ago, she'd been a cheerful, rather innocent trainee, full of enthusiasm. The kind voted Miss Bubbly in high school. She had to be thirty by now, and some of the pixie cuteness had turned to womanly determination. She was petite and fair, with rosy cheeks and straw-colored hair worn in a long soft perm. Her round open face was dominated by hazel saucer eyes and untouched by makeup. She wore no jewelry and her clothes were simple—knee-length navy skirt, short-sleeved blue-and-red plaid blouse, penny loafers. She carried an oversized purse, which she swung up on the desk.

"You look svelte," I said.

"Running. I'm doing long distance, now." She flexed a muscle and laughed.

"Very impressive."

"It helps center me." She sat on the edge of the desk. "What brings you around here after all this time?"

"Raoul wants me to help out with the Swopes."

Her expression changed without warning, the features hardening and gaining a few years. With forced amiability she said, "Good luck."

Raoul stood up and started to lecture.

"Alex Delaware is an expert in the psychosocial care of children with malignant—"

"Raoul," I interrupted, "why don't you let Beverly fill me in on the case. There's no need for you to spend any more time at this point."

He looked at his watch.

"Yes. Of course." To Beverly: "You'll give him a comprehensive rundown?"

"Of course, Dr. Melendez-Lynch," she said sweetly.

"You want me to introduce you to Woody?"

"Don't bother. Bev will handle it."

His eyes darted from me to her and then back to his watch.

"All right. I'm off. Call if you need me."

He removed the stethoscope from around his neck and swung it at his side as he left.

"I'm sorry," I said to her when we were alone.

"Forget it, it's not your fault. He's such an asshole."

"You're the second person he's riled this morning."

"There'll be plenty of others before the day's up. Who was the first?"

"Nona Swope."

"Oh. Her. She's angry at the world."

"It must be rough for her," I said.

"I'm sure," she agreed, "but I think she was an angry young lady long before her brother got cancer. I tried to develop a rapport with her—with all of them—but they shut me out. Of course," she added, bitterly, "*you* may do much better."

"Bev, I've got no stake in being a miracle worker. Raoul called me in a panic, gave me no background, and I tried to do a friend a favor, okay?"

"You should pick your friends with greater care."

I said nothing, just let her listen to the echoes of her own words.

It worked.

"Okay, Alex, I'm sorry for being such a bitch. It's just that he's impossible to work for, gives no credit when you do a good job, and throws these incredible tantrums when things go wrong. I've put in for a transfer, but until they find a sucker to replace me, I'm stuck."

"No one can do this type of work for very long," I said.

"Don't I know it! Life's too short. That's why I got into running—I come home all burnt out and after a couple of hours of pushing my body to the limit I'm renewed."

"You look great."

"Do I? I was starting to worry about getting too thin. Lately I've been losing my appetite—oh, hell, I must sound like a real egomaniac, griping like this when I'm surrounded by people in real crises."

"Griping is a God-given right."

"I'll try to look at it that way." She smiled and pulled out a notebook. "I suppose you want a psychosocial rundown on the Swopes."

"It would help."

"The name of the game is *weird*—these are strange people, Alex. The mother never talks, the father talks all the time, and the sister can't stand either of them."

"Why do you say that?"

"The way she looks at them. And the fact that she's never around when they are. It's like she feels out of place. She doesn't pay much attention to Woody when she's here, keeps strange hours—shows up late at night, or really early in the morning. The night staff says she mostly sits and stares at him—usually he's asleep, anyway. Once in a while she'll go in the unit and read him a book, but that's about it. The father doesn't do much in the way of stimulation, either. He likes to flirt with the nurses, acts like he knows it all."

"Raoul told me the same thing."

"Raoul's not totally incapable of insight." She laughed maliciously. "Seriously, Mr. Swope is a different kind of guy. Big fellow, gray-haired with a beer gut and a little goatee. Kind of like Buffalo Bill without the long hair. He's really cut off from his feelings—I know it's denial and I know it's not unheard of, but he goes beyond what we normally see. His son's diagnosed with cancer and he's laughing and joking with the nurses, trying to be one of the gang, talking about his orchard and his precious plants, throwing around horticultural jargon. You know what can happen to guys like that."

"Sudden breakdown."

"Exactly. All at once it hits them and pow! Pathological grief reaction."

"Doesn't sound like the boy has much support."

"The mother. She's got to be the most unliberated thing I've ever seen—Garland Swope is the *king* of his castle—but she does seem to be a good mother—

nurturant, gives lots of hugs and kisses, goes into the unit a lot, and without any hesitation. You know how scary the spacesuit can be for lots of parents. *She* jumped right in. The nurses see her go off into the corner and cry when she thinks no one's looking, but when Garland comes around she puts on a great big smile, lots of 'Yes, Dears,' and 'No, Dears.' It's really sad."

"Why do you think they want to pull the kid out?" I asked.

"I know Raoul believes it was those people from the Touch—he's so paranoid about anything holistic—but how can he be so sure? Could be he's to blame for the whole thing. Maybe he screwed up communication with them—he's very aggressive when he describes the treatment protocols and lots of people are put off."

"He seemed to think the Fellow was at fault."

"Augie Valcroix? Augie marches to his own drummer but he's a good guy. One of the few docs who actually takes time to sit down with the families and act like a human being. He and Raoul hate each other's guts, which makes sense if you know them. Augie thinks Raoul's a fascist and Raoul sees him as a subversive influence. It's been great fun working in this department, Alex."

"What about those cultists?"

She shrugged.

"What can I say? Another group of lost souls. I don't know much about them—there are so many fringe groups it would take a specialist to understand all of them. Two of them showed up a couple of days ago. The guy looked like a teacher—glasses, scuzzy beard, wimpy manner, brown oxfords. The lady was older, in her forties or fifties, the kind who was probably a hot number when she was younger but lost it. Both of them had that glazed look in their eyes—the

I-know-the-secret-of-the-universe-but-I-won't-tell-you trance. Moonies, Krishnas, esties, Touchers, they're all the same."

"You don't think they turned the Swopes around?"

"They may have been the straw that broke it," she conceded, "but I don't see how they could be entirely responsible. Raoul's looking for a scapegoat, for easy answers. That's his style. Most of the docs are like that. Instant fix-its for complex issues."

She looked away and folded her arms across her chest.

"I'm really tired of all of it," she said softly.

I steered her back to the Swopes.

"Raoul wondered if the parents' being older had anything to do with it. You pick up any hints the boy was an unwanted accident?"

"I didn't get close enough to even touch on stuff like that. I was lucky to get enough for a bare-bones intake. The father smiled and called me 'dear' and made sure I never got enough time alone with his wife to develop a relationship. This family's *armored*. Maybe they've got lots of secrets they don't want coming out."

Maybe. Or maybe they're terrified at being in a strange environment so far from home with a gravely ill child and don't want to strip themselves bare in front of strangers. Maybe they don't like social workers. Maybe they're simply private people. Lots of maybes . . .

"What about Woody?"

"A cutie pie. He's been sick since he got here, so it's hard to judge what kind of kid he really is. Seems like a little sweetie—isn't it always the sweet ones who suffer?" She took out a tissue and blew her nose. "Can't stand the air in here. Woody's a nice little boy who's agreeable and kind of passive. A people pleaser.

He cries during procedures—the spinal tap really hurt him—but he holds still and gives no serious problems." She stopped for a moment and fought tears.

"It's a goddamn crime, their pulling him out of treatment. I don't like Melendez-Lynch, but goddamn it, he's right this time! They're going to kill that little boy because somehow we screwed up, and it's driving me nuts."

She pounded a small fist on the desk, snapped herself to a standing position, and paced the cramped office. Her lower lip quivered.

I stood up and put my arms around her and she buried her head in the warmth of my jacket.

"I feel like such a fool!"

"You're not." I held her tightly. "None if it is your fault."

She pulled away and dabbed at her eyes. When she seemed composed I said, "I'd like to meet Woody."

She nodded and led me to the Laminar Airflow Unit.

There were four modules, placed in series, like rooms in a railroad flat, and shielded from one another by a wall of curtain that could be opened or drawn by pushing buttons inside each room. The walls of the units were transparent plastic and each room resembled an oversized ice cube, eight feet square.

Three of the cubes were occupied. The fourth was filled with supplies—toys, cots, bags of clothing. The interior side of the curtained wall in each room was a perforated gray panel—the filter through which air blew audibly. The doors of the modules were segmented, the bottom half metal and closed, the top plastic, and left ajar. Microbes were kept out of the opening by the high speed at which the air was expelled. Running parallel to all four units were corridors on both sides, the rear passage for visitors, the front for the medical staff.

Two feet in front of the doorway to each module was a no-entry area marked off by red tape on the vinyl floor. I stood just outside the tape at the entrance of Module Two and looked at Woody Swope.

He lay on the bed, under the covers, facing away from us. There were plastic gloves attached to the front wall of the module, which permitted manual entry into the germ-free environment. Beverly put her hands inside them and patted him on the head gently.

"Good morning, sweetie."

Slowly and with seeming effort, he rolled over and stared at us.

"Hi."

A week before Robin left for Japan, she and I went to an exhibition of photographs by Roman Vishniac. The pictures had been a chronicle of the Jewish ghettos of Eastern Europe just before the Holocaust. Many of the portraits were of children, and the photographer's lens had caught their small faces unaware, flash-freezing the confusion and terror it found there. The images were haunting, and afterward we cried.

Now, looking into the large dark eyes of the boy in the plastic room, these same feelings came back in a rush.

His face was small and thin, the skin stretched across delicate bone structure, translucently pale in the artificial light of the module. His eyes, like those of his sister, were black, and glassy with fever. The hair on his head was a thick mop of henna-colored curls. Chemotherapy, if it ever happened, would take care of those curls in a brutal, though temporary, reminder of the disease.

Beverly stopped stroking his hair and held out her glove. The boy took it and managed a smile.

"How we doing this morning, doll?"

"Okay." His voice was soft and barely audible through the plastic.

"This is Dr. Delaware, Woody."

At the mention of the title he flinched and moved back on the bed.

"He's not the kind of doctor who gives shots. He just talks to kids, like I do."

That relaxed him somewhat, but he continued to look at me with apprehension.

"Hi, Woody," I said. "Can we shake hands?"

"Okay."

I put my hand into the glove Beverly relinquished. It felt hot and dry—coated with talc, I recalled. Reaching into the module I searched for his hand and found it, a small treasure. I held it for a moment and let go.

"I see you've got some games in there. Which is your favorite?"

"Checkers."

"I like checkers too. Do you play a lot?"

"Kind of."

"You must be very smart to know how to play checkers."

"Kind of." The hint of a smile.

"I bet you win a lot."

The smile widened. His teeth were straight and white but the gums surrounding them were swollen and inflamed.

"And you like to win."

"Uh huh. I always win my mom."

"How 'bout your dad?"

He gave a perplexed frown.

"He doesn't play checkers."

"I see. But if he did, you'd probably win."

He digested that for a minute.

"Yeah, I pro'ly would. He doesn't know much about playing games."

"Anyone else you play with besides Mom?"

"Jared—but he moved away."

"Anybody besides Jared?"

"Michael and Kevin."

"Are they guys at school?"

"Yeah. I finished K. Next year I go into one."

He was alert and responsive but obviously weak. Talking to me was taxing and his chest heaved with the effort.

"How about you and I play a game of checkers?"

"Okay."

"I could play from out here with these gloves, or I could put on one of those spacesuits and come in the room with you. Which would you like better?"

"I dunno."

"Well, *I'd* like to come in the room." I turned to Bev. "Could somebody help me suit up? It's been a long time."

"Sure."

"I'll be in there in a minute, Woody." I smiled at him and stepped away from the plastic wall. Rhythm-and-blues music blared from the module next door. I glanced over and caught a glimpse of a pair of long brown legs dangling over the foot of a bed. A black boy around seventeen was sprawled atop the covers, staring at the ceiling and moving to the sounds that screamed from the ghetto blaster on his nightstand, seemingly impervious to the I.V. needles imbedded in the crooks of both arms.

"See," said Bev, speaking up to be heard, "I told you. A sweetie."

"Nice kid," I agreed. "He seems bright."

"The parents describe him as having been very

sharp. The fevers have pretty much knocked him out but he still manages to communicate very well. The nurses love him—this whole pullout thing is making everyone very uptight."

"I'll do what I can. Let's start by getting me in there."

She called for help and a tiny Filipino nurse appeared bearing a package wrapped in heavy brown paper and marked STERILE.

"Take off your shoes and stand there," ordered the nurse, pint-sized but authoritative. She pointed to a spot just outside the red taped no-entry zone. After washing her hands with Betadyne, she unwrapped a pair of sterile gloves and slipped them on her hands. Having inspected the gloves and found them free from flaws, she removed a folded spacesuit from the brown paper and placed it inside the red border. It took a bit of playing with the suit—which, in a collapsed state, looked like a heavy paper accordion—but she found the footholes and had me step inside them. Gingerly, she took hold of the edges and pulled it up over me, tying the top seam around my neck. Being so short, she had to stretch to do the job so I bent my knees to make it easier.

"Thanks," she giggled. "Now your gloves—don't touch anything until they're on."

She worked quickly and soon my hands were sheathed in surgical plastic, my mouth concealed behind a paper mask. The headpiece—a hood fashioned of the same heavy paper as the suit attached to a plastic, see-through visor—was slipped over my face and fastened to the suit with Velcro strips.

"How does that feel?"

"Very stylish." The suit was oppressively hot and I knew that within minutes, despite the cool rapid airflow in the unit, I'd be drenched with sweat.

"It's our continental model." She smiled. "You can go in now. Half hour maximum time. The clock's over there. We may be too busy to remind you, so keep an eye on it and come out when the time's up."

"Will do." I turned to Bev. "Thanks for your help. Any idea when the parents will be in?"

"Vangie, did the Swopes say when they'd be in?"

The Filipino nurse shook her head. "Usually they're here in the morning—right around now. If they don't come soon, I don't know when. I can leave a message for them to call you, Doctor—"

"Delaware. Why don't you tell them I'll be here tomorrow at eight thirty and if they arrive earlier, please have them wait."

"Eight thirty you should catch them."

"I'll tell you what," said Bev, "I've got the number of the place they're staying—some motel on the west side. I'll call and leave a message. If they show up to-day do you want to come back?"

I considered it. Nothing on the agenda that couldn't wait. "Sure. Call my exchange. They'll know where to reach me." I gave her the number.

"All right, Alex, you'd better get in there before you truck a few million pathogens over the border. See ya."

She hoisted the large purse over her shoulder and walked out the door.

I stepped into the Laminar Airflow Room.

He'd sat up and his dark eyes followed my entry.

"I look like a spaceman, huh?"

"I can tell who you are," he said gravely, "everyone looks different."

"That's good. I always had trouble recognizing people when they wore these things."

"Ya gotta look close, with strong eyes."

"I see. Thanks for the advice."

I got the box of checkers and unfolded the board on the armlike table that swung across the bed.

"What color do you want to be?"

"Dunno."

"Black goes first, I think. You wanna go first?"

"Uh huh."

He was precociously good at the game, able to plot, set up moves, and think sequentially. A bright little boy.

A couple of times I tried to engage him in conversation but he ignored me. It wasn't shyness or lack of good manners. His attention was focused on the checkerboard and he didn't even hear the sound of my voice. When he completed a move he'd lean back against the pillows with a satisfied look on his grave little face and say, "There! Your turn," in a voice made soft by fatigue.

We were halfway through the game and he was giving me a run for my money when he clutched his abdomen and cried out in pain.

I eased him down and felt his brow. Low-grade fever.

"Your tummy hurts, doesn't it?"

He nodded and wiped his eyes with the back of his hand.

I pressed the call button. Vangie, the Filipino nurse, appeared on the other side of the plastic.

"Abdominal pain. Febrile," I told her.

She frowned and disappeared, returning with a cup of liquid acetaminophen held in a gloved hand.

"Swing that counter over this way, would you."

She set the medicine on the slab of Formica.

"You can take it now and give it to him. The resident's due by within the hour to check him over."

I returned to the boy's bedside, propped him up

with one hand behind his head, and held the liquid to his lips with the other.

"Open up, Woody. This will make it hurt less."

"Okay, Doctor Delaware."

"I think you'd better rest now. You played a good game."

He nodded and the curls bounced. "Tie?"

"I'd say so. Although you were getting me pretty good at the end. Can I come back and play with you again?"

"Uh huh." He closed his eyes.

"Rest up, now."

By the time I was out of the unit and had shed the paper suit, he was asleep, lips parted, sucking gently at the softness of the pillow.

5

The next morning I drove east on Sunset under a sky streaked with tin-strip clouds and thought about last night's dreams—the same kind of spooky, murky images that had plagued my sleep when I first started working in oncology. It had taken a good year to chase those demons away and now I wondered if they'd ever been gone or had just been lurking in my subconscious, ever ready for mischief.

Raoul's world was madness and I found myself resenting him for drawing me back into it.

Children weren't supposed to get cancer.

Nobody was supposed to get cancer.

The diseases that fell under the domain of the marauding crab were ultimate acts of histologic treason, the body assaulting, battering, raping, murdering itself in a feeding frenzy of rogue cells gone berserk.

I slipped a Lenny Breau cassette into the tape deck and hoped that the guitarist's fluid genius would take my mind far away from plastic rooms and bald children and one little boy with henna-colored curls and a Why Me? look in his eyes. But I could see his face and the faces of so many other sick children I'd known, weaving in and out of the arpeggios, ephemeral, persistent, begging for rescue . . .

Given that state of mind, even the sleaze that heralded the entry into Hollywood seemed benign, the half-naked whores nothing more than big-hearted welcome wagoners.

I drove through the last mile of boulevard in a blue funk, parked the Seville in the doctors' lot, and walked through the front door of the hospital with my head down, warding off social overtures.

I climbed the four flights to the oncology ward and was halfway down the hall before hearing the ruckus. Opening the door to the Laminar Airflow Unit turned up the volume.

Raoul stood, bug-eyed, his back to the modules, alternately cursing in rapid Spanish and screaming in English at a group of three people:

Beverly Lucas held her purse across her chest like a shield, but it wouldn't stay in one place because the hands that clutched it were shaking. She stared at a distant point beyond Melendez-Lynch's white-coated shoulder and bit her lip, straining not to choke on anger and humiliation.

The broad face of Ellen Beckwith bore the startled, terrified look of someone caught in the midst of a smarmy, private ritual. She was primed for confession, but unsure of her crime.

The third member of the audience was a tall, shaggy-haired man with a hound dog face and squinty, heavy-lidded eyes. His white coat was unbuttoned and worn carelessly over faded jeans and a cheap-looking shirt of the sort that used to be called psychedelic but now looked merely garish. A belt with an oversized buckle in the shape of an Indian chief bit into a soft-looking middle. His feet were large and the toes were long, almost prehensile. I could tell because he'd encased them, sockless, in Mexican huaraches. His face was clean-shaven and his skin was pale. The shaggy hair was medium brown, streaked with gray, and it hung to his shoulders. A puka shell necklace ringed a neck that had begun to turn to wattle.

He stood impassively, as if in a trance, a serene look in the hooded eyes.

Raoul saw me and stopped his harangue.

"He's gone, Alex." He pointed to the plastic room where I'd played checkers less than twenty-four hours ago. The bed was empty.

"Removed from under the noses of these so-called *professionals*." He dismissed the trio with a contemptuous wave of his hand.

"Why don't we talk about it somewhere else," I suggested. The black teenager in the unit next door was peering out through the transparent wall with a puzzled look on his face.

Raoul ignored me.

"*They* did it. Those quacks. Came in as radiation techs and kidnapped him. Of course, if anyone had possessed the good sense to *read the chart* to find out if radiologic studies had been ordered, they might have prevented this—felony!"

He was boring in on the fat nurse now, and she was on the verge of tears. The tall man came out of his trance and tried to rescue her.

"You can't expect a nurse to think like a cop." His speech was just barely tinged with a Gallic lilt.

Raoul wheeled on him.

"'You! Keep your damned comments to yourself! If you had an iota of understanding of what medicine is all about we might not be in this mess. *Like a cop!* If that means exercising vigilance and care to insure a patient's safety and security, then she damn well does have to think like a cop! This isn't an Indian reservation, Valcroix! It's life-threatening disease and invasive procedures and using the brain that God gave us to make inferences and deductions and *decisions*, for God's sake! It's *not* managing a reverse isolation unit like a bus terminal, where people come in and out and tell you they're someone they're not and whisk your patient away from under your lazy, sloppy, careless nose!"

The other doctor's response was a cosmic smile as he zoned back out into never-never land.

Raoul glared at him, ready to pounce. The gangly black boy watched the confrontation, eyes wide and frightened, from behind his plastic screen. A mother visiting her child in the third module stared, then drew the curtains protectively.

I took Raoul by the elbow and escorted him to the nurses' office. The Filipino nurse was there, charting. After one look at us, she grabbed her paperwork and left.

He picked up a pencil from the desk and snapped it between his fingers. Tossing the broken pieces to the floor, he kicked them into a corner.

"That bastard! The arrogance, to debate me in front of ancillary staff—I'll terminate his fellowship and get rid of him once and for all."

He ran a hand over his brow, chewed on his mustache, and tugged at his jowls until the swarthy flesh turned rosy.

"They took him," he said. "Just like that."

"What do you want to do about it?"

"What I want is to find those Touchers and strangle them with my bare hands and—"

I picked up the phone. "You want me to call Security?"

"Ha! A bunch of senile alcoholics who need help finding their own flashlights—"

"What about the police? It's an abduction now."

"No," he said quickly. "They won't do a damned thing and it will be a freakshow for the media."

He found Woody's chart and leafed through it, hissing.

"Radiology—why would I schedule x-rays for a child whose treatment is up in the air! It makes no sense. Nobody thinks anymore. Automatons, all of them!"

"What do you want to do about it?" I repeated.

"Damned if I know," he admitted and slapped the chart on the desktop.

We sat in glum silence for a moment.

"They're probably halfway to Tijuana," he said, "on a pilgrimage to some damned Laetrile *clinica*—did you ever see those places? Murals of crabs on filthy adobe walls. That's their salvation! Fools!"

"It's possible they haven't gone anywhere. Why don't we check?"

"How?"

"Beverly has the number of the place they're staying. We can call and find out if they've checked out."

"Play detective—yes, why not? Call her in."

"Be civil to her, Raoul."

"Fine, fine."

I beckoned the social worker away from a pow-wow with Valcroix and Ellen Beckwith, who gave me the kind of look usually reserved for plague carriers.

I told her what I wanted and she nodded wearily.

Once in the office she avoided looking at Raoul and silently dialed the phone. There was a brief exchange with the motel clerk, after which she hung up and said:

"The guy was real uncooperative. He hasn't seen them today but they haven't checked out. The car's still there."

"If you'd like," I offered, "I'll go there, try to make contact with them."

Raoul consulted his appointment book.

"Meetings until three. I'll cancel out. Let's go."

"I don't think you should be there, Raoul."

"That's absurd, Alex! I'm the *physician*! This is a medical issue—"

"Only nominally. Let me handle it."

His thick brows curled and fury rose in the coffee bean eyes. He started to say something but I cut him off.

"We have to at least consider the possibility," I said softly, "that this whole thing may be due to a conflict between the family and you."

He stared at me, making sure he'd heard right, purpled, choked on his anger, and threw up his hands in despair.

"How could you even—"

"I'm not saying it's so. Just that we need to consider it. What we want is that boy back in treatment. Let's maximize the probability of success by covering all contingencies."

He was mad as hell but I'd given him something to think about.

"Fine. There's no shortage of things for me to do anyway. Go yourself."

"I want Beverly along. Of anyone she's got the best feel for the family."

"Fine, fine. Take Beverly. Take whomever you want."

He straightened his tie and smoothed nonexistent wrinkles in the long white coat.

"Now, if you'll excuse me, my friend," he said, straining to be cordial, "I'll be off to the lab."

*   *   *

The Sea Breeze Motel was on west Pico, set amid cheap apartments, dusty storefronts, and auto garages on a dingy slice of the boulevard just before L.A. surrenders to Santa Monica. The place was two stories of pitted chartreuse stucco and drooping pink wrought-iron railing. Thirty or so units looked down upon an asphalt motor court and a swimming pool half-filled with algae-clogged water. The only breeze evident was the steaming layer of exhaust fumes that rose from the oily pavement as we pulled in beside a camper with Utah plates.

"Not exactly five star," I said, getting out of the Seville. "And far from the hospital."

Beverly frowned.

"I tried to tell them that when I saw the address but there was no convincing the father. Said he wanted to be near the beach where the air was good. Even launched into a speech about how the whole hospital should move to the beach, how the smog was harmful to patients. I told you, the man is weird."

The front office was a glass booth on the other side of a warped plywood door. A thin, bespectacled Iranian with the numb demeanor of a habitual opium smoker sat behind a chipped, hinged plastic counter poring over the Motor Vehicle Code. A revolving rack of combs and cheap sunglasses took up one corner, a low table covered with ancient copies of throwaway travel magazines squatted in the other.

The Iranian pretended not to notice us. I cleared my throat with tubercular fervor and he looked up slowly.

"Yes?"

"What room is the Swope family in?"

He looked us over, decided we were safe, said, "Fifteen," and returned to the wondrous world of road signs.

There was a dusty brown Chevy station wagon parked in front of Room 15. Except for a sweater on the front seat and an empty cardboard box in the rear deck, the car was empty.

"That's theirs," said Beverly. "They used to leave it parked illegally by the front entrance. One time when the security guard put a warning sticker on the windshield, Emma ran out crying about her sick child and he tore it up."

I knocked on the door. No answer. Knocked again harder. Still no response. The room had a single grimy window, but the view within was blocked by oilcloth curtains. I knocked one more time, and when the silence was unbroken, we returned to the office.

"Excuse me," I said, "do you know if the Swopes are in their room?"

A lethargic shake of the head.

"Do you have a switchboard?" Beverly asked him.

The Iranian raised his eyes from his reading and blinked.

"Who are you? What do you want?" His English was heavily accented, his manner surly.

"We're from Western Pediatric Hospital. The Swopes' child is being treated there. It's important that we speak to them."

"I don't know anything." He shifted his glance back to the vehicle code.

"Do you have a switchboard?" she repeated.

A barely visible nod.

"Then please ring the room."

With a theatrical sigh, he dragged himself up and walked through a door at the rear. A minute later he reappeared.

"Nobody there."

"But their car's there."

"Listen, lady, I don't know cars. You want a room, okay. Otherwise, leave alone."

"Call the police, Bev," I said.

Somehow he must have sneaked in a hit of amphetamine because his face came alive suddenly and he spoke and gesticulated with renewed vigor.

"What for police? What for you cause trouble?"

"No trouble," I said. "We just need to talk to the Swopes."

He threw up his hands.

"They take walk—I see them. Walking that way." He pointed east.

"Unlikely. They've got a sick child with them." To Bev: "I saw a phone at the gas station on the corner. Call it in as a suspicious disappearance."

She moved toward the door.

The Iranian lifted the hinged counter and came around to our side.

"What do you want? Why you make trouble?"

"Listen," I told him, "I don't care what kind of nasty little games you've got going on in the other rooms. We need to talk to the family in fifteen."

He pulled a ring of keys out of his pocket. "Come, I show you, they not here. Then you leave me alone, okay?"

"It's a deal."

His pants were baggy and they flapped as he strode across the asphalt, muttering and jingling the keys.

A quick turn of the wrist and the lock released. The door groaned as it opened. We stepped inside. The desk clerk blanched, Beverly whispered Ohmigod, and I fought down a rising feeling of dread.

The room was small and dark and it had been savaged.

The earthly belongings of the family Swope had

been removed from three cardboard suitcases, which lay crushed on one of the twin beds. Clothing and personal articles were strewn about: lotion, shampoo, and detergent leaked from broken bottles in viscous trails across the threadbare carpeting. Female undergarments hung limply over the chain of the plastic swag lamp. Paperback books and newspapers had been shredded and scattered like confetti. Open cans and boxes of food were everywhere, the contents oozing out in congealing mounds. The room reeked of rot and dead air.

Next to the bed was a patch of carpet that was clear of litter, but far from empty. It was filled with a dark brown amoebalike stain half a foot across.

"Oh no," said Beverly. She staggered, lost her balance, and I caught her.

You don't have to spend much time in a hospital to know the sight of dried blood.

The Iranian's face was waxen. His jaws worked soundlessly.

"Come on," I took hold of his bony shoulders and guided him out, "we have to call the police now."

It's nice to know someone on the force. Especially when that someone is your best friend and won't assume you're a suspect when you call in a crime. I bypassed 911 and called Milo's extension directly. He was in a meeting but I pushed a bit and they called him out.

"Detective Sturgis."

"Milo, it's Alex."

"Hello, pal. You pulled me out of a fascinating lecture. It seems the west side has become the latest hot spot for PCP labs—they rent glitzy houses and park Mercedes in the driveway. Why I need to know all about it is beyond me but tell that to the brass. Anyway, what's up?"

I told him and he turned businesslike immediately.

"All right. Stay there. Don't let anyone touch anything. I'll get everything moving. There's gonna be a lot of people converging so don't let the girl get spooked. I'll crap out of this meeting and be there as soon as I can but I may not be the first, so if someone gives you a hard time, drop my name and hope they don't give you a harder time because you did. Bye."

I hung up and went to Beverly. She had the drained, lost look of a stranded traveler. I put my arm around her and sat her down next to the clerk, who'd progressed to muttering to himself in Farsi, no doubt reminiscing about the good old days with the Ayatollah.

There was a coffee machine on the other side of the counter and I went through and poured three cups. The Iranian took his gratefully, held it with both hands, and gulped noisily. Beverly put hers down on the table, and I sipped as we waited.

Five minutes later we saw the first flashing lights.

6

The two uniformed policemen were muscular giants, one white and blond, the other coal-black, his partner's photographic negative. They questioned us briefly, spending most of their time with the Iranian desk clerk. They didn't like him instinctively, and showed it in the way L.A.P.D. cops do—by being overly polite.

Most of their interrogation had to do with when he'd last seen the Swopes, what cars had come in and out, how the family had been behaving, who had called them. If you believed him, the motel was an oasis of innocence and he was the original see-no-evil, hear-no-evil kid.

The patrolmen cordoned off the area around room fifteen. The sight of their squad car in the center of the motor court must have ruffled some feathers—I saw fingers drawing back corners of curtains in several of the rooms. The policemen noticed, too, and joked about calling Vice.

Two additional black and whites pulled into the lot and parked haphazardly. Out of them stepped four more uniforms, who joined the first two for a smoke and a huddle. They were followed by a crime scene technical van and an unmarked bronze Matador.

The man who got out of the Matador was in his midthirties, big and heavily built, with a loose, ungainly walk. His face was broad and surprisingly unlined, but bore the stigmata of severe acne. Thick drooping brows shadowed tired eyes of a startling bright green hue. His black hair was cut short around the back and sides but worn full on top in defiance of any known style. A thick shock fell across his forehead like a frontal cowlick. Similarly unchic were the sideburns that reached to the bottom of his softlobed ears and his attire—a rumpled checked madras sportcoat with too much turquoise in it, a navy shirt, gray-and-blue striped tie, and light blue slacks that hung over the tops of suede desert boots.

"That one's got to be a cop," said Beverly.

"That's Milo."

"Your friend—oh." She was embarrassed.

"It's okay, that's what he is."

Milo conferred with the patrolmen then took out a pad and pencil, stepped over the tape strung across the doorway to room fifteen, and went inside. He stayed in there awhile and came out taking notes.

He loped over to the front office. I got up and met him at the entrance.

"H'lo, Alex." His big padded hand gripped mine. "Hell of a mess in there. Not really sure what to call it yet."

He saw Beverly, walked over, and introduced himself.

"Stick with this guy," he pointed to me, "and inevitably you're going to get into trouble."

"I can see that."

"Are you in a hurry?" he asked her.

"I'm not going back to the hospital," she said. "All I've got, otherwise, is a run at three thirty."

"Run? Oh, like in cardiovascular stimulation?

Yeah, I tried that but the chest began to hurt and visions of mortality danced before my eyes."

She smiled uneasily, not knowing what to make of him. Milo's great to have around—in more ways than one—when your preconceptions get overly calcified.

"Don't worry, you'll be out of here long before then. Just wanted to know if you could wait while I interview Mr.—" he consulted the pad, "Fahrizbadeh. Shouldn't take long."

"That would be fine."

He escorted the desk clerk outside and over to fifteen. Beverly and I sat in silence.

"This is horrible," she said, finally. "That room. The blood." She sat stiffly in her chair and pressed her knees together.

"He could be okay," I said without much conviction.

"I hope so, Alex. I really do."

After a while Milo returned with the desk clerk, who slunk behind the counter without a glance at us and disappeared into the back room.

"Very unobservant guy," said Milo. "But I think he's on the level, more or less. Apparently his brother-in-law owns the place. He's studying business administration at night and works here instead of sleeping." He looked at Beverly. "What can you tell me about these Swope people?"

She gave him a history similar to the one I'd received in the Laminar Airflow Unit.

"Interesting," he reflected, chewing on his pencil. "So this could be anything. The parents taking the kid out of town in a hurry, which might not be a crime at all unless the hospital wants to make a thing out of it. Except if that was the case, they wouldn't leave the car behind. Hypothesis B is the cultist did the job with the parents' permission, which is still no crime. Or without, which would be good old-fashioned kidnapping."

"What about the blood?" I asked.

"Yeah, the blood. The techs say O positive. That tell you anything?"

"I think I remember from the chart," said Beverly, "that Woody and both of the parents are O. I'm not sure about the Rh factor."

"So much for that. It's not a hell of a lot anyway, not what you'd expect if someone got shot or cut—" He saw the look on her face and stopped himself.

"Milo," I said, "the boy's got cancer. He's not terminally ill—or wasn't as of yesterday. But his disease is unpredictable. It could spread and invade a major blood vessel, or convert to leukemia. And if either of those occur, he could suddenly hemorrhage."

"Jesus," said the big detective, looking pained. "Poor little guy."

"Isn't there something you can do?" demanded Beverly.

"We'll do our best to find them but to be honest it won't be easy. They could be just about anywhere by now."

"Don't you put out A.P.B.s or something like that?" she insisted.

"That's already been done. As soon as Alex called I got in touch with the law in La Vista—it's a one-man show run by a sheriff named Houten. He hasn't seen them but he promised to keep a lookout. He also gave me a good physical description of the family and I put it over the wire. Highway patrol's got it, as well as L.A. and San Diego P.D.s and all the decent-sized departments in between. But we've got no vehicle to look for, no plates. Anything you'd like to suggest in addition to all of that?"

It was a sincere request for ideas, devoid of sarcasm, and it threw her off guard.

"Uh, no," she admitted, "I can't think of anything. I just hope you find him."

"I hope so too—can I call you Beverly?"

"Oh, sure."

"I don't have any brilliant theories about this, Beverly, but I promise to give it a lot of thought. And, if *you* think of anything, call *me*." He gave her a card. "Anything at all, okay? Now, can I have one of the men give you a lift home?"

"Alex could—"

He flashed her a wide, loose-lipped smile. "I'm going to be needing to talk to Alex for a while. I'll get you a ride." He went out to the six patrolmen, selected the best-looking of the bunch, a trim six-footer with curly black hair and shiny teeth, and brought him back to the office.

"Ms. Lucas, this is Officer Fierro."

"Where to, ma'am?" Fierro tipped his hat. She gave him an address in Westwood and he guided her to his squad car.

Just as she was getting in, Milo rummaged in his shirt pocket and called out, "Hey, Brian, hold on."

Fierro stopped and Milo bounded over to the car. I jogged along with him.

"This mean anything to you, Beverly?" He handed her a matchbook.

She examined it. "Adam and Eve Messenger Service? Yeah. One of the nurses told me Nona Swope had gotten a job as a messenger. I remember thinking it was strange—why would she get a job when they were only in town temporarily?" She looked at the matchbook more closely. "What is this, a hooker service or something like that?"

"Something like that."

"I knew she was a wild one," she said angrily, and gave him back the matchbook. "Is that all?"

"Uh huh."

"Then I'd like to go home."

Milo gave the signal and Fierro got behind the wheel and started up the engine.

"Uptight lady," said Milo after they drove away.

"She used to be a sweet young thing," I said. "Too much time on the cancer ward can do things to you."

He frowned.

"Quite a mess in there," he said.

"Looks bad, doesn't it?"

"You want me to speculate? Maybe, maybe not. The room was tossed by someone who was *angry*. But couldn't it have been one of the parents, furious at having a sick kid, all scared and confused about pulling him out? You worked with people in that situation. Ever see anyone freak like that?"

I reeled back a few years.

"There was always anger," I told him. "Most of the time people talked it out. But sometimes it got physical. I can recall at least one intern getting slugged by a father. Plenty of threats. One guy who'd lost his leg in a hunting accident three weeks before his daughter came down with kidney tumors carried a couple of pistols into the hospital the day after she died. It was usually the ones who denied it and held it in and didn't communicate with anyone who were the most explosive." Which fit the description Beverly had given me of Garland Swope. I told him so.

"So that could be it," he said uneasily.

"But you don't think so."

The heavy shoulders shrugged.

"I don't think anything at this point. Because this is a crazy city, pal. More homicides each year and folks are getting wasted for the weirdest reasons. Last week, some old character jammed a steak knife in his neighbor's chest because he was *sure* the guy was killing his tomato plants with evil rays from his navel. Deranged assholes walk into fast-food joints and mow down kids eating *burgers*, for chrissake. When I first went into Homicide things seemed relatively logical, pretty simple, really. Most of the stuff we used to catch was due to love or jealousy or money, family feuds—your basic human conflicts. Not now, *compadre*. Too many holes in the Swiss cheese? Ice the deli man. Looney Tunes."

"And this looks like the work of a crazy?"

"Who the hell knows, Alex? We're not talking hard science. Most probably we'll find it was what I said before. One of them—probably the father—got a good look at the shitty cards he'd been dealt and tossed the room. They left the car behind so it's probably temporary.

"On the other hand, I can't guarantee they didn't happen to be in the wrong place at the wrong time, didn't collide with a nutcase who thought they were Pluto Vampires out to take over his liver." He held the matchbook between thumb and forefinger and waved it like a miniature flag.

"Right now," he said, "all we've got is this. It's not in my ballpark but I'll pay the place a visit and follow it up for you, okay?"

"Thanks, Milo. Getting to the bottom of it would calm a few people down. Want company?"

"Sure, why not? Haven't seen you in a good while. If missing the lovely Ms. Castagna hasn't made you unbearably morose, you might even turn out to be good company."

7

There was a phone number on the matchbook but no address, so Milo called Vice and got one, along with some background on the Adam and Eve Messenger Service.

"They know the operation," he said, tooling onto Pico and heading east. "Owned by a sweetheart named Jan Rambo, has her finger in a little bit of everything. Daddy's a mob biggie in Frisco. Little Jan's his pride and joy."

"What is it, a cover for an outcall service?"

"That and a few other things. Vice thinks sometimes the messengers transport dope, but that's only a sideline—impromptu, when someone needs a favor. They do some relatively legit stuff—party gags, like when it's the boss's birthday and a nubile young thing shows up at the office party, strips and rubs herself all over him. Mostly it's sex for sale, one way or another."

"Which sheds new light on Nona Swope," I said.

"Maybe. You said she was good looking?"

"Gorgeous, Milo. Unusually so."

"So she knows what she's got and decides to profit from it—it might be relevant, but what the hell, when you get right down to it, this town was built on the buying and selling of bodies, right? Small town girl hits glitter-city, gets her head turned. Happens every day."

"That has got to be the most hackneyed soliloquy you've ever delivered."

He broke out laughing and slapped the dashboard with glee, then realized he'd been squinting into the sun and put on a pair of mirrored shades.

"Oka-ay, time to play cop. What do you think?"

"Very intimidating."

Jan Rambo's headquarters were on the tenth floor of a flesh-colored high rise on Wilshire just west of Barrington. The directory in the lobby listed about a hundred businesses, most with names that told you nothing about what they did—a free hand had been used with words like *enterprise, system, communications,* and *network.* A good third of them ended with Ltd. Jan Rambo had outdone them all, christening her meat market, *Contemporary Communications Network, Ltd.* If that didn't convince you it was all very respectable, the brass letters on the teak door and the matching thunderbolt logo were sure to do the trick.

The door was locked but Milo pounded it hard enough for the walls to shake, and it opened. A tall well-built Jamaican in his midtwenties stuck his head out and started to say something hostile, but Milo shoved his badge in the mahogany face and he shut his mouth.

"Hi," said Milo, grinning.

"What can I do for you, Officers?" asked the black, overenunciating in a show of arrogance.

"First, you can let us in." Without waiting for co-operation, Milo leaned on the door. Taken by surprise, the Jamaican stepped back and we walked in.

It wasn't much of a reception room, barely larger than a closet, but Contemporary Communications probably didn't do much receiving. The walls were flat ivory and the only furniture was a chrome and vinyl desk upon which sat an electric typewriter and a phone, and the steno chair behind it.

The wall backing the desk was adorned with a photographic poster of a California surfer couple posing as Adam and Eve, underscored by the legend "Send that Special Message to that Special Person." Eve had her tongue in Adam's ear and though the expression on his face was one of stuporous boredom, his fig leaf bulged appreciatively.

To the left of the desk was a closed door. The Jamaican stood in front of it, arms folded, feet apart, a scowling sentry.

"We want to speak with Jan Rambo."

"You got a warrant?"

"Jesus," said Milo, disgustedly, "everyone in this lousy city thinks he's in the movies. 'You got a warrant?' " he mimicked. "Strictly grade B, dude. C'mon, knock on the door and tell her we're here."

The Jamaican remained impassive.

"No warrant, no entry."

"My, my, an assertive one." Milo whistled. He put his hands in his pockets, slouched and walked forward until his nose was a millimeter short of Eskimo-kissing the Jamaican.

"There's no need to get unpleasant," he said. "I know Ms. Rambo is a busy lady and as pure as the freshly driven snow. If she wasn't, we might be here to search the premises. *Then* we'd need a warrant. All we want to do is *talk* with her. Since you obviously haven't advanced far enough in your legal studies to know this, let me inform you that no warrant is necessary when one simply wants to make conversation."

The Jamaican's nostrils widened.

"Now," Milo continued, "you can choose to facilitate that conversation or continue to be obstructive, in which case I will cause you grievous bodily injury, not to mention significant pain, and arrest you for interfering with a police officer in the performance of his duty. Upon arrest, I will fasten the cuffs tight enough to cause gangrene, see to it that you are body-searched by a sadist, and make sure you are tossed in a holding cell with half a dozen charter members of the Aryan Brotherhood."

The Jamaican pondered his choices. He backed away from Milo, but the detective bird-dogged him, breathing into his face.

"I'll see if she's free," he muttered, opening the door a crack and slithering through.

He reappeared momentarily, eyes smoldering with emasculation, and jerked his head toward the open door.

We followed him into an empty anteroom. He paused before double doors and punched a code into a pushbutton panel. There was a low-pitched buzz and he opened one of the doors.

A dark-haired woman sat behind a marble-topped tubular metal desk in an office as big as a ballroom. The floor was covered with springy industrial carpeting the color of wet cement. To her back was a wall of smoked glass offering a muted view of the Santa Monica mountains and the Valley beyond. One side of the office had been given over to some West Hollywood decorator's fantasies—mercilessly contemporary mauve leather chairs, a lucite coffee table sharp enough to slice bread, an art deco sideboard of rosewood and shagreen similar to one I'd seen recently in a Sotheby's catalogue; that piece had gone for more than Milo took home in a year. Across from this assemblage was the business area: rosewood conference table, bank of black file cabinets, two computers, and a corner filled with photographic equipment.

The Jamaican stood with his back to the door and resumed his sentry pose. He worked at fashioning his face into a war mask but a rosy flush incandesced beneath the dusky surface of his skin.

"You can go, Leon," the woman said. She had a whiskey voice.

The Jamaican hesitated. She hardened her expression and he left hastily.

She remained behind the desk and didn't invite us to sit. Milo sat anyway, stretching out his long legs and yawning. I sat next to him.

"Leon told me you were very rude," said the woman. She was about forty, chunky, with small muddy eyes and short pudgy hands that drummed the marble. Her hair was cut blunt and short. She wore a tailored black business suit. The ruffled bodice of her white crepe de chine blouse seemed out of character.

"Gee," said Milo, "I'm really sorry, Ms. Rambo. I hope we didn't hurt his feelings."

The woman laughed, an adenoidal growl. "Leon's a prima donna. I keep him around for decoration." She pulled out an extra-long black cigarette from a box of Shermans and lit it up. Blowing out a cloud of smoke, she watched it rise to the ceiling. When it had dissipated completely she spoke.

"The answers to your first three questions are: One: They're messengers, not hookers. Two: What they do on their own time is their own business. Three: Yes, he is my father and we talk on the phone every month or so."

"I'm not from Vice," said Milo, "and I don't give a damn if your messengers end up giving fuck shows for horny old men snarfing nose candy and playing pocket pool."

"How tolerant of you," she said coldly.

"I'm known for it. Live and let live."

"What do you want then?"

He gave her his card.

"Homicide?" Her eyebrows rose but she remained impassive. "Who bit it?"

"Maybe no one, maybe a whole bunch of people. Right now it's a suspicious disappearance. Family from down near the border. The sister worked for you. Nona Swope."

She dragged deeply and the Sherman glowed.

"Ah, Nona. The red-haired beauty. She a suspect or a victim?"

"Tell me what you know about her," said Milo, taking out his pad.

She removed a key from a desk drawer, stood, smoothed her skirt, and went to the files. She was surprisingly short—five one or two. "I guess I'm supposed to play hard to get, right?" She inserted the key in the file lock and twisted. A drawer slid open. "Refuse to give you the information, scream for my lawyer."

"That's Leon's script."

That amused her. "Leon's a good guard dog. No," she said, taking out a folder, "I don't care much if you read about Nona. I've got nothing to hide. She's nothing to me."

She settled back behind the desk and passed the folder across to Milo. He opened it and I looked over his shoulder. The first page was an application form filled out in halting script.

The girl's full name was Annona Blossom Swope. She'd listed a birthdate that made her just twenty and physical measurements that matched my memory of her. Under residence she'd claimed a Sunset Boulevard address—Western Pediatric Medical Center—with no phone number to go along with it.

The eight-by-ten glossies had been taken in the office—I recognized the leather furniture—and they'd framed her in a variety of poses, all sultry. The photos were black-and-white and shortchanged her by their inability to capture her dramatic coloring. Nevertheless, she had what professionals call *presence* and it came through in these pictures.

We thumbed through the photos—Nona in a string bikini rolled down over her pelvis, Brazilian style; Nona braless in a sheer tank top and jeans, nipples budding through the fabric; Nona making love to an all-day sucker; Nona, feline, in a filmy negligee with a fuck-you look in her dark eyes.

Milo whistled softly. I felt an involuntary tug below the waist.

"Quite a gal, eh?" asked Jan Rambo. "A lot of skin passes through these portals, gentlemen. She stood out from the rest of them. I started calling her Daisy Mae because there was a naive quality to her. Limited life experience. Despite that, she was a little girl who knew her way around, know what I mean?"

"When were these taken?" asked Milo.

"First day she got here—what's it say, a week ago? I took one look at her and called the cameraman. We shot and developed 'em the same day. I saw her as a good investment, started her off on messenger service."

"Doing what, exactly?" he pushed.

"Doing messenger work, *exactly*. We've got a few basic skits—doctor and nurse, professor and coed. Adam and Eve, dominatrix and slave or vice versa. The old clichés, but your average yahoo can't break out of clichés even when it's fantasy time. The client picks the skit, we send out couples, and they do it like a message—you know, Happy Birthday, Joe Smith, this is from the boys in the Tuesday night poker group and, presto, the show is on. It's all legal—they joke around, but nothing that challenges the penal code."

"How much does that run the poker buddies?"

"Two hundred. Sixty goes to the messengers, split fifty-fifty. Plus tips."

I did some quick mental arithmetic. Working half-time Nona could have pulled in a hundred dollars a day or more. Big bucks for a country girl barely out of her teens.

"What if the client is willing to pay more to see more?" I asked.

She looked sharply at me. "I was wondering if you talked. Like I said before, the messengers are free to do what they want on their own time. Once the skit is over, it's their own time. You like jazz?"

"Good jazz," I answered.

"Me, too. Like Miles and Coltrane and Bird. Know what makes them great? They know how to improvise. Far be it from me to discourage improvisation."

She took out another Sherman and lit it from the one smoldering in her mouth.

"That's all she did, huh?" asked Milo. "Skits."

"She could've done more—I had plans for her. Movies, magazine layouts." The meaty face creased into a smile. "She was cooperative—took off her clothes without batting an eye. They must raise 'em wild in the country." She rolled the cigarette between stubby fingers. "Yeah, I had plans but she split on me. Worked a week and—" She snapped her fingers—"poof."

"Any word where she was going?"

"Not a hint. And I didn't ask. This is no surrogate family. It's a business. I don't play mommy and I don't want to be treated like one. Skin comes and skin goes—this city's full of perfect bodies who think their buns are gonna make 'em rich. Some learn faster than others. High volume, high turnover. Still," she admitted, "that redhead had something."

"Anyone else who'd know anything about her?"

"Can't think of anyone. She kept to herself."

"What about the guys she messengered with?"

"Guy. Singular. She was only here a week. I don't remember his name offhand, and I'm not gonna comb through the files to find it. You guys have just been handed a big freebie." She pointed to the file. "You can even keep it, okay?"

"Tax your memory," pressed Milo. "It's not like it's a big deal—how many studs do you have in your stable?"

"You'd be surprised," she said, stroking the marble desktop. "Meeting adjourned."

"Listen," he persisted, "you've been minimally helpful but it doesn't make you Suzy Citizen. It's hot outside, you've got great air conditioning in here, a fantastic view. Why sweat it at the station, waiting who knows how long for your lawyer to show up?" He held out his hands, palms up, and gave her a boyish grin. "Want to try again?"

The muddy eyes narrowed and her face turned nastily porcine. She pressed a button and Leon materialized.

"Who was the guy teamed up with that redhead, Swope?"

"Doug," he said without hesitation.

"Last name," she snapped.

"Carmichael. Douglas Carmichael."

Turning to us: "Okay?"

"The file." Milo held out his hand.

"Get it." She ordered and the Jamaican fetched. "Let them look at it."

Milo took the folder from him and we walked to the door.

"Hey, wait a minute!" she protested hoarsely. "That's an active one. You can't take it!"

"I'll make a Xerox, mail you back the original."

She started to argue then stopped midsentence. As we left I could hear her screaming at Leon.

8

According to his file, Doug Carmichael lived in the upscale part of Venice, near the Marina. Milo had me call him from a phone booth near Bundy while he used the radio to find out if anything had come in on the Swopes.

A phone machine answered at Carmichael's. Classical guitar music played in the background while a rich baritone said, "Hi, this is Doug," and strove to convince me that receipt of my message was *really* important for his emotional well-being. I waited for the beep, told him it was *really* important to call Detective Sturgis at West L.A. Division, and left Milo's number.

I got back in the car and found Milo with his eyes closed, head tilted back against the seat.

"Anything?" he asked.

"I got a machine."

"Figures. Zilch from this end, too. No Swopes spotted from here to San Ysidro." He yawned and growled and started up the Matador. "Moving right along," he mumbled, steering into the broth of westbound traffic, "I haven't eaten since six. Early dinner or late lunch, take your pick."

We were a couple of miles from the ocean but a

mild easterly wind was blowing and it wafted a hint of brine our way. "How about fish?"

"Righto."

He drove to a tiny place on Ocean at the mouth of the pier that resembles a thirties diner. Some nights during the dinner hour it's hard to find a parking space in the back lot among all the Rolls, Mercedes, and Jags. They don't take reservations or plastic, but people who know seafood are willing to wait and don't mind paying with real money. At lunch it's significantly more relaxed and we were seated at a corner table immediately.

Milo drank two lemonades, which they squeeze fresh and serve unsweetened, and I nursed a Grolsch.

"Trying to cut down," he explained, holding up his glass. "Rick's been on my case. Preaching and showing me slides of what it does to the liver."

"That's good. You were hitting it pretty hard for a while. Maybe we'll have you around a little longer."

He grunted.

The waiter, a cheerful Hispanic, informed us that there'd been a huge albacore run and a prime load had come up from San Diego that morning. We both ordered some and shortly were feasting on huge grilled steaks of the white tuna, baked potatoes, steamed zucchini, and chunks of sourdough bread.

Milo devoured half his meal, took a long swallow of lemonade, and gazed out the window. A chrome sliver of ocean was visible above the rooftops of the ramshackle buildings that hid in the shadow of the sagging pier.

"So how you been, pal?" he asked.

"Not bad."

"What do you hear from Robin?"

"I got a card a few days ago. The Ginza at night.

They're wining and dining her. Apparently it's the first time they've entertained a woman that way."

"What is it they're after, exactly?" he asked.

"She designed a guitar for Rockin' Billy Orleans and he played it onstage in Madison Square Garden. The music trades interviewed him after the concert and he raved about the instrument and the fantastic female luthier who'd created it. The U.S. rep for a Japanese conglomerate picked up on it and sent it to his bosses. They decided it was worth mass-producing as a Billy Orleans model and invited her over there to talk about it."

"Maybe she'll end up supporting you, huh?"

"Maybe," I said glumly and signaled the waiter for another beer.

"I see you're real overjoyed about it."

"I'm happy for her," I said quickly. "It's the big break she's been waiting for. It's just that I miss her like crazy, Milo. It's the longest we've been apart and I've lost my taste for solitude."

"That all of it?" he asked, picking up his fork.

I looked up sharply. "What else?"

"Well," he said, between mouthfuls, "I may be totally off base here, Doctor, but it seems to me that this Japanese thing puts a new perspective on your— pardon the expression—*relationship*."

"How so?"

"Like for the past couple of years, you've been the one with the bread, right? She makes a living, but the life the two of you've been leading—Maui, theater tickets, that incredible garden—who pays for it?"

"I don't get the point," I said, annoyed.

"The point is that despite your pretending it ain't so, you guys have had a traditional setup. Now she's got the chance to become a big shot and it could all change."

"I can handle it."

"Sure you can. Forget I brought it up."

"Consider it forgotten." I looked down at my plate. All of a sudden my appetite was gone. I pushed the food away and fixed my gaze on a flock of gulls raiding the pier for bait scraps. "You insightful bastard," I said. "Sometimes you're spooky."

He reached across the table and patted my shoulder. "Hey, you're not a very subtle guy. Everything registers on that lean and hungry face."

I rested my chin in my hands. "Things were going along so nice and simple. She kept the studio after she moved in, we prided ourselves on giving each other room to move. Lately we'd started talking marriage, babies. It was great, both of us moving at the same pace, mutual decisions. Now," I shrugged, "who knows?" I took a long swallow of the Dutch brew. "I'll tell you, Milo, they don't cover it in the psych books, but there's such a thing as the paternal urge and at thirty-five I'm feeling it."

"I know," he said. "I've felt it, too."

My stare was involuntary.

"Don't look so surprised. Just because it's never gonna happen doesn't mean I don't think about it."

"You never can tell. They're getting pretty liberal."

He loosened his belt a notch and buttered a piece of bread. "Not *that* liberal." He laughed. "Besides, Rick and I are not equipped for motherhood or whatever you wanna call it. Can't you just see it—me shopping at Toys "Я" Us and Dr. Fastidious changing diapers?"

We shared a good laugh over that.

"Anyway," he said, "I didn't mean to bring up a sore point, but it's something you're gonna have to deal with. I did. For most of my life I made my own way. My parents didn't give me squat. I've been working at one dodge or another since eleven, Alex. Paper routes, tutoring, picking pears, construction, a little time out for the M.A., then Saigon and the force. You don't get rich in Homicide, but a single guy can get by nicely. I was lonely as hell but my needs were met. After I met Rick and we started living together, it all changed. You remember my old Fiat—piece of shit that it was. I never drove anything but garbage and unmarkeds. Now we tool around in that Porsche like a pair of coke dealers. And the house—no way I could ever have had a place like that on my salary. He goes shopping at Carrols or Giorgio, picks me up a shirt or tie. I'm not a—kept man, but my lifestyle has changed. For the better, but that hasn't made it easy to accept. Surgeons make more than cops, always have, always will, and I've finally accommodated myself to it. Makes you stop and think about what women go through, huh?"

"Yup." I wondered if Robin had been faced with the type of adjustment he'd described. Had there been a struggle that I'd been too insensitive to notice?

"In the long run," he said, "it's better if both parties feel like adults, don't you think?"

"What I think, Milo, is that you're an amazing guy."

He hid his embarrassment behind the menu. "If I remember correctly the ice cream is good, right?"

"Right."

Over dessert he had me tell him more about Woody Swope and childhood cancer. He was shocked, like most people, that it is the second most common cause of death in children; only accidents kill more.

The mechanics of the Laminar Airflow rooms particularly fascinated him and he asked me detailed, analytical questions until my fund of answers was exhausted.

"Months in that plastic box," he said, troubled. "And they don't freak out?"

"Not if it's handled right. You've got to orient the child to time and space, encourage the family to spend as much time there as possible. You sterilize favorite toys and clothes and bring them in, provide lots of stimulation. The key is to minimize the difference between home and hospital—there's always going to be some, but you can buffer it."

"Interesting. You know what I'm flashing on, don't you?"

"What's that?"

"AIDS. Same principle, right? Lowered resistance to infection."

"Similar but not identical," I said. "The laminar airflow filters out bacteria and fungi in order to protect the kids during treatment. But the loss of immunity is temporary—after chemotherapy's over, their systems rebound. AIDS is permanent and AIDS victims have other problems—Kaposi's Sarcoma, viral infections. The modules might protect them for a while, but not indefinitely."

"Yeah, but you gotta admit, it's a hell of an image: Santa Monica Boulevard lined with thousands of plastic cubes, each one with some poor guy wasting away inside. You could charge admission, raise enough money to find a cure."

He let out a bitter laugh.

"The wages of sin," he shook his head. "Enough to make you a Puritan. I hear the horror stories and thank God I'm monogamous. Rick's been fielding a lot of shit from both sides. Last week a patient came to the E.R. with a mangled arm—bar fight—and glommed onto the fact that Rick was gay. Probably a paranoid guess, be-

cause Rick doesn't exactly swish, but he didn't deny it
when this turkey demanded to know if they were giving
him a faggot doctor. The guy refused to let Rick touch
him, screamed about AIDS—no matter that he's bleeding all over the place. So Rick walked away. But the rest
of the docs were up to their elbows in shit—Saturday
night and they were wheeling 'em in one after the other.
It threw the whole system out of whack. Everyone
ended up getting pissed at Rick. He was a goddamn
leper for the rest of the shift."

"Poor guy."

"Poor guy is right. The man was top of his class,
chief resident at Stanford, and he's taking this kind of
crap? He came home in a *dark* mood. The hell of it is,
night before, *he* was telling *me* that working with gay
patients—especially the ones who came in bleeding—
was making him antsy. I did heavy-duty therapy that
night, Alex."

He spooned the last bit of ice cream into his
mouth.

"Heavy-duty," he repeated and brushed the hair
out of his eyes. "But hey, that's what love's all about,
right?"

9

Milo begged off the case during the drive back to the Sea Breeze Motel.

"I can't take it any further," he said apologetically. "All we've got at this point is a missing persons squeal, and that's stretching it."

"I know. Thanks for coming down."

"No big deal. It was a break from routine. Just so happens I've got a particularly cruddy routine right now. Gang shooting—two *cholos* blown away—liquor store clerk ripped with a broken bottle, and a real sweetheart—a rapist who shits on his victims' abdomens when he's through with them. We know he's attacked at least seven women. The last one ended up more than defiled."

"Jesus."

"Jesus won't forgive this creep." He frowned and turned on Sawtelle toward Pico. "Each year I tell myself I've witnessed the depths of depravity and each year the scumbags out there prove me wrong. Maybe I should have taken the exam."

Fifteen months ago he and I had exposed a prominent orphanage as a brothel catering to pedophiles, solving a handful of murders in the process. He'd been a hero and had been invited to take the lieutenant's exam. There was no doubt he'd have passed, because he's brilliant, and the brass had let him know the city was ready for a gay loot as long as he didn't flaunt it. He'd debated it internally for a long time before turning it down.

"No way, Milo. You would have been miserable. Think back to what you told me."

"What's that?"

"I didn't give up Walt Whitman to push paper."

He chuckled. "Yeah, that's right."

Prior to his hitch in Vietnam, Milo had been enrolled in the graduate program in American Lit at Indiana U., contemplating life as a teacher, hoping the academic world would be a setting where his sexual preference would be tolerated. He'd gotten as far as an M.A. and then the war had turned him into a policeman.

"Just imagine," I reminded him, "endless meetings with desk jockeys, considering the political implications of taking a leak, no contact with the streets."

He held up a hand and feigned suffering.

"Enough, I'm gonna puke."

"Just a little aversive therapy."

He pulled the Matador into the motel lot. The sky had darkened in anticipation of twilight and the Sea Breeze benefited from it aesthetically. Take away the sunlight and the place looked almost habitable.

The office was brightly lit and the Iranian clerk was visible behind the counter, reading. My Seville was the lone occupant of the lot. The half-empty pool looked like a crater.

Milo stopped the car and let the engine idle.

"You understand about my stepping out of this?"

"Of course. No homicide, no homicide detective."

"They'll probably be back for the car. I had it impounded so they'll have to check in to get it back. They do, I'll call you and give you a chance to talk to them. Even if they don't show, we'll probably find out they're back home, no harm done."

He realized what he'd said and grimaced.

"Shit. Where's my head? The kid."

"He could be all right. Maybe they've taken him to another hospital." I wanted to sound hopeful but memories—the pain on Woody's face, the bloodstain on the motel carpet—eroded my faith in a happy ending.

"If they don't treat him that's it, right?"

I nodded.

He stared out the windshield. "That's one kind of murder I've never dealt with."

Raoul had said the same thing in different words. I told him so.

"And this Melendez-Lynch doesn't want to go the legal route?"

"He was trying to avoid it. It may end up in court yet."

He gave his big head a shake and placed a hand on my shoulder. "I'll keep my ears open. Anything comes up I'll let you know."

"I'd appreciate it. And thanks for everything, Milo."

"It was nothing. Literally." We shook hands. "Say hello to the entrepreneur when she gets back."

"Will do. The best to Rick."

I got out of the car. The Matador's headlights striped the gravel as Milo swung out of the lot. The truncated patter of the radio dispatcher created a punk rock concerto that hung in the air after he was gone.

I drove north to Sunset, planning to turn off at Beverly Glen and head home. Then I remembered that the house would be empty. Talking to Milo about

Robin had opened a few wounds and I didn't want to be alone with my thoughts. I realized that Raoul knew nothing about what we'd found at the Sea Breeze, and decided now was as good a time as any to tell him.

He was hunched over his desk scrawling notations on the draft of a research paper. I knocked lightly on the open door.

"Alex!" He rose to greet me. "How did it go? Did you convince them?"

I recounted what we'd found.

"Oh my God!" He slumped in his chair. "This is unbelievable. Unbelievable." He exhaled, compressed his jowls with his hands, picked up a pencil and rolled it up and down the surface of the desk.

"Was there much blood?"

"One stain about six inches wide."

"Not enough for a bleed-out," he muttered to himself. "No other fluids? No bile, no vomitus?"

"I didn't see any. It was hard to tell. The place was a shambles."

"A barbaric rite, no doubt. I told you, Alex, they are madmen, those damned Touchers! To steal a child and then to run amok like that! Holism is nothing more than a cover for anarchy and nihilism!"

He was jumping to conclusions in quantum leaps but I had neither the desire nor the energy to argue with him.

"The police, what did they do?"

"The detective who ran the show is a friend of mine. He came down as a favor. There's an All Points Bulletin out on the family, the sheriff in La Vista has been notified to watch for them. They did a crime scene analysis and filed a report. That's it. Unless you decide to push it."

"Your friend—is he discreet?"

"Very."

"Good. We can't afford a media side show. Have you ever talked to the press? They are idiots, Alex, and vultures! The blonds from the television stations are the worst. Vapid, with paste-on smiles, always trying to trick you into making outrageous statements. Barely a week goes by that one of them doesn't attempt to get me to say that the cure for cancer is just around the corner. They want instant information, immediate gratification. Can you imagine what they'll do with something like this?"

He'd gone quickly from defeatism to rage and the excess energy propelled him out of his chair. He traversed the length of the office with short nervous steps, pounding his fist into his hand, swerved to avoid the piles of books and manuscripts, walked back to the desk, and cursed in Spanish.

"Do you think I should go to court, Alex?"

"It's a tough question. You need to decide if going public will help the boy. Have you done it before?"

"Once. Last year we had a little girl who needed transfusions. The family were Jehovah's Witnesses and we had to get an injunction to give her blood. But that was different. The parents weren't fighting us. Their attitude was, our beliefs don't allow us to give you permission, but if we're forced to comply we will. They *wanted* to save their child, Alex, and were happy when we took the responsibility away from them. That child is alive today and *thriving*. The Swope boy should be thriving, too, not dying in the back room of some scabrous voodoo den."

He thrust his hand into the pocket of his white coat, removed a packet of saltine crackers, tore open the plastic, and nibbled on the crackers until they were consumed. After brushing crumbs out of his mustache he continued.

"Even in the Witness case the media tried to make a cause célèbre of it, implying that we were coercing the family. One of the stations sent around a moron masquerading as a medical reporter to interview me— probably one of those fellows who wanted to be a doctor but flunked his science courses. He swaggered in with a little tape recorder and addressed me by my *first name*, Alex! As if we were buddies! I dismissed him and he made the 'no comment' sound like concealment of guilt. Fortunately the parents took our advice and refused to talk to them, too. At that point the so-called *controversy* died a quick death—no carrion, the vultures go elsewhere."

The door leading to the lab opened and a young woman clutching a clipboard entered the office. She had light brown hair cut in a page boy, round eyes that uncannily matched the hair, pinched features, and a petulant mouth. The hand holding the clipboard was pale, and her nails were gnawed to the quick. She wore a lab coat that reached below her knees and crepe-soled flats on her feet.

She looked through me to Raoul and said, "There's something you should see. Could be exciting." The lack of inflection in her voice belied the content of her message.

Raoul got up. "Is it the new membrane, Helen?"

"Yes."

"Wonderful." He looked as if he were going to hug her then stopped suddenly, remembering my presence. Clearing his throat, he introduced us: "Alex, meet a fellow Ph.D., Dr. Helen Holroyd."

We exchanged the most cursory of pleasantries. She edged closer to Raoul, a proprietary gleam in the beige eyes. He fought, unsuccessfully, to erase the naughty boy look from his face.

The two of them were trying so hard to look platonic that for the first time all day I felt like smiling. They were sleeping together and it was supposed to be a secret. Without a doubt everyone in the department knew about it.

"I've got to get going," I said.

"Yes, I understand. Thank you for everything. I may call you to discuss this further. In the meantime, send your bill to my secretary."

As I walked out the door they were gazing into each other's eyes and discussing the wonders of osmotic equilibrium.

On the way out I stopped in the hospital cafeteria for a cup of coffee. It was after seven and the dining room was sparsely populated. A tall Mexican man wearing a hair net and blue scrubs ran a dry mop over the floor. A trio of nurses laughed and ate doughnuts. I lidded the coffee and was preparing to leave when movement fluttered in the corner of my eye.

It was Valcroix and he was waving me over. I walked to his table.

"Care to join me?"

"All right." I put down my cup and took a chair facing him. The remains of a giant salad sat on his tray along with two glasses of water. He used his fork to move a tumbleweed of alfalfa sprouts around the bowl.

He'd traded his psychedelic sport shirt for a black Grateful Dead T-shirt and had tossed his white coat over the chair next to him. From up close I could see that the long hair was thinning on top. He needed a shave but his beard growth was sparse, spotting only the mustache and chin areas. The drooping face had been worked over by a bad cold; he sniffled, red-nosed and bleary-eyed.

"Any news on the Swopes?" he asked.

I was tired of telling the story but he'd been their doctor and deserved to know. I gave him a brief summary.

He listened with equanimity, no emotion registering in the hooded eyes. When I was finished he coughed and dabbed at his nose with a napkin.

"For some reason I feel an urge to proclaim my innocence to you," he said.

"That's hardly necessary," I assured him. I drank some coffee and put it down quickly, having forgotten how awful it was.

His eyes took on a faraway look and for a moment I thought he was meditating, retreating to an internal world as he'd done during Raoul's harangue. I found my attention wandering.

"I know Melendez-Lynch blames me for this. He's blamed me for everything that's gone wrong in the department since I began my fellowship. Was he that way when you worked with him?"

"Let's just say it took a while to develop a good working relationship."

He nodded solemnly, picked some strands from the ball of sprouts and chewed on them.

"Why do you think they ran away?" I asked him.

He shrugged. "I have no idea."

"No insights at all?"

"None. Why should I have, any more than anyone else?"

"I was under the impression they related well to you."

"Who told you that?"

"Raoul."

"He wouldn't recognize relating if it bit him in the ass."

"He felt you'd developed especially good rapport with the mother."

His hands were scrubbed and pink. They tightened around the salad fork.

"I was a nurse before I became a doctor," he said.

"Interesting."

"Is it?"

"Nurses are always complaining about their lack of status and money and threatening to quit and go to med school. You're the first I've met who actually did it."

"Nurses gripe because their lot in life is shit. But there are insights to be learned at the bottom of the ladder. Like the value of talking to patients and families. I did it as a nurse but now that I'm a doc it makes me a deviate. What's pathetic is that it's viewed as sufficiently deviant to be noticed. Rapport? Hell, no. I barely knew them. Sure I spoke to the mother. I was sticking her son every day with needles, puncturing his bone and sucking out marrow. How could I not speak to her?"

He gazed into the salad bowl.

"Melendez-Lynch can't understand that, my wanting to come across as a human being instead of some white-coated technocrat. He didn't bother to get to know the Swopes but it doesn't occur to him that his remoteness has anything to do with their—defection. I extended myself, so I'm the goat." He sniffed, wiped his nose, and drained one of the water glasses. "What's the use of dissecting it? They're gone."

I remembered Milo's conjecture about the abandoned car.

"They may be back," I said.

"Be serious, man. They see themselves as having escaped to freedom. No way."

"Freedom's going to sour pretty quickly when the disease gets out of control."

"The fact is," he said, "they hated everything about this place. The noise, the lack of privacy, even the sterility. You worked in Laminar Flow, right?"

"Three years."

"Then you know the kind of food the kids in there get—processed and overcooked and dead."

It was true. To a patient without normal immunity a fresh fruit or vegetable is a potential medium for lethal microbes, a glass of milk a breeding pond for lactobacillus. Consequently, everything the kids in the plastic rooms ate was processed to begin with, then heated and sterilized, sometimes to the point where no nutrients remained.

"*We* understand the concept," he said, "but lots of parents have difficulty grasping why this horribly sick kid can have his fill of cola and potato chips and all kinds of junk while carrots are out. It goes against the grain."

"I know," I said, "but most people accept it pretty quickly because their child's life is at stake. Why not the Swopes?"

"They're country folk. They come from a place where the air is clean and people grow their own food. They see the city as a poisonous place. The father used to rail on about how bad the air was. 'You're breathing sewage' he'd tell me every time I saw him. He had a thing for clean air and natural foods. For how healthy it was back home."

"Not healthy enough," I said.

"No, not healthy enough. How's that for a frontal assault on a belief system?" He gave a mournful look. "Isn't there a term in psych for when it all comes tumbling down like that?"

"Cognitive dissonance."

"Whatever. Tell me," he leaned forward, "what do people do when they're in that state?"

"Sometimes change their beliefs, sometimes distort reality to fit those beliefs."

He leaned back, ran his hands through his hair and smiled.

"Need I say more?"

I shook my head and tried the coffee again. It had gotten colder, but no better.

"I keep hearing about the father," I said. "The mother sounds like his shadow."

"Far from it. If anything, she was the tougher of the two. It's just that she was quiet. She let him run off at the mouth while she stayed with Woody, doing what needed to be done."

"Could she have been behind their leaving?"

"I don't know," he said. "All I'm saying is she was a strong woman, not some cardboard cutout."

"What about the sister? Beverly said there was no love lost between her and her parents."

"I wouldn't know about that. She wasn't around much, kept to herself when she was."

He wiped his nose and stood.

"I don't like to gossip," he said. "I've indulged in too much of it already."

He snatched up his white coat, flung it over his shoulder, turned his back and left me sitting there. I watched him walk away, lips moving, as if in silent prayer.

It was after eight by the time I reached Beverly Glen. My house sits atop an old bridle path forgotten by the city. There are no streetlights and the road is serpentine, but I know every twist by heart and drove home by sense of touch. In the mailbox was a love letter from Robin. I got high on it for a while but after the fourth reading, a hazy sense of sadness set in.

It was too late to feed the koi so I took a hot bath, toweled off, put on my ratty yellow robe, and carried a brandy into the small library off the bedroom. I finished writing a couple of overdue forensic reports then settled in an old chair and went through the stack of books I'd promised myself to read.

The first volume I grabbed was a collection of Diane Arbus photographs but the unforgiving portraits of dwarfs, derelicts, and other walking wounded made me more depressed. The next couple of choices were no better so I went out on the deck with my guitar, sat looking at the stars, and forced myself to play in a major key.

10

The next morning I went out on the terrace to get the paper and saw it lying there, sluglike and bloated.

It was a dead rat. A crude noose of hemp had been tied around its neck. Its lifeless eyes were open and clouded, its fur matted and greasy. A pair of disturbingly humanoid forepaws were frozen in supplication. The half-open mouth revealed frontal incisors the color of canned corn.

Underneath the corpse was a piece of paper. I used the *Times* to push the rodent away—it resisted, sticking, then slid like a puck to the edge of the terrace.

It was straight out of an old gangster movie: letters had been cut out of a magazine and pasted up to read:

HERES TO YOU MONEYCHASER HEADSHRINK

I'd probably have figured it out anyway, but that made it a cinch.

Sacrificing the classified section to the task, I wrapped up the rat and carried it down to the garbage. Then I went inside and got on the phone.

Mal Worthy's secretary had a secretary and I had to be assertive with both of them to get through to him.

Before I could speak he said, "I know, I got one, too. What color was yours?"

"Brownish gray, with a noose around its scrawny little neck."

"Count yourself lucky. Mine came decapitated, in a box. I almost lost a damn good mailgirl because of it. She's still washing her hands. Daschoff's was ratburger."

He was trying to make light of it, but sounded shaken.

"I knew the guy was a sicko," he said.

"How'd he find out where I live?"

"Your address on your resumé?"

"Oh shit. What did the wife get?"

"Nothing. Does that make sense?"

"Forget making sense. What can we do about it?"

"I've already begun drafting a restraining order keeping him a thousand yards from any of us. But to be honest, there's no way to prevent him from defying it. If he gets caught at it, that's another story, but we don't want it to get that far, do we?"

"Not too comforting, Malcolm."

"That's democracy, my friend." He paused. "This taped?"

"Of course not."

"Just checking. There is another option, but it would be too risky before the property settlement has been completed."

"What's that?"

"For five hundred dollars I can have him sufficiently damaged so he'll never be able to piss without crying."

"Democracy, huh?"

He laughed.

"Free enterprise. Fee for service. Anyway, it's just an option."

"Don't exercise it, Mal."

"Relax, Alex. Just theorizing."

"What about the police?"

"Forget it. We have no evidence it was him. I mean we both know it but there's no proof, right? And they're not going to fingerprint a rat because sending rodents to your loved ones is no felony. Maybe," he laughed, "we could get Animal Regulation on it. A stern lecture and a night at the pound?"

"Wouldn't they at least go out and talk to him?"

"Not with the workload they've got. If it had been more explicit, something that constituted a threat, maybe. 'Here's to You Motherfucking Shyster' won't do, I'm afraid—the cops feel the same way he does about lawyers. I'm going to file a report just for the record, but don't count on help from the blue guys."

"I know someone on the force."

"Metermaids don't carry much weight, fella."

"How about detectives?"

"That's different. Give him a call. You want me to talk to him, I will."

"I'll handle it."

"Great. Let me know how it goes. And Alex— sorry for the hassle." He sounded eager to get off the phone. At three and a half bucks a minute it doesn't pay to give it away free for any length of time.

"One more thing, Mal."

"What's that?"

"Call the judge. If she hasn't gotten a care package yet, warn her she may."

"I've already called her bailiff. Scratch up a few more brownie points for our side."

* * *

"Describe this asshole as precisely as you can," said Milo.

"My size almost exactly. Say five eleven, one seventy-five. Raw-boned, muscles. Long face, a reddish tan like construction workers get, busted nose, big jaw. Wears Indian jewelry—two rings, one on each hand. A scorpion and a snake. A couple of tattoos on the left arm. Bad dresser."

"Eye color?"

"Brown. Bloodshot. A binge drinker. Brown hair combed back, greasy kid stuff."

"Sounds like a shitkicker."

"Exactly."

"And this Bedabye Motel's where he lives?"

"As of a couple of days ago. He may be living in his truck for all I know."

"I know a couple of guys in Foothill Division. If I can get one of them in particular to go down and talk to this Moody, your troubles'll be over. Guy name of Fordebrand. Has the worst breath you've ever smelled. Five minutes of face to face with him and the asshole will *repent*."

I laughed but my heart wasn't in it.

"He got to you, huh?"

"I've had better mornings."

"If you're spooked and wanna stay at my place, feel free."

"Thanks, but I'll be okay."

"If you change your mind, let me know. Meanwhile, be careful. He may be just an asshole and a wiseguy, but I don't have to tell you about crazies. Keep your eyes open, pal."

I spent most of the day doing mundane things and appearing outwardly relaxed. But I was in what I call my karate state—a heightened level of consciousness typified by perceptual vigilance. The senses are finely tuned to a point, just short of paranoia, where looking over one's shoulder at frequent intervals seems perfectly normal.

To get that way I avoid alcohol and heavy foods, do limbering exercises and practice katas—karate dances—until exhausted. Then I relax with a half hour of self-hypnosis and auto-suggest hyperalertness.

I learned it from my martial arts instructor, a Czech Jew named Jaroslav, who had honed his self-preservation skills fleeing the Nazis. I sought his advice during the first weeks after the Casa de Los Ninos affair, when the wires in my jaw made me feel helpless and nightmares were frequent visitors. The regimen he taught me had helped me mend where it counted—in my head.

I was ready, I told myself, for anything Richard Moody had in store.

I was dressing to go out for dinner when the service called.

"Good evening, Dr. D., it's Kathy."

"Hi, Kathy."

"Sorry to bother you but I've got a Beverly Lucas on the line. She says it's an emergency."

"No problem. Put her on, please."

"Okay. Have a nice night, Doc."

"You too."

The phone hissed as the lines connected.

"Bev?"

"Alex? I've got to talk t'you."

There was loud music in the background—

synthesized drums, screaming guitars, and a heart-stopping bass. I could barely hear her.

"What's up?"

"Can't talk about it here—using the bar phone. Are you busy right now?"

"No. Where are you calling from?"

"The Unicorn. In Westwood. Please. I need to talk to you."

She sounded on edge but it was hard to tell with all that noise. I knew the place, a combination bistro-discotheque (bisco?) that catered to the upscale singles crowd. Once Robin and I had stopped in for a bite after a movie but had left quickly, finding the ambience too nakedly predatory.

"I was just about to have dinner," I said. "Want to meet somewhere?"

"How 'bout right here? I'll put my name down for a table and it'll be ready when you get here."

Dinner at the Unicorn wasn't an appealing prospect—the noise level seemed likely to curdle the gastric juices—but I told her I'd be there in fifteen minutes.

Traffic in the Village was heavy and I was late getting there. The Unicorn was a narcissist's paradise, mirrored on every surface except the floor. Hanging Boston ferns, half a dozen fake Tiffany lamps, and some brass and wood trim had been tossed in, but the mirrors were the essence of the place.

To the right was a smallish restaurant, twenty tables draped with parrot green damask, to the left a glassed-in disco where couples boogied to a live band, the glass shimmying with the backbeat. In between was the lounge. Even the bar was covered with reflective glass, its base a display of trendy footwear.

The lounge was dim and packed with bodies. I edged my way through the throng, surrounded by laughing faces in triplicate, quadruplicate, unsure what was real, what was illusion. The place was a damned funhouse.

She was sitting at the bar next to a chesty guy in a body shirt. He alternated between trying to make time with her, guzzling light beer, and visually trawling the crowd for a more hopeful prospect. She nodded from time to time but was clearly preoccupied.

I elbowed my way next to her. She was staring at a tall glass half-filled with foamy pink liquid, lots of candied fruit, and a paper parasol. One hand twirled the parasol.

"Alex." She wore a lemon-colored Danskin top and matching satin jogging shorts. Her legs were sheathed from ankle to knee with yellow and white warmers that matched her running shoes. She had on lots of makeup and plenty of jewelry—at work she'd always been conservative with both. A glittery sweatband circled her forehead. "Thanks for comin'." She leaned over and kissed me on the mouth. Her lips were warm. Body Shirt got up and left.

"Bet that table's ready," she said.

"Let's check." I took her arm and we wedged through waves of flesh. Plenty of male eyes followed her exit but she didn't seem to notice.

There was a bit of confusion because she'd given the maitre d' the name 'Luke' and hadn't told me, but we got it straightened out and were seated in a corner table under a colossal Creeping Charlie.

"Damn," she said, "left my zinger at the bar."

"How about some coffee?"

She pouted.

"You think I'm drunk or somethin'?"

She was talking clearly and moving normally. Only her eyes gave her away, as they focused and unfocused in rapid succession.

I smiled and shrugged.

"Playing it safe, huh?" She laughed.

I called for the waiter and ordered coffee for myself. She had a glass of white wine. It didn't seem to affect her. She was maintaining as only a heavy drinker can.

A while later the waiter returned. She asked me to order first while she scanned the menu. I kept it simple, choosing a small spinach salad and broiled chicken, because trendy places usually have lousy food and I wanted something they couldn't ruin too easily.

She continued to study the menu as if it were a textbook, then looked up brightly.

"I'll have an artichoke," she said.

"Hot or cold, ma'am?"

"Uh, cold."

The waiter wrote it down and looked at her expectantly. When she didn't say anything he asked if that was all.

"Uh huh."

He left, shaking his head.

"I eat artichokes a lot because when you run you lose sodium and artichokes have lots of sodium."

"Uh huh."

"For dessert I'll have something with bananas because bananas are high in potassium. When you up your sodium you have to up your potassium to put your body in balance."

I'd always seen her as a level-headed young lady, if a bit too hard on herself and prone to self-punishment. The dizzy broad across the table was a stranger.

She talked about running marathons until the food came. When the artichoke was set down before her she stared at it and began picking delicately at the leaves.

My food was unpalatable—the salad gritty, the chicken arid. I played with it to avoid eating.

When she'd dismantled and polished off the artichoke and seemed settled, I asked her what she wanted to talk about.

"This is very difficult, Alex."

"You don't have to tell me if you don't want to."

"I feel like a—traitor."

"Against whom?"

"Shit." She looked everywhere but at me. "It's probably not even important and I'm just shooting off my mouth for nothing but I keep thinking about Woody and wondering how long it'll be before the metastases start popping up—if they haven't already—and I want to do something, to stop feeling so damned helpless."

I nodded and waited. She winced.

"Augie Valcroix knew the couple from the Touch who came to visit the Swopes," she said.

"How do you know?"

"I saw him talking to them, calling them by name, and I asked him about it. He said he visited the place once, thought it was nice. Peaceful."

"Did he say why?"

"Just that he was interested in alternative lifestyles. I know that's true because in the past he'd spoken of checking out other groups—Scientologists, Lifespring, a Buddhist place in Santa Barbara. He's Canadian, thinks the whole California thing is fascinating."

"Did you ever detect any collusion between them?"

"None. Just that they knew each other."

"You said he used their names. Do you remember them?"

"I think he called the guy Gary or Barry. I never

heard the woman's name. You don't really think this was some sort of conspiracy, do you?"

"Who knows?"

She squirmed as if her clothes were too tight, caught the waiter's eye, and ordered a banana liqueur. She sipped it slowly trying to appear relaxed, but she was jumpy and ill-at-ease.

She put the glass down with a furtive look in her eyes.

"Is there anything else, Bev?"

She nodded, embarrassed. When she spoke it was barely a whisper.

"This is probably even less relevant but as long as I'm babbling I might as well spill it all out. Augie and Nona Swope had a thing going. I'm not sure when it started. Not too long ago because the family was only in town a couple of weeks." She fiddled with her napkin. "God, I feel like such a shit. If it weren't for Woody I'd never have opened my mouth."

"I know that."

"I wanted to tell your cop friend about it right there, at the motel—he seemed nice enough—but I just couldn't. Then I got to thinking about it later and I couldn't let go of it. I mean, what if there was a way to help that little boy and I let it go by? But I still didn't want to go to the police. I figured if I told you, you'd know what to do with it."

"You did the right thing."

"I wish doing right didn't feel so wrong." Her voice broke. "I wish I could be sure that my telling you has any meaning."

"All I can do is let Milo know. At this point he's not even convinced a crime's been committed. The only one who seems sure of that is Raoul."

"*He's* always sure of everything," she said angrily. "Ready to assess blame at the drop of a hat. He dumps on everyone but Augie's been his favorite scapegoat since he got here."

She dug the nails of one hand into the palm of the other. "And now I've made things worse for him."

"Not necessarily. Milo may brush it off completely or he may choose to talk to Valcroix. But he doesn't care what Raoul thinks. No one's going to get railroaded, Bev."

That was meager balm for her conscience.

"I still feel like a traitor. Augie's my friend."

"Look at it this way, if Valcroix's sleeping with Nona had anything to do with this mess, you did a good deed. If not, he can endure a few questions. It's not like the guy's a total innocent."

"What do you mean?"

"The way I hear it he makes a habit of sleeping with his patients' mothers. This time it was a sister, for variety. At the very least it's unethical."

"That's so self-righteous," she snapped, turning scarlet, "so damned judgmental!"

I started to reply but before I knew what was happening she got up from the table, grabbed her purse, and ran out of the restaurant.

I pulled out my wallet, threw down a twenty and went after her.

She was half-running, half-walking north on Westwood Boulevard, swinging her arms like a foot soldier, heading into the crush and commotion of the Village at night.

I ran, caught up, and took her arm. Her face was wet with tears.

"What the hell's going on, Bev?"

She didn't answer but let me walk with her. The Village seemed especially Felliniesque that evening, litter-strewn sidewalks clogged with street musicians, grim-faced college students, squealing packs of junior high kids wearing oversized clothes pocked with highpriced holes, empty-eyed bikers, gawking tourists from the exurbs, and assorted hangers-on.

We walked in silence all the way to the southern edge of the UCLA campus. Inside the grounds of the university the pandemonium and bright lights died and were replaced by tree-shadowed darkness and a silence so pure it was startling. Except for an occasional passing car, we were alone.

A hundred yards into the campus I got her to stop and sit on a bench at a shuttle stop. The buses had stopped running for the night and the lights near the stop had been turned off. She turned away and buried her face in her hands.

"Bev—"

"I must be going nuts," she mumbled, "running out like that."

I tried to put my arm around her for comfort but she jerked away.

"No, I'm okay. Let me spit it out, once and for all."

She sucked in her breath, bracing herself for an ordeal.

"Augie and I were—involved. It started pretty soon after he came to Western Peds. He seemed so different from the men I'd been meeting. Sensitive, adventurous. I thought it was serious. I allowed myself the luxury of romance and it turned to shit. When you talked about his sleeping around it brought back all that shit.

"I was a fool, Alex, because he never promised me anything, never lied to me or told me he was anything other than what he was. It was me. I chose to see him as some noble knight. Maybe he came along at a time when I was ready to believe anything, I don't know. We slept together for six months. Meanwhile he was making it with every woman he could find—nurses, lady docs, mothers.

"I know what you're thinking. He's an unethical creep. I doubt I can convince you of this, but he's not a bad man, just a weak one. He was always loving and gentle. And open. When I confronted him with the stories I was hearing he said sure, he was giving pleasure and receiving it in return. What could be wrong with that, especially with all the pain and suffering and death we had to deal with. He was so convincing I didn't stop seeing him even then. It took me a long time to get my head straight.

"I thought I'd gotten over it until a week ago when I saw him with Nona. I was out on a date—a fix-up, a real disaster—at an intimate little Mexican place not far from the hospital. The two of them were across the room, tucked away in a dark little booth. I could barely see them. They were all over each other. Drinking margaritas and laughing. *Tongue-dueling*, for God's sake. Like a couple of reptiles."

She stopped, caught her breath.

"It hurt bad, Alex. She was so confident, so beautiful. The jealousy went through me like a knife. I'd never felt that kind of jealousy before—I was *bleeding*. Their eyes were horribly orange from the candlelight. Two vampires. There I was, stuck with some dull creep, dying for the evening to be over, and they were just about fucking on the table. It was obscene."

Her shoulders shook. She shivered and hugged herself.

"So you can see why I was so torn about telling anyone about it. I'd be seen as the woman scorned, doing it out of spite. That's a degrading role and I've been degraded enough for a lifetime."

Her eyes implored me to understand.

"Everyone takes a bite out of me and I'm fucking

disappearing, Alex. I want to forget him, her, everyone. But I can't. Because of that little boy."

This time she accepted my comfort and put her head on my shoulder, her hand in mine.

"You've got to get some distance from it," I said, "so you can start to see straight again. He may have been gentle and 'honest,' in some perverse way but he's no hero. The guy's got problems and you're best off without him. He's a druggie, isn't he?"

"Yes. How'd you know that?"

I decided not to cite Raoul's suspicions. Mention of his name would set her off. Besides, I had suspicions of my own.

"I talked to him last night. He was sniffing the whole time. At first it looked like a cold but later I started wondering about coke."

"He's into coke pretty heavily. Grass and downers, on the side. Sometimes speed when he's on call. He talked about dropping acid in med school but I don't think he does that anymore. He does booze, too. I started drinking heavily when I was with him and kept it up ever since. I know I have to stop."

I gave her a squeeze.

"You deserve a lot better, hon."

"It's nice to hear that," she said in a small voice.

"I'm saying it because it's true. You're intelligent, you're attractive, and you have a good heart. That's why you're hurting so badly. Get the hell away from all the death and misery. It'll destroy you. I know."

"Oh, Alex," she sobbed into my shoulder, "I'm so cold."

I gave her my jacket. When the tears stopped I walked her back to her car.

1·1

Neither the Swopes' disappearance nor Richard Moody's rat fell under Milo's jurisdiction. Out of friendship he'd helped me with both and I was reluctant to bother him so soon with the information on Valcroix.

But what Beverly had told me the night before was disturbing. As Raoul had claimed, the Canadian was unethical and a drunk, and his familiarity with the Touch visitors fleshed out the suspicion of a conspiracy to remove Woody Swope from treatment. I felt some obligation to let him know what was going on, but I didn't look forward to it because he was sure to flip out. Before the pyrotechnics began I wanted to consult a professional.

Milo, bless his soul, sounded genuinely glad to hear from me.

"No sweat. I was gonna call you anyway. Fordebrand went out to the Bedabye to breathe on Moody but when he got there the asshole was gone. Left behind a room full of b.o.—it would have been a battle of the stinkers—and candy wrappers. Foothill will keep an eye out for him and I'll have the boys here do the same, but be careful. Also, I got a call back from that Carmichael character—the one who messengered with the Swope girl. Normally I might have just talked to him on the phone but this guy sounded *very* uptight. Like he's sitting on something. He's also got a record—busted for prostitution a couple of years ago. So I'm gonna head out and do a face to face. Now what's on your mind?"

"I'll go with you to Carmichael's and tell you in the car."

He absorbed the information on Valcroix while speeding along the Santa Monica Freeway.

"What is he, some kind of stud?"

"Far from it. An old, ersatz hippie. Saggy face, flabby body, kind of a slob really."

"No accounting for taste. Maybe he's hung like a horse."

"I doubt the appeal's strictly physical. He's a scavenger, Milo. Moves in on women when they're under stress, plays Mr. Sensitive, gives them what passes for love and understanding."

He put a finger to his nose and sniffed.

"And a little blow, too?"

"Could be."

"I'll tell you what, after we're finished with Carmichael we'll head out to the hospital and interview him. I've got a little slack because the gang thing resolved nicely—confessions all around. The shooters were fourteen years old. They'll end up at the Youth Authority. The liquor store cutting's due to close any day—Del Hardy's interviewing a snitch who looks promising. The main thing pending is the stomach-shitter. We're praying to the computer on that."

He exited at Fourth Avenue, headed south to Pico, took Pico to Pacific, and continued southward into

Venice. We passed Robin's studio, an unmarked storefront with the windows painted opaque white, but neither of us mentioned it. The neighborhood changed from sleazy to slick as we approached the Marina.

Doug Carmichael's house was on a walk-street west of Pacific, half a block from the beach. It resembled a landlocked cabin cruiser, all peaks and portholes, narrow and high, and wedged into a lot no wider than thirty feet. The exterior was teal blue wood siding and white trim. Fish-scale shingles graced the gablelike peak above the door. A planter brimming with nail-polish pink geraniums hung from the sill of the front window. A white picket fence ringed the dwarf lawn. The door was inlaid with a stained-glass window. Everything looked clean and well tended.

This close to the beach the place had to cost a pretty piece of change.

"Fulfilling fantasies must be paying well," I said.

"Hasn't it always?"

Milo rang the doorbell. It opened quickly and a tall muscular man in a red-and-black plaid shirt, faded jeans, and topsiders flashed us a smile saturated with fear, introduced himself ("Hi, I'm Doug"), and asked us in.

He was about my age. I'd been expecting someone younger and was surprised. He had thick blond hair, layered and blow-dried to look dashingly mussed, a full but neatly trimmed reddish-blond beard, sky blue eyes, artist's model features, and poreless golden skin. An aging beachboy who'd preserved well.

The interior walls of the house had been torn down to create a thousand square feet of skylit living space. The furniture was bleached wood, the walls oyster white. The scent of lemon oil was in the air. There were maritime lithographs, a saltwater aquarium, a small but well-stocked kitchen, a partially folded futon bed. Everything in its place, neat as a pin.

In the center of the room was a sunken area half-filled by a bottle green velvet modular couch. We stepped down and sat. He offered us coffee from a pot that had already been set out on the table.

He poured three cups and sat across from us, still smiling, still scared.

"Detective Sturgis—" he looked from me to Milo who identified himself with a nod—"over the phone you said this had to do with Nona Swope."

"That's correct, Mr. Carmichael."

"I have to tell you at the outset, I'm afraid I won't be of much help. I barely know her—"

"You messengered with her several times." Milo pulled out his pencil and pad.

Carmichael laughed nervously. "Three, maybe four times. She didn't stick around very long."

"Uh huh."

Carmichael drank coffee, put the cup down, and cracked his knuckles. He had iron-pumper's arms, each muscle defined in bas relief and roped with veins.

"I don't know where she is," he said.

"No one said she was missing, Mr. Carmichael."

"Jan Rambo called and told me what it was all about. She said you took my file."

"Does that bother you, Mr. Carmichael?"

"Yes, it does. It's private and I don't see what it has to do with anything." He was trying to assert himself but despite the muscles there was something preternaturally meek and childish about him.

"Mr. Carmichael, you were pretty keyed up over the phone and you're just as nervous in person. Want to tell us why?" Milo sat back and crossed his legs.

It's always pathetic when someone physically impressive starts to fall apart, like watching a monument crumble. I saw the look on the blond man's face and wanted to be somewhere else.

"Tell us about it," said Milo.

"It's my own damned fault. Now I'm going to pay." He got up, went into the kitchen, and came back with a bottle of pills.

"B-twelve. I need it when I'm stressed out." He unscrewed the lid, shook out three capsules, swallowed, and washed them down with coffee. "I shouldn't be taking in so much caffeine but it calms me down. Paradoxical reaction."

"What's on your mind, Doug?"

"My working at Adam and Eve has been a—a secret. Until now. I knew all along it was risky, that I might run into someone who knew me. I don't know, maybe that was part of the thrill."

"We're not interested in your private life. Just in what you know about Nona Swope."

"But if it leads somewhere and ends up in court I'm gonna be subpoenaed, right?"

"Could happen," admitted Milo, "but we're a long way from that. Right now we just want to find Nona and her parents so we can save a little boy's life."

The detective went on in great detail about Woody's lymphoma. He'd retained everything I told him and was throwing it back in Carmichael's handsome face. The blond man tried hard not to listen but failed. He took all of it in, obviously pained. He seemed a sensitive one and I found myself liking him.

"Jesus. She told me she had a sick brother but she never said how sick."

"What else did she tell you?"

"Not much. Really. She didn't say much about anything. Talked about wanting to be an actress—the usual delusional stuff you hear from most of the girls.

But she didn't seem depressed like you'd expect with a brother that sick."

Milo changed the subject.

"What kind of gigs did you two do?"

Returning to the topic of his work made Carmichael anxious again. He tangled his fingers together and twisted. Knots rose on the heavy arms.

"Maybe I should get an attorney before we go any further."

"Suit yourself," said Milo, pointing to the phone.

Carmichael sighed and shook his head. "No. That would only complicate things even more. Listen, I can give you some insights into Nona's personality if that's what you're after."

"It would help."

"But that's all I've got. Insights, no facts. How about you forget where you got them from?"

"Doug," said Milo, "we know who your father is and we know all about the bust, so stop dancing around, okay?"

Carmichael looked like a stallion in a burning stable, ready to bolt despite the consequences.

"Don't panic," said Milo. "We couldn't care less about that stuff."

"I'm not some kind of pervert," Carmichael insisted. "If you traced me that far back you know how it happened."

"Sure. You were a dancer at Lancelot's. After the show one of the ladies in the audience picked you up. Sex for money was discussed and she busted you."

"She entrapped me. The cunt!"

Lancelot's was a male stripper joint in west L.A. catering to women who thought liberation meant aping the crudest aspects of male behavior. The club had long been the object of neighborhood complaints and a couple of years back the police and the fire inspectors had paid it lots of attention. A harassment suit by the owner had ended that.

Milo shrugged. "Anyway, daddy got you off, the file was closed, and you promised to behave yourself."

"Yeah," said Carmichael, bitterly. "End of story, right? Only it wasn't that simple." The blue eyes burned. "Dad commandeered my trust fund—money left to me by my mom. It was illegal, I'm sure of it, but the lawyer in charge of the trust is one of Dad's California Club buddies and before I knew it the old man had all of it under his control. And me by the balls. It was like being a kid again, having to ask permission for everything. He forced me to go to school, said I had to make something of myself. Christ, I'm thirty-six and I'm in junior college! If I get good grades there'll be a place for me at Carmichael Oil. What a crock. Nothing's gonna change me into someone I'm not. What the hell does he want from me?"

He looked at us beseechingly, wanting support. My instinct was to give it to him but this wasn't therapy. Milo let him cool down before he spoke.

"And if he finds out about your current job, kaput, eh?"

"Shit." Carmichael stroked his beard. "I can't help it. I like doing that kind of thing. God gave me a great body and a great face and I get off on sharing it with other people. It's like acting but private, so it's better, more intimate. When I used to dance I could feel the women's eyes on me. I played to them, treated them good. I wanted them to cream right there. It felt so—loving."

"I told this to your boss and I'll tell it to you," said Milo, "we don't give a damn who fucks who in this city. It only becomes a problem when people get cut or shot or strangled in the process."

Carmichael didn't seem to have heard.

"I mean it's not like I'm hooking or anything," he insisted. "I don't need the money—in a good week I pull in six, maybe seven hundred bucks." He dismissed that kind of money with a wave of his hand, operating from the distorted value system of one born into wealth.

"Doug," said Milo, with authority in his voice, "stop defending yourself and listen: we don't care about what you do with your dick. Your file will stay sealed. Just tell us about Nona."

The message finally got through. The look on Carmichael's face was that of a child who'd received an unexpected gift. I realized that I kept thinking of him as a big kid because, except for the manly outer husk, everything about him was childlike, immature. A classic case of arrested development.

"She was a barracuda," he said. "You had to hold her back or she got too aggressive. The last time we worked together was a stag party for an older guy who was getting married for the second time. A bunch of middle-aged men, salesman types, in this apartment in Canoga Park. They'd been drinking hard and watching fuck films before we got there. We were doing jock and cheerleader that night. I had on a football uniform and she was wearing a jersey top, a little pleated skirt, and sneakers. Pompons, her hair in pigtails, the works.

"Those guys were harmless old farts. Before we got there they'd probably been talking big, hooting at the movies like guys do when they're nervous. Then we walked in, they saw her, and I thought a few hearts were gonna give out. She wiggled at 'em, batted her lashes, showed a lot of tongue. We had the skit all planned out but she decided to ad lib. The script says we do a little minor league fondling while trading suggestive lines—you know stuff like I ask her how she'd like to be my wide receiver and she says 'Do it again, we like it, we like it!' She was a lousy actress, by the way, real flat, no emotion. But the audiences seemed to dig her—her looks made up for it, I guess. Anyway, these old guys were eating it up and she got off on it. That's probably what gave her the idea of getting really outrageous.

"All of a sudden she reached into my pants, grabbed my cock, did a bump and grind, started jerking me off, all the time gyrating at them. I wanted to stop her—we're not supposed to go past the script unless we're asked to." He stopped, looked uncomfortable. "And paid to. But I couldn't do it because it would have ruined the skit and been a downer for all those old guys.

"They were staring at her and she was groping me and I was smiling through it all. Then she let go and waltzed over to the guy who was getting hitched—pudgy little fellow with big eyeglasses—and slipped her hand down *his* pants. Everything got real quiet then. He was red as a beet but he couldn't say anything cause it woulda made him look like a wimp in front of his friends. He got a sick look on his face, forced himself to smile. She started tonguing his ear, kept yanking his chain. The other guys started to laugh. To relieve their tension. Soon they were yelling out lewd comments. Nona was high, like she was really getting off on groping the poor sucker.

"Finally I was able to ease her away without it looking like a hassle. We got out of there and I yelled at her in the car. She looked at me like I was nuts, said what was the matter, we got a big tip, didn't we. I could see it was no use talking to her so I gave up. We got on the freeway. I was driving fast because I couldn't wait to get away from her. Then all of a sudden I felt her pulling at my zipper. Before I know it, my cock is out and she's got it in her mouth. We're going seventy and she's sucking me off and telling me to admit it, I love it. I was helpless, just praying the highway patrol wouldn't pull us over—that would be my balls, right? I asked her to stop but she had me and she wouldn't let go until she finished me off."

"The next day I complained to Rambo, insisted I wouldn't work with her anymore. She just laughed, said Nona would be great in films. Later I found out she'd left, just walked out."

Telling the story had made him sweat. He excused himself, went to the bathroom, and came back freshly combed and sprayed and smelling of aftershave. Milo started questioning before he sat back down.

"And you have no idea where she went?"

Carmichael shook his head.

"She ever talk about anything personal?"

"Nope. There was nothing personal about her. She was all on the surface."

"No hint where she might be headed?"

"She never even said where she came from. Like I told you, we did three or four gigs, then she split."

"How'd she connect with Adam and Eve?"

"No idea. Everyone gets into it differently. Rambo called me after she caught my act at Lancelot's. Some find out by word of mouth. She runs ads in the underground papers and skin mags. Gets more applications than she wants."

"All right, Doug," said Milo, standing, "I hope you've been straight with us."

"I really have, Detective. Please don't pull me into this."

"I'll do the best I can."

We left. Back in the car Milo checked in with the dispatcher. There were no important messages.

"So what's the diagnosis on Surfer Boy?" he asked.

"Off the cuff? Personality problems, probably narcissistic."

"Which means?"

"That he's got low self-esteem and it expresses itself in self-obsession—muscles, vitamins, constant attention paid to his body."

"Sounds like half of L.A.," he growled and turned on the ignition. As we pulled away, Carmichael came out of his house in swim trunks carrying a surfboard, a towel, and tanning lotion. He saw us, smiled, waved, and headed toward the beach.

Milo parked in a no parking zone near the entrance to Western Peds. "I hate hospitals," he said, as we boarded the elevator and rode up to the fifth floor. It took a while to locate Valcroix. He was examining a patient and we waited for him in a small conference room off the ward.

He came in fifteen minutes later, gave me a disgusted look, and told Milo to hurry, he was busy. When the detective began talking, he made a show of pulling out a medical chart, perusing it, and writing notes.

Milo's a skilled interrogator but he struck out with the Canadian. Valcroix continued to chart, unflustered, as the detective confronted him with knowing the Touch visitors and his affair with Nona Swope.

"Are you through, Officer?"

"For the time being, Doctor."

"What am I supposed to do, defend myself?"

"You might start by explaining your role in the disappearance."

"That will be quite simple. There is none."

"No collaboration between you and the couple from the Touch?"

"Absolutely not. I visited them once. That's the extent of it."

"What was the purpose of your visit?"

"Educational. I'm interested in communal societies."

"Did you learn much, Doctor?"

Valcroix smiled.

"It was a peaceful place. They have no need for policemen."

"What were the names of the people who visited the Swopes?"

"The man was called Baron, the woman, Delilah."

"Surnames?"

"They don't use them."

"And you've only visited the Touch once or twice."

"Once."

"All right. We'll be verifying that."

"Feel free."

Milo fixed him with a hard stare. The Fellow smiled contemptuously.

"Did Nona Swope tell you anything that would lead us to her family's whereabouts?"

"We didn't talk much. We just fucked."

"Doctor, I suggest you rethink your attitude."

"Oh really?" The squinty eyes became hyphens. "You interrupt my work to ask me stupid questions about my personal life and expect me to have a good attitude?"

"In your case personal and professional seem pretty enmeshed."

"How insightful of you to notice."

"Is that all you have to say, Doctor?"

"What more would you like to hear? That I like to fuck women? All right. I do. I crave it. I'm going to fuck as many women as I can in this life and if there's a life thereafter I hope it will provide an endless chain of warm, willing women so I can keep fucking. Last I heard, fucking was no crime, or have they passed a new law in America?"

"Go back to work, Doctor."

Valcroix gathered his charts and left, dreamy-eyed.

"What an asshole," said Milo walking back to the car. "I wouldn't let him near my hangnail." There was an illegal parking warning from Hospital Security taped on the windshield. He ripped it off and put it in his pocket. "I hope he's not typical of what they're passing off as doctors nowadays."

"He's one of a kind. He won't last much longer here."

We headed west on Sunset.

"You going to check out his story?" I asked.

"I could ask the Touch people how well they know him but if there is some kind of conspiracy they'd lie. Best thing is to call the sheriff down there and find out if the joker's been spotted more than once. Small town like that the law tends to notice things."

"I know someone who might be familiar with the Touch. Want me to call him?"

"Why not? Couldn't hurt."

He drove me home and stayed for a minute to look at the koi. He was transfixed by the colorful fish and smiled as they gobbled down the pellets he tossed them. When he tore himself away to leave, his big body seemed heavy and slow.

"Any longer, I'd stay here till my beard turned white."

We shook hands, he gave a little salute, turned and ambled off for another afternoon of witnessing the human animal at its worst.

12

I phoned Professor Seth Fiacre at UCLA. He's an old classmate from grad school, a social psychologist who'd been studying cults for several years.

"Hi, Alex," he said, cheerful as always, "just got back from Sacramento. Senate hearings. Stultifying."

We reminisced and played catch-up and then I told him why I'd called.

"The Touch? I'm surprised you've even heard of them. They're not well-known and they don't proselytize. They've got a place called the Retreat, used to be a monastery, down near the Mexican border."

"What about the leader—Matthias?"

"Noble Matthias. He was a lawyer originally. Used to call himself Norman Matthews."

"What kind of law did he practice?"

"I don't know. But it was high powered. Beverly Hills."

Attorney to guru seemed an unlikely metamorphosis.

"Why the change of lifestyle?" I asked.

"I don't know, Alex. Most charismatic leaders claim some sort of cosmic vision, usually after a trauma. Your basic voice in the desert stuff. Maybe he ran out of gas in the Mojave and saw God."

I laughed.

"I wish I could tell you more, Alex. The group hasn't attracted much attention because it's so small, maybe sixty members. And like I said, they're not out looking for converts, so it'll probably stay small. Whether or not that'll change if there's increased attrition remains to be seen. They've only been around for three or four years. Another thing that's unusual is that most of their members are middle-aged. Groups that recruit tend to go after young people. In practical terms that means you don't have parents screaming to the cops or calling in the deprogrammers."

"Are they into holistic health?"

"Probably. Most of these groups are. It's part of rejecting the values of the greater society. But I haven't heard about them obsessing on it, if that's what you mean. I think their focus is more on self-sustenance. Growing their own food, making their own clothes. Like the original utopians—Oneida, Ephrata, New Harmony. Can I ask why you want to know all of this?"

I told him about the Swopes' decision not to treat Woody and the family's subsequent disappearance.

"Does that sound like something this group could be involved in, Seth?"

"It doesn't seem likely, because they're reclusive. Taking on the medical establishment would subject them to lots of scrutiny."

"They did visit the family," I reminded him.

"If they wanted to be subversive why do it so publicly? You said the family lived near the Retreat?"

"From what I understand."

"So maybe they were just being neighborly. In a small town like La Vista there's bound to be plenty of distrust of oddballs on the part of the natives. A smart oddball makes a special effort to be friendly. It's good survival strategy."

"Speaking of survival," I asked, "how do they support themselves?"

"My guess is member contributions. On the other hand, Matthews was a rich man. He could be bankrolling the whole thing himself just for the power and prestige. If they're really into self-reliance the overhead wouldn't be that high."

"One more thing, Seth. Why do they call themselves the Touch?"

He laughed. "Damned if I know. I think I'll sic a grad student on it."

Mal Worthy called me later that day.

"It appears that Mrs. Moody didn't get a rat because she was destined for bigger and better things. This morning she found a dog eviscerated, hanging from the front doorknob by its entrails. He castrated it, too, stuffed the balls in its mouth."

Revulsion kept me silent.

"What a guy, huh? On top of that he snuck in a phone call, in defiance of the order, talked to the boy and told him to run away. The kid obeyed and it took seven hours to find him. They finally caught up with him late last night, wandering around the parking lot of some mall, five miles from home. Apparently he thought his father was going to pick him up and take him away. No one showed up and he was scared out of his mind, poor kid. Needless to say Darlene is going bananas, and I'm calling to ask you to see the kids. More for their mental health than anything else."

"Did they see the dog?"

"Thank God, no. She cleaned it up before they had a chance. How soon can you see them?"

"I won't have access to the office until Saturday." I'd been renting space for forensic evaluations in the Brentwood suite of a colleague, but only had use of the office on weekends.

"You can do it here. Just name the time."

"Can you get them down there in a couple of hours?"

"You got it."

The offices of Trenton, Worthy & La Rosa were located on the penthouse floor of a high-prestige building at the intersection of Roxbury and Wilshire. Mal, resplendent in a navy silk and worsted from Bijan, was in the waiting room to greet me personally. He informed me I'd be using his office. I remembered it as a cavernous, dark-walled room with an oversized amorphous desk that looked like a piece of free-form sculpture, saw-toothed abstract prints hanging from the paneling, and shelves full of expensive—and breakable—mementos. Not an ideal place for child therapy but it would have to do.

I rearranged some chairs, moved an end table, and created a play area in the center of the room. Removing paper, pencils, crayons, hand puppets, and a portable playhouse from my carrying case, I placed them on the table. Then I went to fetch the Moody children.

They were waiting in the law library: Darlene, Carlton Conley, and the children, who'd been dressed as if for church.

The three year old, April, wore a white taffeta dress and white patent leather sandals over lace-hemmed socks. Her blond hair had been ribboned and braided. She nestled sleepily in her mother's lap, worrying a knee scab and sucking her thumb.

Her brother'd been costumed in a white western shirt, brown corduroy pants with the cuffs turned up, a snap-on tie and black oxfords. His face had been scrubbed, his dark hair slicked down in an unsuccessful attempt to make it behave. He looked as miserable in the getup as any nine year old could. When he saw me he turned away.

"Now, Ricky, don't be rude to the doctor," admonished his mother. "Say hello, nice and polite. Hello, Doctor."

"Hello, Mrs. Moody."

The boy shoved his hands in his pockets and scowled.

Conley got up from his seat next to her and shook my hand, grinning awkwardly. The judge had been right. Except for being significantly taller, he looked strikingly like the man he'd replaced.

"Doctor," he said weakly.

"Hello, Mr. Conley."

April stirred, opened her eyes, and smiled at me. She'd been the easy one during the evaluation, an expressive, happy child. Because she was a girl her father had chosen to ignore her and she'd been spared his destructive love. Ricky was the favorite; he'd suffered for it.

"Hi, April."

She batted her lashes, lowered her face, and giggled, a natural coquette.

"Remember the toys we played with last time?"

She nodded and giggled again.

"I have them here. Would you like to play with them again?"

She looked at her mother, requesting permission.

"Go 'head, honey."

The little girl climbed down and took my hand.

"I'll see you in a while, Ricky," I said to the sullen boy.

I spent twenty minutes with April, mostly observing as she manipulated the miniature inhabitants of the playhouse. Her play was organized and structured and relatively untroubled. Though she enacted several episodes of parental conflict, she was able to resolve them by having the father leave and the family live happily ever after. For the most part, hope and determination emanated from the scenarios she constructed.

I drew her out about the situation at home and found that she had an age-appropriate understanding of what was going on. Daddy was angry at mommy, mommy was angry at daddy, so they weren't going to live with each other anymore. She knew it wasn't her fault or Ricky's and she liked Carlton.

Everything was consistent with what I'd learned during the initial evaluation. At that time she'd expressed little anxiety over her father's absence and had seemed to be growing attached to Conley. When I questioned her about him now her face lit up.

"Carlton's so nice, Docka Alek. He take me to da zoo. We saw da diraffe. An da cockadile." Her eyes widened with wonder, the memory alive.

She went on singing his praises and I prayed Judge Severe's cynical prophecy would be proved wrong. I'd treated countless girls who'd suffered tortured relationships with their fathers or no relationship at all, and had witnessed the psychic damage they'd incurred, grievously handicapped in the relationship game. This little sweetheart deserved better.

When I'd observed long enough to convince myself she was functioning reasonably well, I took her back. She stood on tippy toes and reached out toothpick arms. I bent and she kissed my cheek.

"Bye, Docka Alek."

"Bye, honey. If you ever want to talk to me, tell your mommy. She'll help you call."

She said okay and crawled back to the pillowy sanctuary of her mother's thighs.

Ricky'd moved to a far corner where he stood alone, staring out the window. I walked over to him, put my hand on his shoulder, and spoke softly so only he could hear: "I know you're really mad about having to do this."

He thrust out his lower lip, stiffened his neck, and crossed his arms across his chest. Darlene got up, still holding April, and started to say something but I motioned her down.

"It must be real hard not to see your dad," I said.

He stood as straight as a Marine, trying hard to look tough and grim.

"I heard you ran away."

No reply.

"That must have been a real adventure."

The hint of a smile danced across his lips and escaped.

"I knew you had strong legs, Ricky, but to go five miles all by yourself. Whew!"

The smile returned, staying a little longer this time.

"See anything interesting?"

"Uh huh."

"Can you tell me about it?"

He looked back at the others.

"Not here," I assured him. "Let's go to another room. We can draw and play like the last time. Okay?"

He frowned but followed me.

Mal's office amazed him and he circled the immense room several times before settling down.

"Ever see a place like this?"

"Uh huh. In a movie."

"Oh yeah? Which one?"

"It was about bad guys who were taking over the world. They had an office with lasers and stuff. It looked like this."

"Bad guy headquarters, huh?"

"Yeah."

"Do you think Mr. Worthy's a bad guy?"

"My dad said he was."

"Did he tell you anyone else was a bad guy?"

He looked uneasy.

"Like me? And Dr. Daschoff?"

"Uh huh."

"Do you understand why your father said that?"

"He's mad."

"That's right. He's really mad. Not because of anything you or April did, but because he doesn't want your mom and him to get divorced."

"Yeah," the boy said with sudden ferocity, "it's her damn fault!"

"The divorce?"

"Yeah! She kicked him out and he even paid for the house with his money!"

I sat him down, took a chair opposite him, and put my hands on his small shoulders as I spoke:

"Ricky, I'm sorry everything is so sad. I know you want your mom and dad to get back together. But that's not going to happen. Do you remember how they used to fight all the time?"

"Yeah, but then they'd stop fighting and be happy to us."

"When that happened it was nice."

"Yup."

"But the fighting got worse and worse and there wasn't much happiness left."

He shook his head.

"Divorce is terrible," I said. "Like everything's falling apart."

He looked away.

"It's okay to be angry, Ricky. I'd be angry, too, if my parents were getting divorced. But it's not okay to run away because you could get hurt that way."

"My dad'll take care of me."

"Ricky, I know you love your dad very much. You should. A dad is someone special. And a dad should be able to be with his children, even after a divorce. I hope some day your dad can see you a lot, and take you places and do fun stuff with you. But right now— and this is really sad—it's not a good idea for him to spend a lot of time with you and April. Do you understand why?"

"Cause he's sick?"

"Right. Do you know what kind of sickness?"

He ruminated on the question.

"He gets mad?"

"That's part of it. He gets real mad or real sad or real happy all of a sudden. Sometimes without a good reason. When he's real mad he could do mad things that wouldn't be right, like fight with somebody. That could be dangerous."

"Uh *uh*! He could beat'em up!"

"That's true, but it would be dangerous for the person he beat up. And you or April could get hurt, accidentally. Do you understand?"

A grudging nod.

"I'm not saying he'll always be sick. There are medicines he can take that can help. And talking to doctors, like me, can help, too. But right now your dad doesn't want to admit that he needs help. So the judge said he couldn't see you until he got better. That made him really mad and now he thinks everyone is a bad guy trying to hurt him. But we're really trying to help him. And to protect you."

He stared at me, stood, found the drawing paper, and proceeded to construct a fleet of paper airplanes. For the next quarter hour he waged a solitary battle of epic proportions, destroying entire cities, massacring thousands, stomping and shouting and shredding paper until Mal's antique Saruk was covered with confetti.

After that he drew for a while but wasn't happy with any of his creations and tossed them, crumpled, in the trash. I tried to get him to talk about the runaway episode but he refused. I reiterated the danger and he listened, looking bored. When I asked him if he'd do it again he shrugged.

I brought him back and took Darlene into the office. She wore a pink pantsuit with a faint diamond pattern and silver sandals. Her dark hair was piled high and sprayed in place. She'd spent a lot of time on her makeup but still looked tired and worn and scared. After seating herself she pulled a handkerchief out of her purse and passed it from hand to hand, kneading and squeezing.

"This must be really hard on you," I said.

Tears oozed out of her eyes. Up went the handkerchief.

"He's a crazy man, Doctor. He's been getting crazier all along and now he won't let me go without doing something really crazy."

"How have the kids been doing?"

"April's a little clingy—you saw her out there. She gets up a couple of times at night, wants to come into our bed. But she's a sweet thing. *He*'s my problem, just angry all the time, refusing to mind. Yesterday he said the ef word to Carlton."

"What did Carlton do?"

"Told him he'd whip him if he did it again."

Great.

"It's not a good idea to get Carlton involved in discipline at this point. Having him there is a big adjustment for the kids in the first place. If you let him take over they'll feel abandoned."

"But Doctor, he can't use language like that!"

"Then you need to handle it, Mrs. Moody. It's important for the children to know that you're there for them. That you're in charge."

"Okay," she said, without enthusiasm, "I'll try it."

I knew she wouldn't comply. The word *try* was the tipoff. In a couple of months she'd be wondering why both children were ornery and miserable and impossible to manage.

I did my job anyway, telling her that both of the children could benefit from professional help. April, I explained, showed no serious problems but was insecure. Therapy for her was likely to be short-term and could reduce the risk of more severe problems in the future.

Ricky, on the other hand, was a troubled little boy, full of anger and likely to run away again. She interrupted at that point to blame the running away on the boy's father and said that come to think of it he reminded her of his father.

"Mrs. Moody," I said, "Ricky needs the chance to blow off steam on a regular basis."

"You know," she said, "Carlton and him are starting to get along better. Yesterday they were playing catch in the backyard and having a great time. I know Carlton's gonna be a good influence on him."

"Great. But that won't take the place of professional help."

"Doctor," she said, "I'm broke. Do you know how much lawyers cost? Just being here today is draining me dry."

"There are clinics that operate on a sliding scale based on ability to pay. I'll give some numbers to Mr. Worthy."

"Are they far? I don't drive freeways."

"I'll try to find one close to you, Mrs. Moody."

"Thank you, doctor." She sighed, picked herself up, and let me hold the door for her.

Watching her trudge down the hall like an old woman it was easy to forget she was twenty-nine years old.

I dictated my findings to Mal's secretary as she typed silently on a court stenographer's machine. When she left he brought out a bottle of Johnny Walker Black and poured us each a couple of fingers.

"Thanks for coming by, Alex."

"No problem, but I don't know that it did any good. She won't follow through."

"I'll see to it that she does. Tell her it's important for the case."

We sipped Scotch.

"Incidentally," he said, "the judge hasn't gotten any nasty surprises so far—apparently Moody's crazy but not stupid. But she's mega-pissed about the whole thing. She called the D.A. and ordered him to get someone on it. He dumped it on Foothill Division."

"Who said they'd been looking for him already."

"Right." He looked surprised. I told him about Milo's call to Fordebrand.

"Very impressive, Alex. More?" He picked up the bottle. I declined a refill. Good Scotch is hard to resist but talking about Moody reminds me of the importance of staying clear-headed.

"Anyway, Foothill claims to be looking for him seriously but they think he's gone into Angeles Crest."

"Wonderful."

Angeles Crest National Forest is 600,000 acres of wilderness bordering the city to the north. The Moodys had lived in nearby Sunland, and the forest would be familiar territory to Richard, a natural place to escape. Much of the acreage was impenetrable except on foot and a man could stay lost there for as long as he pleased. It was a haven for hikers, campers, naturalists, and climbers, as well as for packs of outlaw bikers who partied all night and sacked out in caves. And its ravines and washes were favorite dumping spots for bodies.

Just before we'd scuffled in the court parking lot, Moody'd talked about surviving in the wilderness, clearly including his children in the fantasy. I let Mal know that.

He nodded grimly.

"I've instructed Darlene to take the kids and get out of town for a while. Her folks have a farm up near Davis. They're leaving today."

"Won't he be able to figure that out?"

"If he comes out in the open. I'm hoping he decides to play mountain man for a while."

He threw up his arms.

"It's the best I can do, Alex."

The conversation was taking an unsettling turn. I got up to go and we shook hands. At the door I asked him if he'd ever heard of a lawyer named Norman Matthews.

"Stormin' Norman? That's a golden oldie. I went up against him at least a dozen times. Biggest ballbreaker in Beverly Hills."

"He was a divorce lawyer?"

"The best. Super-aggressive, had a reputation for getting his clients what they wanted no matter who he offended in the process. Handled lots of Hollywood dissolutions with big bucks at stake and got to thinking of himself as a star. Very image conscious—an Excalibur *and* a Corniche, conspicuous clothes, blonds on each arm, blew Dunhill latakia through a thousand-dollar meerschaum."

"He's a bit more spiritual nowadays."

"Yeah, I heard. Got a weird group down on the border. Calls himself Grand Noble Poobah or something like that."

"Noble Matthias. Why'd he leave law?"

He laughed uneasily.

"You might say it left him. This was five or six years ago. It was in the papers. I'm surprised you don't remember. Matthews was representing the wife of some playwright. The guy had just hit it big—a smash on Broadway—after ten years of eating air sandwiches. At that point the wife found another loser to mother and filed. Matthews got her everything—a huge chunk of royalties from the play and a healthy percentage of everything the guy would bring in for the next ten years. It was a publicized case and there was a press conference scheduled on the courtroom steps. Matthews and the wife were headed there when hubby came out of nowhere with a twenty-two. He shot them both in the head. She died but Matthews squeaked by after half a year of touch and go. Then he dropped out of sight, resurfaced a couple of years later as a maharishi. Your basic California story."

I thanked him for the information and turned to leave.

"Hey," he asked, "why the interest?"

"Nothing important. His name came up in conversation."

"Stormin' Norman," he smiled. "Sanctification through brain damage."

13

The next morning, Milo knocked on my door and woke me at six forty-five. The sky was alley-cat gray. It had rained all night and the air smelled like damp flannel. The glen harbored a relentless chill that seeped into my bones the moment I opened the door.

He wore a thin shiny black raincoat over a wrinkled white shirt, a brown and blue tie, and brown slacks. His chin was blued with stubble, his eyelids weighted by fatigue. There was mud on his brogues, which he scraped off along the edge of the terrace before coming in.

"We found two of the Swopes, the mother and father, up in Benedict Canyon. Shot in the head and back."

He talked rapidly without making eye contact and walked past me into the kitchen. I followed him and put up coffee. While it brewed I washed my face in the kitchen sink and he chewed on a log of French bread. Neither of us spoke until we'd sat down at my old oak table and punished our gullets with large swallows of scalding liquid.

"Some old character with a metal detector found them a little after one a.m. He's a rich guy, a retired dentist, has a big house off Benedict but likes to roam around in the dark prospecting. His gizmo picked up the coins in the father's pockets—the two of them weren't buried very deep. The rain had washed away some of the dirt and he could see part of a head in the moonlight. Poor fellow was shaking."

He looked downward, dispiritedly.

"Another detective picked up the squeal but when they identified the bodies he remembered my involvement and called me. He was scheduled for vacation anyway and more than happy to hand it over. I've been there since three."

"No sign of Woody and Nona?"

Milo shook his head.

"*Nada*. We combed the immediate area. The place we found them is just before the road climbs toward the Valley. Most of Benedict's pretty well built up but there's a small gully on the west side that the developers haven't gotten to. It's concave, kind of like a saucer in the ground, covered with brush and layered with about a foot of dead leaves. Easy to miss if you drive by quickly 'cause it's blocked from the road by big eucalyptus. We used the grid approach, went over it foot by foot. Funny thing is, we did dig up another body, but this one was all bones. From the shape of the pelvis, the M.E. says a woman. Been there for at least a couple of years."

He was concentrating on details to avoid dealing with the emotional impact of the murders. Taking a large gulp of coffee, he rubbed his eyes and shivered.

"I'm soaked. Lemme peel out of this."

He pulled off the raincoat and draped it over a chair.

"Let's hear it for sunny goddamn California," he snarled. "I feel like I've been marinating in a rice paddy."

"Want a warm shirt?"

"Nah." He rubbed his hands together, drank more coffee, and got up for a refill.

"Not a sign of the kids," he reiterated upon returning to the table. "Several possibilities present themselves: one, they weren't with the parents and escaped what went down. When they got back to the motel, they saw the blood and ran scared."

"Why wouldn't the family stick together if they were returning home?" I asked.

"Maybe she took him for an ice cream. While the parents packed."

"No way, Milo. He was too sick for that."

"Yeah, I keep forgetting that. Must be unconscious repression, huh?"

"Must be."

"Okay, hypothesis two, then. They weren't together because the sister snatched the kid. You told me Bev said she didn't like the parents. Could be it came to a head."

"Anything Bev has to say about her needs to be taken with a shaker of salt, Milo. Nona made it with a man she once loved. Down deep she hates the girl's guts."

"You told me yourself the kid was pissed the time you met her, how she lit into Melendez-Lynch. And the picture we get of her after talking to Rambo and Carmichael is one strange little girl."

"That's true. She sounds like she's got plenty of problems. But why would she abduct her brother? All indications are that she was self-centered, cut off from family feelings. She and Woody didn't have a close relationship. She rarely visited and when she did it was at night when he was asleep. Her not being there with the others makes sense. But not the rest of it."

"Gee, you're fun to be with," said Milo. "I'll call you next time I need a yes man."

His face opened in a giant yawn. When he'd taken in enough air he continued. "Everything you say is logical, pal, but I've gotta touch all bases. I called Houten in La Vista just before I came here. Woke the poor devil up and told him to scour the town for her and the kid. He was pretty broken up hearing about the parents, said he'd already searched carefully the first time I asked, but agreed to do it again."

"Including the Touch's place?"

"Especially there. Melendez-Lynch may have been right from the beginning. Even if Houten comes up empty they're sweet suspects. I'm heading down there today to check them out. Especially the two that visited the Swopes. A couple of my guys are going to the hospital to interview anyone who took care of the Swopes. With special emphasis on squeezing that asshole Valcroix."

I told him about Seth Fiacre's assessment of the Touch as a reclusive group that shunned the limelight and tacked on Mal's account of the greening of Norman Matthews.

"They don't seek converts," I pointed out. "They seclude themselves. What motivation would there be for them to get involved with outsiders?"

Milo seemed to ignore the question and expressed surprise at Noble Matthias's identity.

"Matthews is the guru? I always wondered what happened to him. I remember the case. It went down in Beverly Hills so we weren't involved. They locked the husband up in Atascadero and six months later he mixed himself a Draino cocktail." He smiled mirthlessly. "We used to call Matthews the 'Shyster to the Stars.' What do you know?"

He yawned again and drank more coffee.

"Motivation?" he repeated. "Maybe they thought they'd convinced the parents to treat the kid their way, there was a change of heart and things got out of control."

"That's pretty far out of control," I said.

"Don't forget what I told you in the motel room. About the world getting crazier and crazier. Besides, maybe the cultists were camera-shy when your professor friend studied them but not anymore. Weirdos change, like anyone else. Jim Jones was everyone's hero until he turned into Idi Amin."

"It's a good point."

"Of course it is. I'm a pro-fesh-you-nole." He laughed, a good warm sound soon replaced by silence made cold by unspoken words.

"There's another possibility," I said, finally.

"Now that you've mentioned it, yes." His green eyes darkened with melancholia. "The kids are buried somewhere else. Whoever did it got scared before he could finish dumping them at Benedict and took off. There are coyotes and all sorts of creepy crawlies out there. You could see a pair of eyes and easily get spooked."

I'd been heartsick and numb since learning of the killings, my attention vacillating between Milo's words and the images they evoked. But now the full impact of what he was saying slammed straight into me and I mustered up a wall of denial to block it out.

"You're still going to look for him, aren't you?"

He looked up at the urgency in my voice.

"We're canvassing Benedict from Sunset up into the Valley, Alex, doing door-to-doors on the chance someone saw something. But it was dark so an eyewitness is unlikely. We're also going to cruise the other canyons—Malibu, Topanga, Coldwater, Laurel, right here in the Glen. About a thousand man hours and unlikely to be productive."

I got back on the subject of the parents' murders because grim as it was, it was preferable to fantasizing about Woody's fate.

"Were they shot right there, in Benedict?" I asked.

"Not likely. There was no blood on the ground and we couldn't find any spent shells. The rain introduces a little uncertainty, but each of them had half a dozen bullet holes. That much shooting would make a lot of noise and there'd have to be some shells left behind. They were killed somewhere else, Alex, and then dumped. No footprints or tiretracks, but that you can definitely put down to the rain."

He ripped viciously at the French bread with small, sharp teeth, and chewed noisily.

"More coffee?" I offered.

"No thanks. My nerves are scraped raw as it is." He leaned forward, thick, spatulate fingers splayed on the table. "Alex, I'm sorry. I know you cared about the kid."

"It's like a bad dream," I admitted. "I'm trying not to think of him." Perversely, the small pale face floated into consciousness. A game of checkers in a plastic room . . .

"When I saw the motel room I really thought they'd gone home, that it was a family thing," he was saying morosely. "From the looks of the bodies, the M.E. guessed they were murdered a couple of days ago. Probably not too long after the kid was pulled out of the hospital."

"Hindsight is twenty-twenty, Milo," I said, trying to sound supportive. "There was no way anyone could have known."

"Right. Let me use your john."

*   *   *

After he left I set about pulling myself together—
with meager success. My hands were unsteady and my
head buzzed. The last thing I needed was to be left
alone with my helplessness and my anguish. I searched
for absolution through activity. I'd have gone to the
hospital to tell Raoul about the murders but Milo had
asked me not to. I paced the room, filled a cup with
coffee, tossed it down the sink, snatched up the paper
and turned to the movie section. A revival house in
Santa Monica was featuring an early matinee, a docu-
mentary on William Burroughs, which sounded sufficiently bizarre to crowd out reality. Just as I was
stepping out the door Robin called from Japan.

"Hello, lover," she said.

"Hello, babe. I miss you."

"Miss you, too, sweetie."

I took the phone to the bed and sat down facing
a framed picture of the two of us. I remember the day
it had been taken. We'd gone to the arboretum on a
Sunday in April and had asked a passing octogenarian
to do us the favor. Despite his trembling hands and
protestation of ignorance about modern cameras it had
come out beautifully.

We held each other against a backdrop of royal
purple rhododendrons and snowy camelias. Robin
stood in front, her back to my chest, my arms around
her waist. She wore tight jeans and a white turtleneck
that showed off her curves. The sun had picked up the
auburn highlights in her hair, which hung long and
curly, like coppery grapes. Her smile was wide and
open, the perfect teeth a crescent of white. Her face
was a valentine, her dark eyes liquid and dancing.

She was a beautiful woman, inside and out. Hearing the sound of her voice was sweetly painful.

"I bought you a silk kimono, Alex. Gray-blue, to match your eyes."

"Can't wait to see it. When are you coming home?"

"About another week, honey. They're tooling up to actually manufacture a gross of instruments and they want me here to inspect them."

"Sounds like things are going well."

"They are. But you sound distant. Is something wrong?"

"No. Must be the connection."

"You sure, baby?"

"Yes. Everything's fine. I miss you, that's all."

"You're mad at me, aren't you? For staying so long."

"No. Really. It's important. You have to do it."

"It's not like I'm having fun, you know. The first couple of days they entertained me, but after the amenities were over it was strictly business. Design studios and factories all day. And no male geishas to help me unwind at night!"

"Poor baby."

"You bet." She laughed. "I have to admit, though, it's a fascinating country. Very tense, very structured. Next time I go you have to come with me."

"Next time?"

"Alex, they love my designs. If the Billy Orleans does well they're sure to want another. We could go during cherry blossom time. You'd love it. They've got beautiful gardens—larger versions of ours—in the public parks. And I saw a koi almost five feet long. Square watermelons, sushi bars you wouldn't believe. It's incredible, hon."

"Sounds like it."

"Alex, what's wrong? And stop saying nothing."

"Nothing."

"Come on. I was so lonely, sitting by myself in this sterile hotel room, drinking tea and watching 'Kojak' with Japanese subtitles. I thought talking to you would help me feel alive again. But it's only made me sadder."

"I'm sorry, babe. I love you and I'm really proud of you. I'm trying really hard to be noble, to put my needs aside. But as it turns out, I'm just another selfish, sexist bastard, threatened by your success and worried that it won't be the same."

"Alex, it'll always be the same. The most precious thing in my life is us. Didn't you once tell me that all the busy little things we do—career, achievement—are just trim around the edges? That what's important is the intimacy we establish in our lifetime? I bought it. I really believe that."

Her voice broke. I wanted to hold her near.

"What's this about square watermelons?" I said.

We laughed together and the next five minutes were long-distance heaven.

She'd been traveling around the country but was now settled in Tokyo and would be there until returning to the States. I took down the address of her hotel and her room number. Her travel plan included an overnight stopover in Hawaii before the final flight back to L.A.. The idea of my flying to meet her in Honolulu and our spending a week together on Kauai came up as a lark but ended up as a serious possibility. She promised to call when her departure date had been determined.

"Do you know what's been keeping me going?" she giggled. "Remembering that wedding we went to last summer in Santa Barbara."

"The Biltmore, room three fifty-one?"

"I'm getting wet right now just thinking about it."

"Stop or I'll be limping all day."

"That's good. You'll appreciate me."

"Believe me, I already do."

We prolonged the good-byes and then she was gone.

I hadn't told her about my involvement with the Swopes. We'd always had an open relationship and I couldn't help feeling that holding back had been an unfaithful act of sorts. Still, I rationalized, it had been the right thing to do, because hearing about such horror from so great a distance would only have burdened her with intractable anxiety.

In an attempt to quell my guilt I spent a long time on the phone with a histrionic florist, arranging for a dozen coral roses to be sent halfway around the world.

14

The person on the phone was female, agitated, and vaguely familiar.

"Dr. Delaware, I need your help!"

I tried to place her. A patient from years back reaching out in the throes of crisis? If so, not being remembered would only compound her anxiety. I'd fake it until I figured out who it was.

"What can I do for you?" I said soothingly.

"It's Raoul. He's gotten himself into terrible trouble."

Bingo. Helen Holroyd. Her voice sounded different when heated by emotion.

"What kind of trouble, Helen?"

"He's in prison, down in La Vista!"

"What!"

"I just spoke to him—they allowed him one call. He sounds terrible! Heaven knows what they're doing to him! A genius locked up like a common criminal! Oh God, please help!"

She was falling apart, which didn't surprise me. Icy people often freeze themselves in order to hold in check a volcanic stew of disturbing and conflictual feelings. Emotional hibernation, if you will. Crack the ice and the stuff inside comes pouring out with all the discipline of molten lava.

She was sobbing and began to hyperventilate.

"Calm down," I said. "We'll clear it up. But first tell me how it happened."

It took a couple of minutes for her to regain control.

"The police came to the lab late yesterday afternoon. They told him about those people being killed. I was there, working on the other side of the room. Hearing about it didn't seem to affect him. He was at the computer, typing in data, and he didn't stop the entire time they were there. Just kept on working. I knew something was wrong. It's not like him to be that impassive. He had to be really upset. When they were gone I tried to talk to him but he shut me out. Then he left, just walked out of the building without telling anyone where he was going."

"And drove to La Vista."

"Yes! He must have thought about it all night and left early in the morning because he got there by ten and had some kind of altercation with someone. I'm not sure who, they wouldn't let us talk long and he was so agitated he wasn't making much sense. I called back and talked to the sheriff but he said they were holding Raoul for the Los Angeles police to question. He wouldn't tell me more, said I was free to get a lawyer, and hung up. He was rude and insensitive, talking about Raoul as if he were a criminal and my knowing him made me a criminal, too."

She sniffled, remembering the indignity.

"It's all so—Kafkaesque! I'm so confused, don't know how to help him. I thought of you because Raoul said you had connections with the police. Please tell me, what should I do?"

"Nothing for the time being. Let me make a few

calls and get back to you. Where are you calling from?"

"The lab."

"Don't go anywhere."

"I rarely do."

Milo wasn't available and the desk man at the station wouldn't tell me where he was so I asked for Delano Hardy, my friend's occasional partner, and was connected to him after being put on hold for ten minutes. Hardy is a dapper, balding black man with an easy wit and a ready smile. His skill with a rifle had once saved my life.

"Hey, Doc."

"Hi, Del. I need to talk to Milo. The guy at the desk was all hush-hush. Isn't he back from La Vista?"

"He's not back because he never went. Change of plans. We've been working on a very hot case and a big break came through yesterday."

"The stomach-shitter?"

"Yeah. We've got him cold and Milo and another guy have been locked up with the prick all morning playing good-cop, bad-cop."

"Congratulations on the bust. Could you give him a message to call me when he's free?"

"What's the trouble?"

I told him.

"Hold on. Lemme see if he's gonna break soon."

He returned to the phone moments later.

"He said give him another half hour. He'll call you."

"Thanks a lot, Del."

"No sweat. By the way, I'm still digging that Strat."

Hardy was a fellow guitarist, a first-rate musician who gigged with an R & B group after hours. I'd

bought him a vintage Fender Stratocaster in gratitude
for his marksmanship.

"Glad you're enjoying it. Let's jam again."

"Absolutely. Come by the club and bring your
axe. Gotta go now."

I called Helen and told her it would take time. She
sounded shaky so I talked her through it by getting her
to tell me about her work. When the chill came back
into her voice I knew she'd be okay. At least for a
while.

Milo called an hour later.

"Can't talk long, Alex. We've got the asshole
nailed. A Saudi Arabian student, related to the royal
family. It's gonna get hairy but I'll be damned if this
one is gonna slither away on diplomatic immunity."

"How'd you get him?"

"I wish I could say it was brilliant police work.
He attacked another woman and she had mace in her
purse. Sprayed the fucker until he shrieked, knee-
dropped him, and called us. Little wisp of a thing,
too," he added, with admiration. "We found articles
belonging to the other victims in his apartment. The
guy shits his pants when he gets excited. It's been a giggle interrogating him. Only cheerful note is that his
asshole lawyer has to sit there and smell it, too."

"Sounds like fun. Listen, if you can't talk now—"

"It's okay. I took a break. Gotta come up for air.
Del told me about the Cuban. I called Houten and he
told me what happened. Seems your friend is a hot-
head. Drove into town this morning like Gary Cooper
before the big showdown. Barged in on Houten, demanded he arrest the Touch people for the murder of
the Swopes, and claimed the boy and Nona were being
held captive at their place. Houten told him they'd already been questioned by him, that I was planning to
come down and do it again, and that the premises had

been thoroughly searched. Melendez-Lynch wouldn't listen, got really abusive and eventually Houten had to basically kick him out. He got in his car and drove straight to the Retreat."

I groaned.

"Wait, it gets better. Apparently they have big iron gates at the front entrance that they keep locked. Melendez-Lynch drove up and started screaming for them to let him in. A couple of them came out to calm him down and it got physical. He absorbed most of the damage. They went back in, he started up his car and rammed the gate. At that point they called Houten and he busted Melendez-Lynch for disturbing the peace, malicious mischief, and who knows what else. Houten said the guy seemed like a lunatic and he got to wondering if we'd be interested in interviewing him. So he locked him up, offered him an attorney, which he refused, and gave him the proverbial one phone call."

"Unbelievable."

Milo laughed.

"Isn't it? Between him and Valcroix and the stories Rick tells me, I'm losing what little faith I had in modern medicine. I mean, these guys are *not* confidence inspiring."

"Maybe the Swopes didn't think so either."

"That's right. If they saw the kind of flakiness we've been uncovering I can understand them wanting out."

"Not as far out as they got."

"Yeah. Once we're sure the Saudi's off the streets their case will be my number one problem. But it's going to have to wait awhile because if we don't pay close attention to Shitpants, he'll weasel out and be back in Riyadh before we know it."

His words chilled me. Human life meant a lot to Milo, and if he thought Woody and Nona were alive he'd find a way, Saudi or not, to pursue their case aggressively.

I fought back my anger.

"When did you decide they were dead?"

"What?—Jesus, Alex, stop analyzing! I haven't decided a goddamn thing. I've got *platoons* going through the canyons, I check the APBs at least two, three times a day. So, it's not like I'm sitting on my ass. But the fact is I've got a suspect in custody in one case and zilch on the other. Where would *you* put your priorities?"

"Sorry. I was way out of line. It's just that it's hard to think of that little boy as beyond hope."

"I know, pal." His tone softened. "I'm on the rag, too. Too much time spent with blood and crud. Just be careful you're not getting overinvolved. Again."

Unconsciously, I fingered my jaw.

"Okay. Now what's the story with Raoul? I need to tell his girlfriend something."

"No story. I told Houten we didn't care if he let him go. The guy may be whacko but right now he's not a suspect. Houten says he wants him escorted out of there. Melendez-Lynch hasn't stopped ranting since they locked him up, and they don't want him causing trouble the minute they let him out. If you think you can keep him calm, I'll tell Houten to release him to your custody. Your being a shrink would make it look better, too."

"I don't know," I said. "I've seen Raoul pull tantrums but never like this."

"Up to you. Unless the guy calms down and agrees to talk to a lawyer or someone comes to get him, he could be there for a while."

If word got out about Melendez-Lynch's incarceration, his professional reputation would be compromised. I knew of no one close to him except Helen

Holroyd and she was definitely not up to the task of dragging him away from La Vista.

"They're calling me back, Alex," Milo was saying, "gotta hold my nose and jump into it."

"All right. Call the sheriff. Tell him I'll get down there as soon as I can."

"What a nice guy. Bye."

I called Helen again and told her I'd secured the release of the esteemed Dr. Melendez-Lynch. She thanked me effusively and was starting to lapse into tears before I cut her off. For her own good.

15

The Seville glided onto the interstate shortly past noon. The first half of the two-hour journey to La Vista was a southward slice through the industrial underbelly of California. I sped past stockyards and freight docks, mammoth auto dealerships, grimy warehouses, and factories belching effluvia into a sky obscured by billboards. I kept the windows closed, the air conditioning on, and Flora Purim on the tape deck.

At Irvine the terrain shifted suddenly to endless expanses of green—fields of rich, dark soil stitched precisely with emerald rows of tomatoes, peppers, strawberries, and corn, spasmodically bathed by whirligig sprinklers. I opened the window and let in the good stench of manure. A while later the highway edged closer to the ocean and the fields gave way to the affluent suburbs of Orange County, then thinned to miles of empty scrub enclosed by barbed chain-link fence—government land, rumored to harbor secret nuclear testing plants.

Just past Oceanside, traffic going the other way slowed to a crawl: the Border patrol had set up a spot check for illegal aliens. Gray-uniformed officers in Smoky the Bear hats peered into each vehicle, waving on the majority, pulling a few over for closer scrutiny. The process had a ceremonial look to it, which was appropriate, for stemming the tide of those yearning for the good life was as feasible as capturing the rain in a thimble.

I exited a few miles later, heading east on a state highway that slogged through blocks of fast-food joints and self-serve gas stations before turning into two-lane blacktop.

The road rose, climbing toward mountains veiled by lavender mist. Twenty minutes out of the junction and there wasn't another vehicle in sight. I passed a granite quarry where mantislike machines dipped into the earth and brought up piles of rocks and dirt, a horse ranch, a field of grazing Holsteins, then nothing. Dusty signs heralded the construction of "luxury planned communities" and "town-homes," but apart from one abandoned project—the roofless remains of a warren of small houses crammed into a sun-baked gully—it was empty, silent land.

As the altitude increased the scenery grew lush. Acres of eucalyptus-shaded citrus groves and a mile of avocado preceded the appearance of La Vista. The town sat in a valley at the foot of the mountains, surrounded by forest, vaguely alpine. A wayward glance and I would have missed it.

The main drag was Orange Avenue and a good part of it was given over to a sprawling gravel yard filled with somnolent threshers, tillers, bulldozers, and tractors. A long, low, glass-fronted structure occupied one end of the yard and a worn wooden sign above the entrance announced sales, rental, and repair of farm equipment and power tools.

The street was quiet and ribbed with diagonal parking lines. Few of the spaces were occupied, those that were housed half-ton pickups and old sedans. The posted speed limit was 15 m.p.h. I decelerated and coasted past a dry-goods store, a market, an eight-dollar-a-visit chiropractor ("no appointment necessary"), a barbershop complete with spinning pole, and a windowless tavern named Erna's.

City Hall was a two-story square of pink cinder block midway through the town. A concrete walkway ran down the center of a well-tended lawn, flanked by towering date palms, and leading to brass double doors, propped open. Weathered brass rods bearing Old Glory and the flag of California jutted out above the entrance.

I parked in front of the building, stepped out into the dry heat, and walked to the door. A plaque commemorating La Vista's World War II dead and dated 1947 was inlaid in the block at eye level, just left of the doorpost. I stepped into an entry hall containing a pair of slat-backed oak benches and nothing else. I looked for a directory, saw none, heard the sound of typing and walked toward it, footsteps echoing in the empty corridor.

There was a woman pecking at a Royal manual in a stuffy room full of oak file cabinets. Both she and her machine were of antique vintage. An electric fan perched atop one of the files spun and blew, causing the ends of the woman's hair to dance.

I cleared my throat. She looked up with alarm, then smiled, and I asked her where the sheriff's office could be found. She directed me to a rear stairwell leading to the second floor.

At the top of the stairs was a tiny courtroom that looked as if it hadn't been used in a long time. The word SHERIFF had been painted in glossy black on lime green plaster. Underneath it, was an arrow pointing to the right.

La Vista law enforcement was headquartered in a small dark room containing two wooden desks, an unmanned switchboard, and a silent teletype machine. A map of the county covered one wall. Wanted posters and a well-stocked gun rack rounded out the decor. At the center of the rear wall was a metal door with a four inch wire-glass window.

The beige-uniformed man at one of the desks looked too young to be a peace officer—pink chipmunk cheeks and guileless hazel eyes under brown bangs. But he was the only one there and the nametag over his breast pocket said Deputy W. Bragdon. He was reading a farm journal and when I entered, looked up and gave me a cop's stare: wary, analytic, and inherently distrustful.

"I'm Dr. Delaware, come to pick up Dr. Melendez-Lynch."

W. Bragdon stood, hitched up his holster, and disappeared through the metal door. He returned with a man in his fifties who could have stepped off a Remington canvas.

He was short and bow-legged, but broad shouldered and rock-solid, and he walked with a hint of a bantam swagger. His razor-creased trousers were of the same tan material as the deputy's uniform, his shirt green plaid and pearl buttoned. A crisp, wide-brimmed Stetson rested squarely atop his long head. The suggestion of vanity was confirmed by his tailoring: the shirt and slacks had been tapered to hug a trim physique.

The hair under the hat was dun and cropped close to narrow temples. His facial features were prominent and somewhat avian. A thick gray handlebar mustache flared under a strong beakish nose.

I was drawn to his hands, which were unusually thick and large. One rested on the butt of a long-barreled Colt.45 nestling in a hand-tooled holster, the other extended in a handshake.

"Doctor," said a deep mellow voice, "Sheriff

Raymond Houten." His grip was solid but he didn't exert pressure—a man well aware of his own strength.

He turned to Bragdon. "Walt." The baby-faced deputy looked me over once more and returned to his desk.

"Come on in, Doctor."

On the other side of the tiny mesh window were ten feet of corridor. To the left was a bolted metal door, to the right his office, high-ceilinged, sunlit, and redolent of tobacco.

He sat behind an old desk and motioned me to a scarred leather armchair. Removing his hat, he tossed it on a rack fashioned from elk antlers.

Pulling out a pack of Chesterfields, he offered me one and when I declined, lit up, leaned back, and looked out the window. A large bay window afforded a view of Orange Avenue and his eyes followed the path of a semi hauling a load of produce. He waited until the big truck had rumbled out of sight before speaking.

"You're a psychiatrist?"

"Psychologist."

He held the cigarette between thumb and forefinger and inhaled.

"And you're here as Dr. Lynch's friend, not in a professional capacity."

His tone implied the latter would have been more than appropriate.

"That's correct."

"I'll take you to see him in just a minute. But I want to prepare you. He looks like he fell into a combine. We didn't do it."

"I understand. Detective Sturgis said he started a fight with members of the Touch and came out the worse for it."

Houten's mouth twisted under his mustache.

"That about sums it up. From what I understand Dr. Lynch is a prominent man," he said skeptically.

"He's an internationally renowned expert on children's cancer."

Another look out the window. I noticed a diploma hanging on the wall behind the desk. He'd earned a bachelor's degree in criminology from one of the state colleges.

"Cancer." He mouthed the word softly. "My wife had it. Ten years ago. It ate her up like some wild animal before it killed her. The doctors wouldn't tell us anything. Hid behind their jargon till the end."

His smile was frightful.

"Still," he said, "I don't recall any of them quite like Dr. Lynch."

"He's one of a kind, Sheriff."

"Seems to have a temper problem. What is he, Guatemalan?"

"Cuban."

"Same thing. The *latino* temperament."

"What he did here wasn't typical. To my knowledge he's never been in trouble with the law."

"I know that, Doctor. We ran him through the computer. That's one reason I'm willing to be lenient and let him go with just a fine. I've got enough to hold him over for quite a while—trespassing, assault, malicious mischief, interfering with an officer. Not to mention the damage he did to their gate with his car. But the circuit judge doesn't get up this way until winter and we'd have to ship him to San Diego. It would be complicated."

"I appreciate your leniency and I'll write a check for any damages."

He nodded, put out his cigarette, and got on the phone.

"Walt, write up Dr. Lynch's fines and include the estimate on the gate ... No need, Dr. Delaware will come by and pay for it." A glance in my direction. "Take his check, he looks like an honest man."

When he hung up he said, "It's going to be a sizable sum. The man created lots of problems."

"He must have been traumatized hearing about the Swope murders."

"We were all *traumatized*, Doctor. Nineteen hundred and seven people live in this town, not counting migrants. Everyone knows everyone. Yesterday we flew the flag at half mast. When little Woody got sick it was a kick in the gut for all of us. Now this . . ."

The sun had changed position and it flooded the office. Houten squinted. His eyes disappeared in a thatch of crow's feet.

"Dr. Lynch seems to have gotten it into his head that the children are here, over in the Retreat," he said expectantly. I got the feeling I was being tested, and turned it back on him.

"And you feel that's out of the question."

"You bet. Those Touch people are—unusual—but they're not criminals. When folks found out who bought the old monastery, there was one hell of an uproar. I was supposed to play Wyatt Earp and run 'em out of town." He smiled sleepily. "Farmers don't always grasp the finer points of due process, so I had to do a bit of educating. The day they drove into town and actually moved in, it was a circus, everyone gawking and pointing.

"That very day I went over and had a chat with Mr. Matthias, gave him a sociology lesson. Told him they'd do best to keep a low profile, patronize local businesses, make timely contributions to the church auxiliary."

It was precisely the strategy Seth Fiacre had described.

"They've been here three years, without a traffic

ticket. Folks have grown used to them. I drop in on them when I please, so that everyone knows there's no witchcraft brewing behind those gates. They're just as strange as the day they moved in. But that's all. Strange, not criminal. If felonies were being committed, I'd know about it."

"Any chance Woody and Nona could be somewhere else around here?"

He lit up again and regarded me coldly.

"Those children were raised here. They played in the fields and explored the dirt roads and never fell into harm's way. One trip to your big city and all that's changed. A small town is like a family, doctor. We don't murder each other, or kidnap each other's young."

His experience and training should have taught him that families are the cauldrons in which violence is brewed. But I said nothing.

"There's one more thing I want you to hear so that you can pass it along to Dr. Lynch." He got up and stood in front of the window. "This is one giant TV screen. The show is called La Vista. Some days it's a soap opera, other times a comedy. Once in a while there's action and adventure. No matter what's on, I watch it every day."

"I understand."

"I thought you would, Doctor."

He retrieved his hat and put it on.

"Let's go see how the renowned expert is doing."

The bolt on the metal door responded noisily to Houten's key. On the other side were three cells in a row. I thought of the Laminar Airflow rooms. The jail was hot and humid, and it stank of body odor and solitude.

"He's in the last one," said Houten.

I followed his bootsteps down the windowless passageway.

Raoul was sitting on a metal bench bolted to the wall, staring at the floor. His cell was seven feet square and contained a bed, also bolted down and covered by a thin, stained mattress, a lidless toilet, and a zinc washbasin. From the smell of things the toilet wasn't in peak condition.

Houten unlocked the door and we walked in.

Raoul looked up with one eye. The other was blackened and swollen shut. A crust of dried blood had formed under his left ear. His lip was split and the color of raw steak. Several buttons were missing from his white silk shirt, which hung open, exposing his soft hairy chest. There was a blue-black bruise along his ribcage. A shirtsleeve had been ripped at the seam and it dangled vestigially. His belt, tie, and shoelaces had been taken from him and I found the sight of his alligator shoes, caked with dirt, the tongue protruding, especially pathetic.

Houten saw my expression and said, "We wanted to clean him up but he started fussing so we let it be."

Raoul muttered something in Spanish. Houten looked at me, his expression that of a parent faced with a tantruming child.

"You can go now, Dr. Lynch," he said. "Dr. Delaware will drive you home. You can have your car towed back to Los Angeles at your expense, or leave it here to be fixed. Zack Piersall knows foreign ca—"

"I'm not going anywhere," snapped Raoul.

"Dr. Lynch—"

"It's *Melendez*-Lynch, and your deliberate failure to remember that doesn't intimidate me. I'm not leaving until the truth comes out."

"Doctor, you're in a lot of trouble, potentially. I'm

letting you go with fines in order to simplify things for all of us. I'm sure you've been under a lot of strain—"

"Don't patronize me, Sheriff. And stop covering for those murderous quacks!"

"Raoul—" I said.

"No, Alex, you don't understand. These people are closed-minded imbeciles. The tree of knowledge could sprout on their doorstep and they wouldn't pick the fruit."

Houten moved his jaws as if trying to bring up a cud of patience.

"I want you out of my town," he said softly.

"I won't go," Raoul insisted, gripping the bench with both hands to demonstrate his intransigence.

"Sheriff," I said, "let me speak to him alone."

Houten shrugged, left the cell, and locked me in. He walked away, and after the metal door closed behind him I turned to Raoul.

"What the hell's the matter with you!"

"Don't lecture me, Alex." He stood and shook a fist in my face.

I stepped back instinctively. He stared at his upraised hand, dropped it to his side and mumbled an apology. Collapsing as if he'd been fileted, he sat back down.

"What in the world possessed you to conduct a one-man invasion of this place?" I asked him.

"I know they're in there," he panted. "Behind those gates. I can feel it!"

"You turned the Volvo into an assault tank because of feelings? Remember when you called intuition 'just another form of soft-headed hocus-pocus'?"

"This is different. They wouldn't let me in. If that's not proof they're hiding something I don't know what it is!" He punched his palm with his fist. "I'll get in there somehow and tear that place apart until I find him."

"That's crazy. What is it about the Swopes that's turned you into a damned cowboy?"

He covered his face with his hands.

I sat down next to him and put my arm around his shoulder. He was soaked with sweat.

"Come on, let's get out of here," I urged.

"Alex," he said hoarsely, his breath sour and strong, "oncology is a specialty for those who are willing to learn how to lose graciously. Not to love failure or accept it, but to suffer with dignity, as a patient must. Did you know that I was first in my medical school class?"

"I'm not surprised."

"I had my pick of residencies. Many oncologists are the cream of medicine. And yet we confront failure each day of our lives."

He pushed himself up and walked to the bars, running his hands up and down the ragged and rusty cylinders.

"Failure," he repeated. "But the victories are uncommonly sweet. The salvage and reconstruction of a life. What could create greater illusions of omnipotence, eh, Alex?"

"There'll be many more victories," I assured him. "You know that better than anyone. Remember the speech you used to give at fund raisers—the slide show with all those pictures of cured kids? Let this one go."

He swiveled around and faced me, eyes blazing.

"As far as I'm concerned that boy is alive. Until I see his corpse I won't believe otherwise."

I tried to speak but he cut me off.

"I didn't go into this field because of mawkish sentimentality—no favorite cousin died of leukemia, no grandpapa wasted away of carcinoma. I became an oncologist because medicine is the science—and the art—of *fighting death*. And cancer is death. From the first time, as a medical student, when I viewed those monstrous, primitive, *evil* cells under the microscope, I was seized with that truism. And I knew what my life's work would be."

Beads of perspiration had collected on his high dark forehead. The coffee bean eyes glistened and roamed the cell.

"I won't give up," he said, radiating defiance. "Only the conquest of death, my friend, allows a glimpse of immortality."

He was unreachable, caught up in his own frantic vision of the world. Obsessive and quixotic and denying what was most probable: Woody and Nona were dead, buried somewhere in the shifting mulch beneath the city.

"Let the police handle it, Raoul. My friend's due to come down here soon. He'll check everything out."

"The police," he spat. "A lot of good they've been. Bureaucratic pencil pushers. Mediocre minds of limited vision. Like that stupid cowboy out there. Why aren't they here right now—every day is crucial for that little boy. They don't care, Alex. To them he's just another statistic. But not to me!"

He folded his arms in front of him, as if warding off the indignity of confinement, unaware of his derelict appearance.

I'd long thought that a surfeit of sensitivity could be a killing thing, too much insight malignant in its own right. The best survivors—there are studies that show it—are those blessed with an inordinate ability to deny. And keep on marching.

Raoul would march till he dropped.

I'd always considered him a touch manic. Perhaps as manic at the core as Richard Moody, but more generously endowed intellectually so that the excess energy was channeled honorably. For the good of society. Now, too many failures had converged upon him:

the Swopes' rejection of treatment, which, because he lived his work, was seen as a rejection of *him*, an atheism of the worst sort. The abduction of his patient—humiliation and loss of control. And now, death, the ultimate insult.

Failure had made him irrational.

I couldn't leave him there but didn't know how to get him out.

Before either of us could speak, the sound of approaching footsteps punctuated the silence. Houten peered into the cell, keys in hand.

"Ready, gentlemen?"

"I've had no luck, Sheriff."

The news deepened the worry lines around his eyes. "You're choosing to stay with us, Dr. *Melendez-Lynch*?"

"Until I've found my patient."

"Your patient isn't here."

"I don't believe that."

Houten's mouth tightened and his eyebrows lowered. "I'd like you out of there, Dr. Delaware."

He turned a key, held the door barely open and kept a watchful eye on Raoul as I slipped through.

"Good-bye, Alex," said the oncologist with a martyr's solemnity.

Houten spoke to him in clipped cadence.

"If you think prison is fun, sir, you're going to learn different. I promise you that. In the meantime, I'm getting you a lawyer."

"I refuse legal services."

"I'm getting you one anyway, Doctor. Whatever happens to you is going to be by the book."

He turned on his heel and stomped away.

As we left the jail I caught a last glimpse of Raoul behind the bars. There wasn't any good reason for me to feel unfaithful, but I did.

16

Houten made a phone call out of earshot. Ten minutes later a man in shirtsleeves showed up and the sheriff came forward to greet him.

"Thanks for coming on such short notice, Ezra."

"Pleased to help, Sheriff." The man's voice was soft, modulated, and even.

He looked to be in his late forties, medium-sized but sparely built, with a scholar's stoop. Everything about him was compact and neat. The smallish head was covered with thin salt-and-pepper hair combed straight back. The ears were elfin and close set. His facial features were regular but too delicate to be handsome. His short-sleeved white shirt was spotless and, despite the heat, free of wrinkles. His khaki trousers seemed freshly laundered. He wore rimless octagonal eyeglasses and carried a clip-on case for them in his breast pocket.

He looked like a man who never perspired.

I stood up and he appraised me mildly. ·

"Ezra," said Houten, "this is Dr. Delaware, a psychologist from Los Angeles. Came all the way down to take back the one I told you about. Doctor, meet Mr. Ezra Maimon, the best lawyer in town."

The neat man laughed gently.

"The Sheriff's engaging in a bit of hyperbole," he said and held out a thin callused hand. "I'm the *only* attorney in La Vista, and the cases I usually work with are made of wood."

"Ezra owns a rare fruit nursery just out of town," explained Houten. "Claims he's retired but we still get him to do a bit of lawyering from time to time."

"Wills and small estates are comparatively simple matters," said Maimon. "If this turns into criminal defense you'll have to bring in a specialist."

"That's all right," Houten twirled one of his mustaches. "This is no criminal case. Yet. Just a little problem, like I told you over the phone."

Maimon nodded.

"Tell me the details," he said.

He listened quietly and impassively, turning once or twice to smile at me. When Houten was through, the attorney placed a finger to his lips and gazed up at the ceiling, as if doing mental arithmetic. After a minute of silent contemplation he said, "Let me see my client."

He spent half an hour in the cell. I tried to kill the time by reading a magazine for highway patrolmen until I found that it specialized in graphic photoessays of fatal road wrecks accompanied by detailed descriptions of the vehicular horrors. I couldn't imagine why those who witnessed such carnage as part of their daily routine would be attracted to a photographic reprise. Perhaps it provided distance—the true solace of the voyeur. I put the magazine aside and contented myself with watching W. Bragdon read about alfalfa culture while he picked at his cuticles.

Finally a buzzer rang.

"Go in and get him, Walt," ordered Houten.

Bragdon said yessir, left, and came back with Maimon.

"I think," said the attorney, "we may be able to reach a compromise."

"Run it by me, Ezra."

The three of us sat around one of the desks.

"Dr. Melendez-Lynch is a very intelligent man," said Maimon. "Perhaps overly persistent. But not, in my opinion, at all malicious."

"He's a pain in the butt, Ezra."

"He's been a little overzealous in his attempts at fulfilling his medical obligations. But, as we all know, Woody's deathly ill. Dr. Melendez-Lynch feels he has the means to cure him and he sees himself as trying to save a life."

Maimon spoke with quiet authority. He could have acted as Houten's mouthpiece but instead seemed to be functioning as a true advocate. I didn't think it was for my benefit and I was impressed.

Houten's face darkened with anger.

"The boy's not here. You know that as well as I do."

"My client is an empiricist. He wants to see that for himself."

"No way is he going near that place, Ezra."

"I agree with you. That would be inviting trouble. However he did agree to Dr. Delaware's conducting a search of the Retreat. Promised to pay his fines and leave without a fuss if the good doctor finds nothing suspicious."

It was a simple solution. But neither Houten nor I had come up with it. He, because his appetite for concession wasn't hearty in the first place and he'd already had his fill. And I'd been too overwhelmed by Raoul's fanaticism to think straight.

The sheriff digested it.

"I can't force Matthias to open the place up."

"Of course not. He has every right to refuse. If he does we'll reapproach the problem."

An eminently logical man.

Houten turned his attention to me.

"What about it? You up for it?"

"Sure. Whatever works."

Houten went into his office and returned saying Matthias had okayed the visit. Maimon had another talk with Raoul, buzzed, was retrieved by Bragdon and left, telling the sheriff to call him if he was needed. Houten put on his hat and absently touched the butt of his Colt. He and I climbed down the stairs and out of the building. We got into a white El Camino decaled on the door with the sheriff's star. He gunned the engine, which sounded supercharged, and turned right in front of city hall.

The road forked a half mile out of town. Houten headed right, driving quickly and smoothly, accelerating around turns that would have given a stranger pause. The road narrowed and grew dim in the shadows of bordering conifers. The El Camino's tires churned up dust as it sped past. A jackrabbit in our path froze, quivered, and bounded into the shelter of the tall trees.

Houten managed to pull out a Chesterfield and light it without reducing speed. He drove another two miles, sucking in smoke and surveying the countryside with a cop's scanning eyes. At the top of a rise he turned abruptly, drove a hundred feet, and braked to a stop in front of a pair of black-painted arched iron gates.

The entrance to the Retreat was unlabeled as such.

Prickly mounds of cactus squatted at the outer edges of both gates. A tide of electric pink bougainvillaea flowed over one of the adobe gateposts. A single climbing rosebush awash with scarlet blooms and studded with thorns embraced the other. He turned off the engine and we were greeted by silence. And all around, the deep, secretive green of the forest.

Houten stubbed out his cigarette, dismounted the truck, and strode up to the entrance. There was a large columnar lockbox affixed to one gate, but when he pushed the iron door, it swung open.

"They like it quiet," he said. "We'll walk from here."

An unpaved path lined with smooth brown stones and meticulously barbered beds of succulents had been excised from the forest. It climbed and we moved briskly, the pace set by Houten. He hiked rather than walked, muscles swelling through the tautness of his slacks, arms swinging by his sides, military fashion. California jays squawked and fussed. Large fuzzy bees nuzzled up to the labia of wildflowers. The air smelled meadow-fresh.

The sun bore down relentlessly on the unshaded path. My throat was dry and I felt the sweat trickle down my back. Houten seemed as crisp as ever. Ten minutes of walking brought us to the top of the road.

"That's it," said Houten. He stopped to pull out another cigarette and light it in the shelter of cupped hands. I mopped my brow and gazed down at the valley below.

I saw perfection and it unnerved me.

The Retreat still looked like a monastery, with its towering cathedral and high walls. An assortment of smaller buildings sat behind the walls and created a maze of courtyards. A large wooden crucifix topped the belfry of the churchtower, a brand burned into the azure flanks of the sky. The front windows were leaded and supported by wooden balconies. The roofs and the tops of the walls were layered with red clay tile. The walls were fresh vanilla stucco splashed dove white where the sun hit. A great deal of care had been taken to preserve the intricate moldings and borders scored into the stucco.

A running brook circled the compound like a moat. Above it floated an arched viaduct that bled into a brick pathway at the point where solid ground reasserted itself. The path was hooded by a stone arbor caressed by tendrils of grape vine, ruby clusters of fruit ponderous amid the green leaves.

To the front of the compound was a small patch of lawn shaded by ancient gnarled oaks. The big twisted trees danced like witches around a fountain that spat into an enormous stone urn. Beyond the buildings were acres of farmland. I made out corn, cucumbers, groves of citrus and olive, a sheep pasture and vineyards, but there was plenty more. A handful of white-garbed figures worked the land. Heavy machinery buzzed wasplike in the distance.

"Pretty, isn't it?" asked Houten resuming the hike.

"Beautiful. Like out of another time."

He nodded. "When I was a kid I used to climb around the hills, try to get a peek at the monks—they wore heavy brown robes no matter how hot it got. Never talked to anyone or had anything to do with folks in town. The gates were always locked."

"Must have been nice growing up here."

"Why's that?"

I shrugged.

"The open air, the freedom."

"Freedom, huh?" His smile was abrupt and bitter. "Farming is just another word for bondage."

His jaw set and he kicked at a rock with sudden

savagery. I'd hit some kind of nerve and quickly changed the subject.

"When did the monks leave?"

He sucked on his cigarette before answering.

"Seven years ago. The land went fallow. Scrub and brambles. Couple corporations thought of buying it—executive resort and all that—but all of 'em backed out. The buildings weren't suited to it—rooms like cells, no heat, looked like a church any way you cut it. The cost of renovation would have been too high."

"But perfect for the Touch."

He shrugged.

"Something for everyone in this world."

The front door was rounded at the top, a slab of stout boards braced by wide iron bands. Inside was a three-story white-walled entrance floored with Mexican pavers and skylit from above. A smear of color reflected from the stained-glass windows rainbowed the tiles. The spicy aroma of incense suggested itself. The air was cool, almost to the point of refrigeration.

A woman in her sixties sat at a wooden table in front of a pair of oversized doors that were rounded and banded like the one out front. Above them was a wooden sign that said SANCTUARY. The woman's hair had been tied back in a ponytail and fastened with a leather thong. She wore a sack dress of raw white cotton and sandals on her feet. Her face was weathered, bland and pleasant, and free of makeup or other pretense. Her hands were in her lap and she smiled, reminding me of a well-behaved schoolchild. The teacher's pet.

"Good afternoon, Sheriff."

"Hello, Maria. Like to see Matthias."

She rose gracefully. The skirt reached below her knees.

"He's waiting for you."

She led us to the left of the sanctuary down a long hallway unadorned except for potted palms placed at ten-foot intervals. There was a single door at the end, which she held open for us.

The room was dim and lined with books on three walls. The floor was pine plank. The incense smell was stronger. There was no desk, only three plain wooden chairs arranged in an isosceles triangle. At the peak of the triangle sat a man.

He was long, lean, and angular and wore a tunic and drawstring trousers of the same raw cotton as Maria's dress. His feet were bare, but a pair of sandals lay on the floor by his chair. His hair was the waxy, amber-tinted white that is the heritage of some blonds grown to maturity, and was cropped short. His beard was a shade darker—more amber and less snow—and hung across his chest. It curled luxuriantly and he stroked it as if it were a pet. His brow was high and domed and I saw the crease just below the hairline, an indentation you could rest your thumb in. The eyes, cradled in deep sockets, were gray-blue in color, not dissimilar from mine. But I hoped mine gave off more warmth.

"Please sit." His voice was powerful and somewhat metallic.

"This is Dr. Delaware, Matthias. Doctor, Noble Matthias."

The imperial title sounded silly. I searched for mirth on Houten's face but he looked dead-serious.

Matthias kept stroking his beard. He sat meditatively still, a man not uncomfortable with silence.

"Thanks for cooperating," said Houten stiffly. "Hopefully we can clear this thing up and move along."

The white head nodded. "Whatever will help."

"Dr. Delaware would like to ask you a few questions and then we'll take a stroll around."

Matthias remained in repose.

Houten turned to me.

"It's your show."

"Mr. Matthias," I began.

"Just Matthias, please. We eschew titles."

"Matthias, I'm not here to intrude upon you or your—"

He interrupted me with a wave of his hand.

"I'm well aware of the nature of your visit. Ask what you need to ask."

"Thank you. Dr. Melendez-Lynch feels you had something to do with the removal of Woody Swope from the hospital and the family's subsequent disappearance."

"Urban madness," said the guru. "Madness." He repeated the word as if testing it for suitability as a mantra.

"I'd appreciate hearing any theories you might have about it."

He inhaled deeply, closed his eyes, opened them, and spoke.

"I can't help you. They were private people. As are we. We barely knew them. There were brief encounters—passing each other on the road, perfunctory smiles. Once or twice we purchased seeds from them. In the summer of our first season the girl worked for us as a scullery maid."

"Temporary job?"

"Correct. In the beginning we were not yet self-sufficient and we hired several of the local youngsters to help. Her duties were in the kitchen, as I recall. Scrubbing, scouring, readying the ovens for use."

"How was she as a worker?"

A smile vented the cotton-candy beard.

"We are rather ascetic by contemporary standards. Most young people would not be attracted to that."

Houten broke in. "Nona was—is a live one. Not a bad kid, just a little on the wild side."

The message was clear: she'd been a problem. I remembered Carmichael's story about the stag party. That kind of spontaneity could wreak havoc in a place that prized discipline. She'd probably come on to the men. But if that had anything to do with the issue at hand I couldn't see it.

"Anything else you could tell me that might help?"

He stared at me. His gaze was intense, almost tangible. It was hard not to look away.

"I'm afraid not."

Houten shifted restlessly in his chair. Nicotine fidgets. His hand went up to his cigarette pocket then stopped.

"I'm gonna take some air," he said and walked out. Matthias didn't seem to notice his exit.

"You didn't know the family well," I went on. "Yet two of your people visited them at the hospital. I'm not doubting your word but it's a question you're bound to be asked again."

He sighed.

"We had business in Los Angeles. Baron and Delilah were assigned to handle it. We felt it would be gracious for them to visit the Swopes. They brought the family fresh fruit from our orchards."

"Not," I smiled, "for medicinal purposes."

"No," he said, amused. "For nourishment. And pleasure."

"So this was a social call."

"In a sense."

"What do you mean?"

"We're not sociable. We don't make small talk. Visiting them was an act of good will, not part of some nefarious scheme. No attempt was made to interfere with the child's medical care. I've notified Baron and Delilah to join us momentarily so you'll have a chance to obtain additional details."

"I appreciate that."

A vein throbbed in the center of the crater in his brow. He held out his hands as if to ask, What next? The remote look on his face reminded me of someone else. The association triggered my next question.

"There's a doctor who treated Woody by the name of August Valcroix. He told me he visited here. Do you remember him?"

He twirled the ends of his beard around one long finger.

"Once or twice a year we offer seminars on organic gardening and meditation. Not to proselytise, but to enlighten. He may have attended one of those. I don't remember him specifically."

I gave him a physical description of Valcroix but it didn't evoke recognition.

"That's it, then. I appreciate your help."

He sat there, unblinking and unmoving. In the stingy light of the room his pupils had expanded so that only a thin rim of pale iris was visible. He had hypnotic eyes. A prerequisite for charisma.

"If you have any more questions you may ask them."

"No questions, but I would like to hear more about your philosophy."

He nodded.

"We are refugees from a former life. We've chosen a new life that emphasizes purity and industry. We avoid environmental poisons and seek self-sufficiency.

We believe that by changing ourselves we increase the positive energy in the world."

Standard stuff. He rattled it off like some New Age pledge of allegiance.

"We're not killers," he added.

Before I could reply, two of them came into the room.

Matthias stood up and left without acknowledging their presence. The man and woman took the two empty seats. The transaction was oddly mechanical, as if the people were interchangeable parts in some smoothly functioning apparatus.

They sat, hands in laps—more good schoolkids— and smiled with the maddening serenity of the born-again and the lobotomized.

I was far from serene. Because I recognized both of them, though in quite different ways.

The man who called himself Baron was medium-sized and thin. Like Matthias, his hair was cut short and his beard left untrimmed. But in his case the effect was less dramatic than untidy. His hair was medium brown and wispy. Patches of skin showed through the sparse frizzy chin whiskers and his cheeks were covered with soft fuzz. It was as if he'd forgotten to wash his face.

In graduate school I'd known him as Barry Graffius. He was older than I, in his early forties, but had been a class behind, a late starter who'd decided to become a psychologist after trying just about everything else.

Graffius's family was wealthy, big in the movie business, and he'd been one of those rich kids who couldn't seem to settle down—inadequate drive level because he'd never been deprived of anything. The consensus was that family money had gotten him in, but that may have been a jaundiced view. Because

Barry Graffius had been the most unpopular person in the department.

I've always tended to be charitable in my evaluations of others but I'd despised Graffius. He was loud-mouthed and contentious, dominating seminars with irrelevant quotes and statistics aimed at impressing the professors. He insulted his peers, bullied the meek, played devil's advocate with malicious glee.

And he loved to flaunt his money.

Most of us were struggling to get by, working extra jobs in addition to our teaching assistantships. Graffius delighted in coming to class in hand-tailored leather and suede, complaining about the repair bill on his XKE, lamenting the tax bite. He was an outrageous name dropper, recounting lavish Hollywood parties, offering a teasing glimpse into a glamorous world beyond the grasp of the rest of us.

I'd heard that after graduating he'd gone into practice on Bedford Drive—Beverly Hills Couch Row—planning to capitalize on his connections and become Therapist to the Stars.

I could see where he'd run into Norman Matthews.

He recognized me, too. I could tell by the flurry of activity behind his watery brown eyes. As we looked at each other that activity crystallized: fear. The fear of being discovered.

His former identity was no secret in the strict sense. But he didn't want to be confronted by it: for those who imagine themselves reborn, bringing up the past has all the appeal of exhuming one's own moldering corpse.

I said nothing, but wondered if he'd told Matthias about knowing me.

The woman was older, but uncommonly pretty despite the ponytail no-makeup look that seemed to be *de rigueur* for Touch women. Madonna-faced with ivory skin, raven hair now streaked with silver, and brooding gypsy eyes. Beverly Lucas had called her a hot number who'd lost it but that seemed unfairly bitchy. Perhaps knowing the woman's true age would have softened the critique.

She looked a well-preserved fifty but I knew she was at least sixty-five.

She hadn't made a film since 1951, the year I was born.

Desiree Layne, Queen of budget films noirs. There'd been a revival of her movies when I was in college, with free screenings during finals week. I'd seen them all: *Phantom Bride, Darken My Doorstep, The Savage Place, Secret Admirer.*

An eon ago, before my early retirement, I'd been a frantic, lonely man, with little free time. But one of the few pleasures I'd allowed myself was a Sunday afternoon in bed with a tall glass of Chivas and a Desiree Layne flick.

It hadn't mattered who the leading man was as long as there were lots of closeups of those beautiful evil eyes, the dresses that looked like lingerie. The voice husky with passion . . .

She emitted no passion now, sitting statue-still, white-garbed, smiling vacantly. So goddamned *harmless*.

The place was really starting to spook me. It was like walking through a wax museum . . .

"Noble Matthias told us you have questions," said Baron.

"Yes. I just wanted to hear more about your visit to the Swopes. It could help explain what's happened, aid in locating the children."

They nodded in unison.

I waited. They looked at each other. She spoke.

"We wanted to cheer them up. Noble Matthias had us pick fruit—oranges, grapefruit, peaches, plums—the best we could find. We put it all in a basket, wrapped it with gay paper."

She stopped talking and smiled, as if her narrative had explained everything.

"Was your graciousness well received?"

Her eyes widened.

"Oh yes. Mrs. Swope said she was hungry. She ate a plum—a Santa Rosa plum—right there. Said it was delicious."

Baron's face hardened as she prattled on. When she paused he said, "You want to know if we tried to talk them out of treating the boy." He sat passively but there was an aggressive edge to his voice.

"Matthias told me you didn't. Did the subject of medical treatment come up?"

"It did," he said. "She complained about the plastic room, said she felt cut off from the boy, that the family was being divided."

"Did she explain what she meant?"

"No. I assumed she was talking about the physical separation—not being allowed to touch him without gloves, only one person in the room at a time."

Delilah nodded in assent.

"Such a cold place," she said. "Physically and spiritually." To illustrate she gave a little shudder. Once an actress . . .

"They didn't feel the doctors treated them like human beings," added Baron. "Especially the Cuban."

"Poor man," said Delilah. "When he tried to force his way in this morning I couldn't help feeling sorry for him. Overweight and flushed red as a tomato—he must have high blood pressure."

"What were their complaints about him?"

Baron pursed his lips.

"Just that he was impersonal," he said.

"Did they mention a doctor named Valcroix?"

Delilah shook her head.

Baron spoke again.

"We didn't talk about much of anything. It was just a brief visit."

"I couldn't wait to get out of there," recalled Delilah. "Everything was so mechanical."

"We dropped off the fruit, left, and drove back home," Baron said with finality.

"A sad situation," she sighed.

17

A group of Touch people were sitting yoga-style on the grass when I came out, eyes closed, palms pressed together, faces glowing in the sun. Houten leaned against the fountain, smoking, eyes drifting idly in their direction. He saw me coming, dropped the butt, stomped on it, and tossed it in an earthenware trashbasket.

"Learn anything?"

I shook my head.

"Like I told you," he cocked his head toward the meditators who had now started to hum, "strange but harmless."

I looked at them. Despite the white costumes, the sandals, and the untrimmed beards, they resembled participants in a corporate seminar, one of those glossy pop-psych affairs promoted by management to increase productivity. The faces gazing heavenward were middle-aged and well-fed, suffused with an executive look that bespoke prior lives of comfort and authority.

Norman Matthews had been described to me as an aggressive and ambitious man. A hustler. As Matthias he'd tried to come across as a holy man but there was enough cynicism in me to wonder if he hadn't simply traded one hustle for another.

The Touch was a gold mine: offer the prosperous simplicity amid lush surroundings, remove the burden of personal responsibility, substitute an ethos that equated health and vitality with righteousness, and pass the collection plate. How could it miss?

But even if the whole thing was a scam it didn't spell kidnapping and murder. As Seth had pointed out, loss of privacy was the last thing Matthias wanted, be he prophet or con man.

"Let's take a look around," said Houten, "and be done with it."

I was allowed free access to the grounds, permitted to open any door. The sanctuary was domed and majestic, with clerestory windows and biblical murals on the ceiling. The pews had been removed and the floor covered with padded mats. There was a rough pine table in the center of the room and little else. A woman in white dusted and swept, stopping only to smile at us maternally.

The sleeping rooms were indeed cells—no larger than the one in which Raoul was confined—low-ceilinged, thick-walled, and cool, with a single window the size of a hardbound book and grilled with wood. Each room was furnished with a cot and a chest of drawers. Matthias's differed only in that it had a small bookcase. His literary taste was eclectic—the Bible, the Koran, Perls, Jung, Cousins's *Anatomy of An Illness*, Toffler's *Future Shock*, the Bhagavad-Gita, several texts on organic gardening and ecology.

I took a tour of the kitchen, where cauldrons of broth simmered on industrial stoves and bread baked sweetly in brick ovens. There was a member's library, its stock leaning toward health and agriculture, and a conference room with textured adobe walls. And everywhere people in white working, smiling, bright-eyed and friendly.

Houten and I traipsed through the fields, watching Touch members tend the grapes. A black-bearded giant put down his shears and offered us a freshly picked cluster. The fruit was moist to the touch and it burst electrically upon my tongue. I complimented the man on the flavor. He nodded and returned to his work.

It was well into the afternoon but the sun continued to rage. My unprotected head began to ache and after cursorily inspecting the sheepyard and the vegetable plots I told Houten I'd had enough.

We turned and walked back toward the viaduct. I wondered what I'd accomplished, for the search had been symbolic, at best. There wasn't any reason to believe the Swope children were there. And if they were, there'd be no way to find them. The Retreat was surrounded by hundreds of acres, much of it forest. Nothing short of a bloodhound pack could cover it all. Besides, monasteries are secret places, designed for refuge, and the compound might very well harbor a maze of underground caverns, secret compartments, and hidden passages that only an archaeologist could unravel.

It had been a futile day, I thought, but if it helped Raoul confront reality it was worth it. Then I realized what *reality* meant and craved the balm of denial.

Houten had Bragdon bring Raoul's personal effects in a large manila envelope. In the end he'd agreed to accept the oncologist's check for six hundred eighty-seven dollars worth of fines and while he recorded the amount in triplicate, I walked around the room restlessly, eager to get going.

The county map caught my eye. I located La Vista and noticed a back road to the east that seemed to skirt the town, allowing entry to the region from the outlying woodlands without actually passing through the commercial district. If that was the case, avoiding Houten's scrutiny was easier than he'd let on.

After some hesitation I asked him about it. He fiddled with a piece of carbon paper and continued writing.

"Oil company bought up the land, got the county to seal off the road. There was big talk of deep deposits, prosperity just around the corner."

"Did they strike it rich?"

"Nope. Bone dry."

The deputy brought Raoul out. I told him about my visit to the Retreat and the negative findings. He took it in, looking downcast and beaten, and offered no protest.

The sheriff, pleased with his passivity, treated him with exquisite courtesy while he signed him out. He asked Raoul what he wanted to do about his Volvo, and the oncologist shrugged and said to have it fixed, he'd pay for it.

I led him out of the room and down the stairs.

He was silent throughout the ride home, not even losing his cool when a chubby female border guard pulled us over and asked for his identification. He accepted the indignity with a mute acquiescence that I found pitiful. Two hours ago he'd been aggressive and poised for battle. I wondered if he'd been laid low by the accumulated stress or if cyclical mood swings were a part of his makeup I'd never noticed.

I was famished but he looked too grungy to take to a restaurant so I bought a couple of burgers and

Cokes at a stand in Santa Ana and pulled to the side of the road near a small municipal park. I gave Raoul his food and ate mine while watching a group of teenagers play softball, racing to finish before nightfall. When I turned to look at him, he was asleep, the food still wrapped and lying in his lap. I took it, stowed it in a trashcan and started up the Seville. He stirred but didn't awaken and by the time I got back on the freeway he was snoring peacefully.

We reached L.A. by seven, just as traffic on the downtown interchange was untangling. When I turned off at the Los Feliz exit he opened his eyes.

"What's your address?"

"No, take me back to the hospital."

"You're in no shape to go back there."

"I must. Helen will be waiting."

"You'll only scare her looking like that. At least go home and freshen up first."

"I have a change of clothes in my office. Please, Alex."

I threw up my hands and drove to Western Peds. After parking in the doctors' lot I walked him to the front door of Prinzley.

"Thank you," he said, looking at his feet.

"Take care of yourself."

On the way back to the car I met Beverly Lucas leaving the wards. She looked tired and worn, the oversized purse seeming to weigh her down.

"Alex, I'm so glad to see you."

"What's the matter?"

She looked around to make sure no one was listening.

"It's Augie. He's been making my life miserable ever since your friend interrogated him, calling me unfaithful, a quisling. He even tried to embarrass me on rounds but the attending doc stopped it."

"Bastard."

She shook her head.

"What makes it hard is that I see his point. We were—close, once. What he did in bed was nobody's business."

I took her by the shoulders.

"What you did was right. If you got enough distance to see straight that would be obvious. Don't let him get to you."

She flinched at the harshness in my voice.

"I know you're right. Intellectually. But he's falling apart and it hurts me. I can't help my feelings."

She started to cry. A trio of nurses walked our way. I steered her off the walkway and into the stairwell to the doctors' level.

"What do you mean falling apart?"

"Acting strange. Doping and drinking more heavily than usual. He's bound to get caught. This morning he pulled me off the ward and into a conference room, locked the door, and came on to me."

She lowered her eyes in embarrassment.

"He told me I was the best he'd ever had, actually tried to get physical. When I stopped him he looked crushed. Then he started to rant about Melendez-Lynch—how he'd scapegoated him and was going to try to use the Swope case to terminate the fellowship. He started to laugh—it was a freaky laugh, Alex, full of anger. He said he had an ace up his sleeve. That Melendez-Lynch would never get rid of him."

"Did he say what that was?"

"I asked him. He just laughed again and walked out. Alex, I'm worried. I was just on my way to the residents' dorm. To make sure he was okay."

I tried to talk her out of it but she was resolute. She had an infinite capacity for guilt. Someday she'd make someone a wonderful doormat.

It was clear she wanted me to accompany her to his apartment, and tired as I was, I agreed to go with her, in case things got hairy. And on the off-chance Valcroix really had an ace and might show it.

The residents' dorm across the boulevard from the hospital was a utilitarian affair, three stories of unfinished concrete over a subterranean parking lot. Some of the windows had been brightened up with plants and flower arrangements resting on sills or hanging from macrame harnesses. But that didn't stop it from looking like what it was: low-cost housing.

An elderly black guard was stationed at the door—there had been rapes in the neighborhood and the residents had screamed for security. He looked at our hospital badges and let us pass.

Valcroix's apartment was on the second floor.

"It's the one with the red door," said Beverly, pointing.

The corridor and all the other doors were beige. Valcroix's was scarlet and stood out like a wound.

"Amateur paint job?" I ran my hand over the wood, which was rough and bubbled. A segment from a doper comic had been pasted to the door—furry people popping pills and hallucinating in technicolor, their fantasies sexually explicit and excessive.

"Uh huh."

She knocked several times. When there was no answer she bit her lip.

"Maybe he went out," I suggested.

"No. He always stays home when he's not on call. That was one thing that bothered me about our relationship. We never went out."

I didn't remind her that she'd spotted him in a restaurant with Nona Swope. No doubt he was one of those men as stingy about giving as he was greedy about taking. He'd do the least amount possible to enter a woman's body. With her lowered expectations, Beverly would have been his dream. Until he got bored with her.

"I'm worried, Alex. I know he's in there. He could be OD'ed on something."

Nothing I said alleviated her anxiety. Finally, we went downstairs and convinced the guard to use his master key on the red door.

"I don't know 'bout this, Doctor," he said, but he unlocked the apartment.

The place was a sty. Dirty laundry was piled on the grubby carpet. The bed was unmade. On the nightstand was an ashtray brimming with marijuana roaches. Nearby was an engraved roach clip in the shape of a pair of female legs. Medical books and more doper comics coexisted in the paper blizzard that covered half the living room floor. The kitchen sink was a swamp of dirty dishes and cloudy water. A fly circled overhead.

No one was home.

Beverly walked through and unconsciously began straightening up. The guard looked at her quizzically.

"Come on," I said with surprising vehemence. "He's not here. Let's get out."

The guard cleared his throat.

She covered the bed, took a last look around, and left.

Outside the dorm she asked if we should call the police.

"What for?" I demanded sharply. "A grown man leaves his apartment? They'd never take it seriously. And for good reason."

She looked wounded and wanted to discuss it further but I begged off. I was weary, my head hurt, my joints were sore; it felt like I was coming down with something. Besides, my altruism account was already badly overdrawn.

We crossed the street in silence and parted ways.

By the time I got home I felt really lousy—feverish, logy, and aching all over. There was a bright spot—an express letter from Robin confirming her departure from Tokyo in a week. One of the Japanese executives owned a condo on Kauai and he'd offered her the use of it. She was hoping I could meet her flight in Honolulu and set aside two weeks for fun and sun. I called Western Union and wired a Yes on all accounts.

A hot bath didn't make me feel any better. Neither did a cool drink or self-hypnosis. I dragged myself downstairs to feed the koi but didn't linger to watch them eat. Back in the house I fell into bed with the paper, the rest of the mail, and Leo Kottke on the stereo. But I found myself too drained to concentrate, and surrendered to sleep without a struggle.

18

By morning my malaise had matured to influenza. I took aspirin, drank lemon tea, and wished Robin were there to take care of me.

I kept the TV on for background noise and slept, on and off, all day. By evening I was feeling well enough to hobble out of bed and eat Jell-O. But even that tired me and soon I was back asleep.

In my dream I was adrift on an Arctic ice floe, seeking shelter from a violent hailstorm in a meager cardboard lean-to. Each new fusillade shredded the cardboard, leaving me increasingly terrified and exposed.

I awoke naked and shivering. The hailstorm continued. Digital numbers glowed in the dark: 11:26. Through the window I saw clear black skies. The hail turned into bullets. Shotgun fire stinging the side of the house.

I dove to the floor, lay flat, belly-down, breathing hard.

More gunfire. A percussive pop, then the tinkle of broken glass. A cry of pain. A sickening dull sound, like a melon bursting under a sledgehammer. An engine starting. Automotive escape.

Then silence.

I crawled to the phone. Called the police. Asked for Milo. He was off-shift. Del Hardy, then. *Please.*

The black detective came to the phone. Between gasps I told him about the nightmare that had turned real.

He said he'd call Milo, both of them would be there code three.

Minutes later the wail of sirens stretched up the glen, trombones gone mad.

I put on a robe and stepped outside.

The redwood siding on the front of the house was peppered with holes and splintered in a dozen places. One window had been blown out.

I smelled hydrocarbons.

On the terrace were three open cans of gasoline. Wadded rags had been fashioned into oversized wicks and stuffed into the spouts. Oily footprints led to the edge of the landing and ended in a single smear of a skidmark. I looked over the railing.

A man sprawled face down and motionless in the Japanese garden.

I climbed down just as the black and whites pulled up. Walked barefoot to the garden, the stone cool under feet burning with fever. I called out. The man didn't respond.

It was Richard Moody.

Half his face had been blown away. What remained was dog food. Or more precisely, fish food, for his head was submerged in my pond and the koi nibbled at it, sucking up the bloody water, relishing the novelty of a new snack.

Sickened, I tried to wave them away but the sight of me was a conditioned stimulus for feeding and they grew more enthusiastic, feasting and slurping, scaly gourmands. The big black and gold carp came half out of the water to get a mouthful. I could swear he grinned at me with whiskered lips.

Someone was at my side. I jumped.

"Easy, Alex."

"Milo!"

He looked as if he'd crawled out of bed. He wore a lifeless windbreaker over a yellow Hang-Ten polo shirt and baggy jeans. His hair was a fright wig and his green eyes gleamed in the moonlight.

"Come on," he took my elbow. "Let's go upstairs, get something liquid in you and then you can tell me what happened."

As the crime scene crew busied themselves with the technical minutiae of murder I sat on my old leather sofa and drank Chivas. The shock was beginning to slough off; I realized I was still sick—chilled and weak. The Scotch went down warm and smooth. Across from me sat Milo and Del Hardy. The black detective was dapper, as always, in a shaped dark suit, peach-colored shirt, black tie, and spit-polished demiboots. He put on a pair of reading glasses and took notes.

"On the surface," said Milo, "it looks like Moody had plans to torch your place and somebody followed him, caught him in the act, and took him out." He thought for a moment. "There was a triangle, right? How do you like the boyfriend for the shooter role?"

"He didn't seem the type to stalk a man like that."

"Full name," said Hardy, pen poised.

"Carlton Conley. He's a carpenter for Aurora Studios. He and Moody were friends before it triangulated."

Hardy scribbled. "Did he move in with the wife?"

"Yes. They're all supposed to be up near Davis. On the advice of her lawyer."

"The lawyer's name?"

"Malcolm J. Worthy. Beverly Hills."

"Better call him," said Milo. "If Moody had a list he'd be on it. Find out the number up in Davis and check out if anything went down there—she's still next of kin, has to be notified anyway. Have the local law go over there and read her face—see if she's surprised by the news. Call the judge, too. Anyone else you can think of, Alex?"

"There was another psychologist involved in the case. Dr. Lawrence Daschoff. Lives in Brentwood. Office in Santa Monica." I knew Larry's office number by heart and gave it to them.

"What about Moody's own lawyer?" asked Del. "If the joker thought his case had been botched he might lash out, right?"

"True. The guy's name is Durkin. Emil or Elton or something like that."

A grimace of recognition crossed the black detective's face.

"Elridge," he growled. "Fucker represented my ex-wife. Cleaned me out."

"Well, then," laughed Milo, "you can have the pleasure of interviewing him. Or consoling his widow."

Hardy grumbled, closed his pad, and went into the kitchen and left to make the calls.

A crime scene tech beckoned from the door and Milo patted my shoulder and went out to talk to him. He returned in a few minutes.

"They found tire tracks," he said. "Fat ones, like on a hot rod. Ring any bells?"

"Moody drove a truck."

"They already looked at his wheels. No match."

"Nothing else comes to mind."

"There were six more gas cans in the truck, which supports the hit list theory. But it also doesn't make sense. He was going to use three cans here. Let's assume that he planned this out as some kind of structured revenge ritual, three cans per victim. Given a minimum of five victims—you, the other shrink, both lawyers, and the judge, that adds up to fifteen cans. Six left means nine used. Not counting you, that makes two prior attempts. If he planned on torching the family home, make it twelve and three possible priors. Even if the numbers are wrong it's unlikely you were singled out for more gas than anyone else. Which means you probably weren't his first stop. Why would the shooter follow him around town, watch him set two or three fires, risk being seen, and wait until the third to do the job?"

I puzzled over that.

"Only thing I can think of," I said, "is this is a pretty secluded area. Lots of big trees, easy for a sniper to hide."

"Maybe," he said skeptically. "We'll pursue the tire angle. The Hot Rod Killer. Catchy."

He chewed on a hangnail, looked at me gravely.

"Got any enemies I don't know about, pal?"

My stomach lurched. He'd put into words what had been fulminating in my mind. That I was the intended victim . . .

"Just the Casa de Los Ninos guys, and they're behind bars. No one on the streets that I know of."

"Way the system runs you never know whether they're on the streets or not. We'll run parole checks on all of them. Which'll be in my best interests, too."

He sipped coffee and leaned forward.

"I don't want to raise your anxiety level, Alex, but there's something we should deal with. Remember when you called me about the rat and I asked you to describe Moody? You told me you and he were almost exactly the same size and coloring."

I nodded numbly.

"You've been in the house all day, sick in bed. Someone arriving after dark wouldn't have known that. From a distance, the mistake would be easy to make."

He waited a moment before continuing.

"It's not pretty to think about, but we've got to consider it," he said, almost apologetically. "In my gut I don't think the Casa thing'll pan out. What about the jokers you've run into on the Swope case?"

I thought of the people I'd encountered during the last couple of days. Valcroix. Matthias and the Touchers. Houten—did the sheriff's El Camino have fat tires? Maimon. Bragdon. Carmichael. Rambo. Even Beverly and Raoul. None seemed remotely likely as suspects and I told Milo so.

"Of all of them, I like that asshole Canadian the best," he said. "Guy's a Class A bad actor."

"I don't see it, Milo. He resented being interrogated and could have held that against me. But resentment isn't hatred and whoever fired those shots did it out of blood lust."

"You told me he was a heavy doper, Alex. They've been known to get paranoid."

I thought of what Beverly had said about Valcroix's increasingly strange behavior and repeated it to Milo.

"There you go," he said. "Cokehead madness."

"I guess it's possible, but it still doesn't feel right. I wasn't that important to him. Anyway, he seems more of an escapist, someone who'd retreat rather than act out. The peace-love-Woodstock type."

"So were the Manson family. What kind of car does he drive?"

"No idea."

"We'll run it through D.M.V., then pick the guy up for questioning. Talk to the others, too. Hopefully the whole thing will boil down to Moody. When you get down to it he sounds like an easy one to hate."

He stood and stretched.

"Thanks for everything, Milo."

He waved it off. "Haven't done a damn thing so don't thank me yet. And I probably won't be able to handle it myself. Gotta travel."

"Where to?"

"Washington, D.C. On the rape-murder. The Saudis have one of those slick public relations firms on retainer. Been putting millions into commercials showing they're just plain folks. Prince Stinky's exploits could make them look like the enemy again. So there's been pressure from the top to let him slink out of town to avoid a trial and all the publicity. The department won't let go of this one cause the crimes were too damned ugly. But the Arabs keep pushing and the politicos have to do a bit of symbolic brownnosing."

He shook his head in disgust.

"Other day a couple of gray suits from the State Department came down and took Del and me out to lunch. Three martinis and haute cuisine at the taypayer's expense, followed by congenial chitchat about the energy crisis. I let them talk, then I shoved a bunch of pictures of the girl Stinky killed right in front of them. Foreign Service types must have delicate constitutions. They almost heaved right into the coq au vin. That afternoon I got volunteered to fly to D.C. and discuss it further."

"That'll be something to see," I said. "You and a room full of bureaucrats. When are you leaving?"

"Don't know. I'm on call. Could be tomorrow or

the day after. Going first class for the first time in my deprived life."

He looked at me with concern.

"At least Moody's out of the way."

"Yeah," I sighed. "I wish it could have happened another way." I thought of April and Ricky, what this would do to them. If Conley turned out to have been the one who blew away their father, the tragedy would be compounded. The entire case had a raw, primal stink that foreshadowed tragic endings for generations to come.

Hardy came back from the kitchen and gave his report.

"Coulda been worse than it was. Half of Durkin's house is up in smoke. He and his wife suffered second-degree burns and some smoke inhalation but they're gonna live. Worthy had smoke alarms and caught it in time. He lives in the Palisades, big property with lots of trees. Couple of 'em burned down."

Which meant plenty of hiding places. Milo glanced at me meaningfully. Hardy kept on talking.

"The judge's and Daschoff's places haven't been touched so the cans in the car were probably meant for them. I sent uniforms to check out all of their offices."

Richard Moody had ended his tormented life in a blaze of twisted passion.

Milo whistled and told Hardy the Delaware-as-victim scenario. Hardy found merit to it, which did nothing to improve my state of mind.

They thanked me for the coffee and stood. Hardy left the house and Milo lingered behind.

"You can stay here if you want," he said, "because most of the forensic work will go on outside. But if you want to go somewhere else, that's okay, too." It was intended more as advice than the granting of permission.

The glen was filled with blinking lights, footsteps,

and muted human conversation. Safe, for now. But the police wouldn't be there forever.

"I'll move out for a couple of days."

"If you wanna stay at my place, the offer's still open. Rick'll be on call next couple days, it'll be quiet."

I thought for a moment.

"Thanks, but I really want to be alone."

He said he understood, drained his coffee mug, and came closer.

"I see that gleam in your eyes and it worries me, pal."

"I'm fine."

"So far. I'd like to see it stay that way."

"There's nothing to worry about, Milo. Really."

"It's the kid, isn't it? You haven't let go of it."

I was silent.

"Look, Alex, if what happened tonight has anything to do with the Swopes, that's all the more reason for you to stay out of it. I'm not saying cut off your feelings, just cover your ass."

He touched my bad jaw gently. "Last time you were lucky. Don't push it."

I packed an overnight bag and drove around awhile before deciding on the Bel-Air Hotel as a good place to recuperate. And hide. It was just minutes away, quiet and secluded behind high stucco walls and towering subtropical shrubbery. The ambience—pink exterior, forest green interiors, swaying coconut palms, and a pond in which flamingos floated—had always reminded me of the old mythical Hollywood— romance, sweet fantasy, and happy endings. All of which seemed in short supply.

I headed west on Sunset, turned north at Stone Canyon Road, and drove past immense gated estates until coming to the hotel's entrance. No one was parking cars at one forty in the morning; I slipped the Seville between a Lamborghini and a Maserati and left it looking like a dowager escorted by two gigolos.

The night clerk was a brooding Swede who didn't look up when I paid in advance with cash and registered as Carl Jung. Then I noticed he'd recorded it as Karl Young.

A tired-looking bellman took me to a bungalow overlooking a pool, which was lit up like an aquamarine. The room was understated and comfortable, with a big soft bed and heavy dark forties furniture.

I slid my body between cool sheets and remembered the last time I'd been there: the previous July, on Robin's twenty-eighth birthday. We'd heard the philharmonic do Mozart at the Music Center and followed the concert with a late supper at the Bel-Air.

The dining room had been dark and quiet, our booth private and next to a picture window. Between the oysters and the veal a stately older woman in a formal gown had glided regally across the palm court.

"Alex," Robin had whispered, "look—no it couldn't be . . ."

But it was. Bette Davis. We couldn't have custom-ordered it.

Thinking of that perfect night helped keep the ghastliness of this quite imperfect one at bay.

I slept until eleven, dialed room service and ordered fresh raspberries, an herb omelette, bran muffins, and coffee. The food came on china and silver and was superb. I chased images of death from my mind and ate heartily. Soon, I started to feel like a human being again.

I slept some more, woke, and called West L.A. Division at two. Milo had flown to Washington so I checked in with Del Hardy. He informed me that Conley was out as a suspect. While Moody was being blown apart, he'd been on location in Saugus for a night shoot on a new TV series. I took the news with equanimity, never having seen him as a calculating killer. Besides, I'd already convinced myself I was the sniper's intended victim. Accepting the role didn't make for tranquillity but at least I'd be vigilant.

I went for a swim at four, more for exercise than pleasure, returned to my room, and called for the evening paper and a Grolsch. The flu seemed to have surrendered. I sank into an armchair to read and drink.

The news of Valcroix's death was a two-inch filler piece on page twenty-eight entitled DOCTOR LOSES LIFE IN AUTO CRASH. From it I learned the genre, if not the make, of the car the Canadian had driven ("foreign compact") before crashing it into an abutment near the Wilmington harbor. He'd been pronounced dead at the scene and relatives in Montreal had been notified.

Wilmington is midway between L.A. and San Diego if you take the coastal route, a drab section of warehouses and shipyards. I wondered what he'd been doing there and which direction he'd been headed before the collision. He'd visited La Vista before. Was he returning from there when he crashed?

I thought of his boasts to Beverly about having an ace up his sleeve with regard to the Swopes. More questions reverberated relentlessly: was the crash an accident, the result of drug-numbed reflexes, or had he tried to play that ace and lost his life in the process? And what was the secret he'd considered his salvation? Could it solve the murder of the Swopes? Or help locate their children?

I turned it over, again and again, until my head

hurt, sitting tensely on the edge of the chair, groping haphazardly like a blind man in a maze.

It wasn't until I realized what was missing that I was able to focus on what had to be done. Had I looked at it *clinically*, as a psychologist, clarity of purpose might have come sooner.

I'd been trained in the art of psychotherapy, the excavation of the past as a means of untangling the present and rendering it livable. It's detective work of sorts, crouching stealthily in the blind alleys of the unconscious. And it begins with the taking of a careful and detailed history.

Four people had perished unnaturally. If their deaths seemed a jumble of unrelated horrors, I knew it was because such a history was missing. Because insufficient respect had been paid to the past.

That had to be remedied. It was more than an academic exercise. There were lives at stake.

I refused to compute the odds on the Swope children being alive. For the time being, it was sufficient that they were greater than zero. I thought, for the hundredth time, of the boy in the plastic room, helpless, dependent, potentially curable but harboring an internal time bomb . . . He had to be found or he'd die in pain.

Seized with anger at my helplessness, I shifted from altruism to self-preservation. Milo had urged me to be careful but sitting still could be the most dangerous act of all.

Someone had hunted me. The news of my survival would eventually emerge. The hunter would return to claim his prey, taking his time so as to do it right. I wouldn't, couldn't play that waiting game, living like a man on death row.

There was work to be done. Exploration. Exhumation.

The compass pointed south.

19

To trust someone is to take the greatest risk of all. Without trust nothing ever happens.

The issue, at this juncture, wasn't whether or not to take the risk. It was who could be trusted.

There was Del Hardy of course, but I didn't see him, or the police in general, as being much help. They were professionals who dealt with facts. All I had to offer were vague suspicions and intuitive dread. Hardy would hear me out politely, thank me for my input, tell me not to worry, and that would be it.

The answers I needed had to come from an insider; only someone who had known the Swopes in life could shed light on their deaths.

Sheriff Houten had seemed straight. But like many a large frog in a small pond, he'd overidentified with his role. He *was* the law in La Vista and crime was a personal affront. I recalled his anger at my suggestion that Woody and Nona might be somewhere in town. Such things simply didn't happen on *his* turf.

That kind of paternalism bred a make-nice approach exemplified by the formal coexistence between the town and the Touch. On the positive side it could lead to tolerance, on the negative, tunnel vision.

I couldn't turn to Houten for help. He wouldn't welcome inquiries by outsiders under any circumstances and the hassles with Raoul were certain to have firmed his defenses. Neither could I waltz into town and strike up conversations with strangers. For a moment it seemed hopeless, La Vista a locked box.

Then I thought of Ezra Maimon.

There'd been a simple dignity and independence of spirit about the man that had impressed me. He'd walked into a mess and cleaned it up within minutes. Representing an outside troublemaker's interests against those of the sheriff could have proved intimidating to a less resolute man. Maimon had taken the job seriously and had done it damn well. He had spine and smarts.

Equally important, he was all I had.

I got his number from information and dialed it.

He answered the phone "Rare Fruit and Seed Company" in the same quiet voice I remembered.

"Mr. Maimon, Alex Delaware. We met at the sheriff's station."

"Good afternoon, Dr. Delaware. How is Dr. Melendez-Lynch?"

"I haven't seen him since that day. He was pretty depressed."

"Yes. Such a tragic state of affairs."

"That's why I called you."

"Oh?"

I told him of Valcroix's death, the attempt on my life, and my conviction that the situation would never be resolved without delving into the history of the Swopes, finishing with a straight-out plea for help.

There was silence on the other end and I knew he was deliberating, just as he had after Houten presented his case. I could almost hear the wheels turning.

"You've got a personal stake in this," he said finally.

"That's a big part of it. But there's more. Woody Swope's disease is curable. There's no reason for him to die. If he's alive I want him found and treated."

More silent cerebration.

"I'm not sure I know anything that will help you."

"Neither am I. But it's worth a try."

"Very well."

I thanked him profusely. We agreed that meeting in La Vista was out of the question. For both our sakes.

"There's a restaurant in Oceanside named Anita's where I dine regularly," he said. "I'm a vegetarian and they serve fine meatless cuisine. Can you meet me there at nine tonight?"

It was five forty. Given even the heaviest traffic, I'd make it with time to spare.

"I'll be there."

"All right, then, let me tell you how to find the place."

The directions he gave were as expected: simple, straightforward, precise.

I paid for another two nights at the Bel Air, returned to my room and called Mal Worthy. He was out of the office but his secretary volunteered his home number.

He picked up on the first ring, sounding weary and drained.

"Alex, I've tried to get you all day."

"I'm in seclusion."

"Hiding? Why? He's dead."

"It's a long story. Listen, Mal, I called for a couple of reasons. First, how did the children take it?"

"That's what I wanted to talk to you about. To get your advice. What a goddamned mess. Darlene didn't want to tell them but I told her she had to. I spoke to her afterward, and she said April cried a lot, asked questions, wouldn't let go of her skirt. She couldn't get Ricky to talk. Kid clammed up, went into his room and wouldn't come out. She had lots of questions and I tried my best to answer them but it's not my area of expertise. Do those reactions sound normal?"

"Normal or abnormal isn't the issue. Those kids have had to deal with more trauma than most people encounter in a lifetime. When I examined them in your office I felt they needed help and said so. Now it's absolutely necessary. Make sure they get it. In the meantime keep an eye on Ricky. He identified strongly with his father. Imitative suicide isn't out of the question. Neither is arson. If there are guns in the house get rid of them. Tell Darlene to watch him closely—keep him away from matches, knives, ropes, pills. At least until she gets him into therapy. After that she should do what the therapist says. And if the kid starts expressing his anger she should make sure not to clamp down. Even if it gets abusive."

"I'll pass it on. I'd like you to see them once they get back to L.A."

"I can't, Mal. I'm too close to the whole thing." I gave him the names of two other psychologists.

"All right," he said, with some reluctance. "I'll give her the referrals, make sure she calls one of them." He paused. "I'm staring out the window. Place looks like a barbecue pit. Firemen sprayed it with something that's supposed to make the smell go away but it still stinks. I keep wondering if it could have turned out differently."

"I don't know. Moody was programmed for violence. He had a violent upbringing. You remember the history—his own father was explosive, died in a brawl."

"History repeats itself."

"Get that boy in therapy and maybe it won't."

The whitewashed walls of Anita's Café were backlit by lavender-tinted bulbs and trimmed with used brick. The entrance was through a lattice-wood arch. Dwarf lemon trees had been espaliered to the lattice and the fruit glowed turquoise in the artificial light.

The restaurant was tucked away, incongruously, in an industrial park, flanked on three sides by black-glass office buildings, acres of parking lot on the fourth. The songs of nightbirds mingled with the distant roar of the highway.

Inside, it was cool and dim. Baroque harpsichord music issued forth at low volume. The aroma of herbs and spices—cumin, marjoram, saffron, basil—saturated the air. Three quarters of the tables were occupied. Most of the diners looked young, hip, affluent. They spoke earnestly in subdued tones.

A stout blond woman in peasant blouse and embroidered skirt showed me to Maimon's table. He rose in a courtly gesture and sat when I did.

"Good evening, Doctor." He was dressed as before: spotless white shirt, pressed khaki trousers. His eyeglasses had slid down his nose and he pushed them back into place.

"Good evening. Thank you very much for seeing me."

He smiled.

"You stated your case eloquently."

The waitress, a slender girl with long dark hair and a Modigliani face, came to our table.

"They make an excellent lentil wellington," said Maimon.

"That sounds fine." My mind wasn't on food.

He ordered for both of us. The waitress returned with ice water in cut-crystal goblets, pillowy slices of whole-wheat bread and two small tubs of vegetable pâté that tasted uncannily like the real thing. A paper-thin lemon slice floated in each glass.

He spread pâté on bread, took a bite, chewed slowly and deliberately. After he swallowed he asked, "How can I help you, Doctor?"

"I'm trying to understand the Swopes. What they were like before Woody's illness."

"I didn't know them well. They were secretive people."

"I keep hearing that."

"I'm not surprised." He sipped his water. "I moved to La Vista ten years ago. My wife and I were childless. After she died I retired from my law practice and opened up the nursery—horticulture had been my first love. One of the things I did after settling in was to contact the other growers in the area. For the most part I was welcomed warmly. Traditionally, horticulturists and orchardists are cordial people. So much of our progress depends upon cooperation—one grower will obtain seeds from an unusual species and distribute it to the others. It's in the best interests of all—scientifically and economically. A fruit that no one tastes will eventually die out, as did so many of the old American apples and pears. One that achieves some degree of circulation will survive.

"I'd expected to be welcomed warmly by Garland Swope, because he was my neighbor. It was a naive expectation. I dropped in on him one day and he stood by his gate, not inviting me in, curt, almost to the point of hostility. Needless to say, I was taken aback. Not only by the unfriendliness but also by his lack of desire to show off—most of us love to exhibit our prize hybrids and rare specimens."

The food came. It was surprisingly good, the lentils intriguingly spiced and wrapped in filo dough. Maimon ate sparingly then put his fork down before speaking again.

"I left quickly and never went back, though our properties are less than a mile apart. There were other growers in the area interested in collaboration and I quickly forgot about Swope. About a year later I attended a convention in Florida on the cultivation of subtropical Malaysian fruits. I met several people who'd known him and they explained his behavior.

"It seems the man was a grower in name only. He'd been prominent at one time, but hadn't done anything for years. There's no nursery behind his gates, only an old house and acres of dust."

"What did the family live on?"

"Inheritance. Garland's father was a state senator, owned a large ranch and miles of coastal land. He sold some to the government, the rest to developers. Much of the proceeds were immediately lost to bad investments, but apparently there was enough left to support Garland and his family."

He looked at me with curiosity.

"Does any of this help you?"

"I don't know. Why did he give up horticulture?"

"Bad investments of his own. Have you heard of the cherimoya?"

"There's a street in Hollywood by that name. Sounds like a fruit."

He wiped his lips.

"You're correct. It is a fruit. One that Mark Twain called 'deliciousness of deliciousness.' Those who've tasted it are inclined to agree. It's subtropical in nature, native to the Chilean Andes. Looks somewhat like an artichoke or a large green strawberry. The skin is inedible. The pulp is white and textured like custard, laced with many large, hard seeds. Some joke that the seeds were put there by the gods so the fruit wouldn't be consumed with undue haste. One eats it with a spoon. The taste is fantastic, Doctor. Sweet and tangy, with perfumed overtones of peach, pear, pineapple, banana, and citrus, but a totality that is unique.

"It's a wonderful fruit, and according to the people in Florida, Garland Swope was obsessed with it. He considered it the fruit of the future and was convinced that once the public tasted it, there would be instant demand. He dreamed of doing for the cherimoya what Sanford Dole had done for the pineapple. Even went so far as to name his first child after it—*Annona cherimola* is the full botanical name."

"Was it a realistic dream?"

"Theoretically. It's a finicky tree, requiring a temperate climate and constant moisture, but adaptable to the subtropical strip that runs along the coast of California from the Mexican border up through Ventura County. Wherever avocadoes grow so can the cherimoya. But there are complications that I'll come to.

"He bought up land on credit. Ironically, much of it had originally been owned by his father. Then he went on expeditions to South America and brought back young trees. Propagated seedlings and planted his orchard. It took several years for the trees to reach fruiting size, but finally he had the largest cherimoya grove in the state. During all this time he'd been traveling up and down the state, talking up the fruit with produce buyers, telling them of the wonders that would soon be blossoming in his groves.

"It must have been an uphill battle, for the palate of the American public is quite unadventurous. As a nation, we don't consume much fruit. The ones we do eat have gained familiarity over centuries. The tomato was once believed poisonous, the eggplant thought to cause madness. Those are just two examples. There are literally hundreds of tantalizing food plants that would thrive in this climate but are ignored.

"However, Garland was persistent and it paid off. He received advance orders for most of his crop. Had the cherimoya caught on he would have cornered the market on a gourmet delicacy and ended up a rich man. Of course, the corporate growers would have moved in eventually and coopted everything, but that would have taken years and even then, his expertise would have been highly marketable.

"Almost a decade after he conceived his plan the first year's crop set—that in itself was an achievement. In its native habitat the cherimoya is pollinated by an indigenous wasp. Duplicating the process requires painstaking hand pollination—pollen from the anthers of one flower is brushed on the pistils of another. Time of day is important as well, for the plant undergoes fertility cycles. Garland babied the trees almost as if they were human infants."

Maimon took off his glasses and wiped them. His eyes were dark and unblinking.

"Two weeks before harvest a killing frost borne by frigid air currents crept up from Mexico. There'd been a rash of tropical storms that had battered the Caribbean and the frost was an aftershock. Most of the trees died overnight and the ones that survived dropped their fruit. There was a frantic attempt at rescue. Several of the people I met in Florida had been there to help. They described it to me: Garland and Emma running through the groves with smudgepots and blankets, trying to wrap the trees, warm the soil, do anything to save them. The little girl watching them and crying. They struggled for three days but it was hopeless. Garland was the last to accept it."

He shook his head sadly.

"Years of work were lost in a span of seventy hours. After that he withdrew from horticulture and became a virtual hermit."

It was a classic tragedy—dreams savaged by the Fates. The agony of helplessness. Terminal despair.

I began to catch a glimpse of what Woody's diagnosis must have meant to them:

Cancer in a child was never less than monstrous. For any parent it meant confronting a sickening sense of impotence. But for Garland and Emma Swope the trauma would be compounded, the inability to save their child evoking past failures. Perhaps unbearably . . .

"Is all of this well-known?" I asked.

"To anyone who's lived here for a while."

"What about Matthias and the Touch?"

"That I couldn't tell you. They moved here a few years ago. May or may not have found out. It's not a topic of public conversation."

He smiled the waitress over and ordered a pot of herb tea. She brought it, along with two cups, which she filled.

He sipped, put his cup down, and looked at me through the steam.

"You still harbor suspicions about the Touch," he said.

"I don't know," I admitted. "There's no real reason to. But something about them is spooky."

"Somewhat contrived?"

"Exactly. It all looks too programmed. Like a movie director's version of what a cult should be."

"I agree with you, Doctor. When I heard Norman Matthews had become a spiritual leader I was rather amused."

"You knew him?"

"By reputation only. Anyone in the legal profession had heard of him. He was the quintessential Beverly Hills attorney—bright, flamboyant, aggressive, ruthless. None of which jibed with what he presently claims to be. Still, I suppose odder transformations have taken place."

"Someone took a pot shot at me yesterday. Can you see them doing that kind of thing?"

He thought about it.

"Their public face has been anything but violent. If you told me Matthews was a swindler I'd believe it. But a murderer . . ." He looked doubtful.

I took a different tack.

"What kind of relationship was there between the Touch and the Swopes?"

"None, I would imagine. Garland was a recluse. Never came to town. Occasionally I'd see Emma or the girl out shopping."

"Matthias told me Nona worked for the Touch one summer."

"That's true. I'd forgotten." He turned away and fiddled with a container of unfiltered honey.

"Mr. Maimon, forgive me if this sounds rude, but I don't see you forgetting anything. When Matthias talked about Nona, the sheriff got uncomfortable, as you just did. Broke in with a comment about what a wild kid she was, as if to end the discussion. You've been very helpful until now. Please don't hold back."

He put his glasses back on, stroked his chin, started to lift his teacup but thought better of it.

"Doctor," he said evenly, "you seem a sincere young man and I want to help you. But let me explain the position I'm in. I've lived here for a decade but still consider myself an outsider. I'm a Sephardic Jew, descended from the great scholar Maimonides. My ancestors were expelled from Spain in 1492, along with all the Jews. They settled in Holland, were expelled from there, went to England, Palestine, Australia, America. Five hundred years of wandering gets into the blood, makes one reluctant to think in terms of permanence.

"Two years ago, a member of the Ku Klux Klan was nominated for state assembly from this district. Part of it was subterfuge—the man concealed his membership— but too many people knew who he was to make the nomination an accident. He lost the election but shortly afterward there were cross-burnings, anti-Semitic leafleting, an epidemic of racist graffiti and harassment of Mexican-Americans along the border.

"I'm not telling you this because I think La Vista is a hotbed of racism. On the contrary, I've found it an extremely tolerant town, as witnessed by the smooth integration of the Touch. But attitudes can change rather quickly—my forebears were court physicians to the Spanish royal family one week, refugees the next." He warmed both hands on his cup. "Being an outsider means exercising discretion."

"I know how to keep a secret," I said. "Anything you tell me will be kept confidential unless lives are at stake."

He engaged in another bout of silent contemplation, the delicate features solemn and still. We locked eyes for a moment.

"There was some kind of trouble," he said. "Exactly what kind was never publicized. Knowing the girl, it had to be of a sexual nature."

"Why's that?"

"She had a reputation for promiscuity. I don't seek out gossip, but in a small town one overhears things. There's always been something libidinous about the girl. Even at twelve or thirteen when she walked through town every male head would turn. She exuded—physicality. I'd always thought it strange that she sprang from such a withdrawn, isolated family—as if somehow she'd sucked the sexual energy from the others and ended up with more than she could handle."

"Do you have any idea what happened at the Retreat?" I asked, though from Doug Carmichael's story, I had a strong hypothesis.

"Only that her job was terminated abruptly and snickers and whispers circulated around town for the next few days."

"And the Touch never hired town kids again."

"Correct."

The waitress brought the check. I put down my credit card. Maimon thanked me and called for another pot of tea.

"What was she like as a little girl?" I asked.

"I have only vague memories—she was a pretty little thing—that red hair always stood out. Used to pass by my place and say hello, always very friendly. I don't think the problems started until she was twelve or so."

"What kinds of problems?"

"What I told you. Promiscuity. Wild behavior. She started running with a bunch of older kids—the ones with fast cars and motorcycles. I suppose things got out of hand because they sent her away to boarding school. That I remember vividly because on the morning she left Garland's car broke down on the way to the train station. Just gave out in the middle of the road, a few yards from my nursery. I offered to give them a lift but of course he refused. Left her sitting there with her suitcase until he came back with a truck. She looked like a sad little child, though I suppose she must have been at least fourteen. As if all the mischief had been knocked out of her."

"How long was she away?"

"A year. She was different when she returned—quieter, more subdued. But still sexually precocious, in an angry kind of way."

"What do you mean?"

He flushed and drank tepid tea.

"Predatory. One day she walked into my nursery wearing shorts and a halter top. Out of the blue. Said she'd heard I had a new kind of banana and she wanted to see it. It was true—I'd brought in several fifteen-gallon Dwarf Cavendish plants from Florida and had taken a lovely bunch of fruit to the town market for display. I wondered why she'd be interested in something like that, but showed her the plants anyway. She looked them over in a cursory manner and smiled—lasciviously. Then she leaned over and gave me a frank view of her chest, picked a banana and began eating it in a rather crude manner—" He stopped, stammered—"You'll have to excuse me, Doctor, I'm sixty-three, from another generation, and it's hard for me to be as uninhibited about this kind of thing as is fashionable."

I nodded, trying to seem empathetic. "You look much younger."

"Good genes." He smiled. "Anyway, that's the story. She made a production out of eating the banana, smiled at me again and told me it was delicious. Licked her fingers and ran off down the road. The encounter unnerved me because even as she vamped there'd been hatred in her eyes. A strange mixture of sex and hostility. It's hard to explain."

He sipped his tea, then asked, "Has any of this been relevant?"

Before I could answer the waitress returned with the charge slip. Maimon insisted upon leaving the tip. It was a generous one.

We walked out to the parking lot. The night was cool and fragrant. He had the springy step of a man a third his age.

His truck was a long-bed Chevy pickup. Conventional tires. He took out his keys and asked, "Would you like to stop by and visit my nursery? I'd like to show you some of my most fascinating specimens."

He seemed eager for companionship. He'd unloaded a lot of alienation, probably for the first time. Self-expression can become habit forming.

"It would be my pleasure. Could being seen with me cause problems for you?"

He smiled and shook his head.

"Last I heard, Doctor, this was still a free country. I'm located several miles southeast of town. Up in the foothills where most of the big groves are. You'll follow me, but in case we disconnect I'll give you directions. We'll cut under the freeway, ride parallel with it, and turn right on an unmarked road—I'll slow down so you don't miss it. At the foot of the mountains there'll be a left turn onto an old utility trail. Too narrow for commercial vehicles and it floods when the rains come. But this time of year it's a handy shortcut."

He went on for a while before I realized he was directing me to the back road I'd seen on the county map in the sheriff's office. The one that bypassed the town. When I'd asked Houten about it he'd said it was sealed off by the oil company. Perhaps he considered a utility trail too insignificant to be thought of as a road. Or maybe he'd lied.

I wondered about it as I got into the Seville.

20

The turnoff was sudden. The road, apart from being unmarked, was hardly a road at all. Just a narrow dirt ribbon, at first glance one furrow of many that cut through the vast table of farmland. Anyone unfamiliar with the area would have missed it. But Maimon drove slowly and I followed his taillights through moonlit fields of strawberries. Soon the freeway sounds were behind us, the night hushed and aglitter with moths spiraling up toward the stars, pressing frantically and hopelessly for the heat of distant galaxies.

The mountains hovered above us, grim hulking masses of shadow. Maimon's truck was old and it lurched as he shifted into low gear and began the climb into the foothills. I stayed several car-lengths behind and trailed him into darkness so dense it was palpable.

We climbed for miles, finally reaching a plateau. The road veered sharply to the right. To the left was a broad mesa surrounded by chain-link fence. Pyramidal towers rose from the flatlands, skeletal and still. The abandoned oilfields. Maimon turned away from them and resumed the ascent.

The next few miles were groves, unbroken stretches of trees recognizable as such by the serrated silhouette of star-kissed leaves, shiny satin against the velvet of the sky. Citrus, from the perfume in the air. Then came a series of homesteads, farmhouses on one-acre plots shadowed by sycamore and oak. The few lights that were on blurred as we drove by.

Maimon's turn signal went on two hundred feet before he swung left through an open gate. An unobtrusive sign said RARE FRUIT AND SEED CO. He pulled up in front of a big two-story frame house girdled by a wide porch. On the porch were two chairs and a dog. The dog rose on its haunches and nuzzled Maimon's hand as he climbed out of the truck. A Labrador, heavy and stolid, seemingly unimpressed by my presence. Its master petted it and it went back to sleep.

"Come around to the back," said Maimon. We walked along the left side of the house. There was an electrical junction box hanging from the rear wall. He opened it, flicked a switch, and a series of lights came on in sequence, as if choreographed.

What unfolded before my eyes was as textured and verdant as a painting by Rousseau. A masterpiece entitled *Variations on the Theme of Green.*

There were plants and trees everywhere, many in bloom, all thick with foliage. The larger ones sat in five and fifteen gallon containers, a few were rooted in the rich dark soil. Smaller plants and seedlings in peat pots rested on tables shielded by canopies of mesh. Beyond the canopies were three glass greenhouses. The air was a cocktail of mulch and nectar.

He gave me a guided tour. Initially I recognized most of the species but found the varieties novel. There were unusual strains of peach, nectarine, apricot, plum, low-chill apples, and pears. Several dozen fig trees in pots were lined up against a fence. Maimon picked two figs from one of them, handed one to me and popped the other in his mouth. I'd never cared for raw figs but ate the fruit to oblige him. I was glad I did.

"What do you think?"

"Wonderful. Tastes like a dried fig."

He was pleased.

"Celeste. Best taster by my standards, though some prefer Pasquale."

It continued like that, Maimon pointing out choice hybrids with unconcealed pride, sometimes stopping to pick one and offer me a taste. His fruit was unlike anything I'd found on the produce shelves, larger, juicier, more vividly colored and intensely flavored.

Finally we came to the exotic specimens. Many were aflame with orchidlike blossoms in shades of yellow, pink, scarlet, and mauve. Each group of plants was accompanied by a wooden sign staked into the ground. On the sign was a color photograph of fruit, flower, and leaf. Under the illustration were botanical and common names in neatly lettered text, along with geographic, horticultural, and culinary details.

There were species with which I was vaguely familiar—litchies, unusual varieties of mango and papaya, loquats, guavas, and passion fruits—and many others I'd never known existed—sapotes, sapodillas, acerola cherries, jujubes, jaboticaba, tamarinds, tree tomatoes.

One section was devoted to vines—grapes, kiwis, raspberries hued from black to gold. In another, stocked with rare citrus, I saw Chandler pommelos three times the size of grapefruit and sugary sweet, Moro, Sanguinelli, and Tarocco blood oranges with pulp and juice the color of burgundy wine, tangors, limequats, sweet limes, and Buddha's Finger citrons resembling eight-digited human hands.

The greenhouses protected seedlings of the most

fragile plants in the collection, those Maimon had obtained from young adventurers who explored the remote tropical regions of the world for new species of flora. By manipulating light, heat, and moisture he'd constructed microclimates that assured high success in propagation. He became animated as he described his work, tossing out esoterica followed by patient explanations.

Half of the last greenhouse was given over to stacks of carefully labeled boxes. On the table were a postage meter, scissors, tape, and padded envelopes.

"Seeds," he said. "The mainstay of my business. I ship all over the world."

He held open the door and took me to a cluster of small trees.

"Family *annonaceae*." He poked among the leaves of the first tree and uncovered a large yellow-green fruit covered with fleshy spines. "*Annona muricata*, the soursop. And this red one is *Annona reticulata*, the custard apple, Lindstroms variety. There are no fruit on this one here, won't be until August—*Annona squamosa*, sweetsop or custard apple, seedless Brazilian variety. And these," he indicated half a dozen trees with drooping, elliptical leaves, "are the cherimoyas. Right now I've got several varieties—Booth, Bonita, Pierce, White, Deliciosa."

I reached out and touched a leaf. The underside was fuzzy. An orangelike scent issued forth.

"Lovely fragrance, isn't it?" More probing among the branches. "This is the fruit."

It didn't look like the stuff of which dreams were made—a large, globose, heart-shaped mound, pale green and dotted with protrusions, resembling a leathery green pine cone. I touched it gingerly. Firm and gently abrasive.

"Come inside. I'll open a ripe one."

His kitchen was big and old and spotless. The refrigerator, oven, and sink were white enamel, the floor, linoleum waxed to a gleam. A table and chairs fashioned from rock maple occupied the center. I pulled up a chair and sat down. The big Lab had moved indoors and lay snoring at the base of the stove.

Maimon opened the refrigerator, pulled out a cherimoya, and brought it, two bowls, two spoons, and a knife, to the table. The ripe fruit was mottled with brown and soft to the touch. He sliced it in two, put each half in a bowl, skin down. The pulp was a creamy off-white, the color and consistency of fresh custard.

"Dessert," said Maimon and spooned out a shimmering mouthful. He held it aloft then ate.

I put my spoon to the fruit. It slid in and sank. I pulled it out filled with custard and put it to my lips.

The taste was incredible, bringing to mind the flavors of many other fruits yet different from each; sweet, then tart, then sweet again, shifting elusively on the tongue, as subtle and satisfying as the finest confection. The seeds were plentiful, beanlike and hard as wood. An annoyance, but tolerable.

We ate in silence. I savored the cherimoya, knowing it had brought heartbreak to the Swopes, but not permitting that to adulterate my pleasure until all that was left was an empty green shell.

Maimon ate slowly and finished a few minutes later.

"Delicious," I said when he put down his spoon. "Where can you get them?"

"Generally two places. At Hispanic markets they're comparatively cheap but the fruit is small and irregular. If you go to a gourmet grocer you'll pay fifteen dollars for two good-sized ones wrapped in fancy tissue paper."

"So they're being grown commercially?"

"In Latin America and Spain. On a more limited basis here in the U.S., mostly up near Carpenteria. The climate there's too cool for true tropicals but it's even more temperate than what we get down here."

"No frosts?"

"Not yet."

"Fifteen dollars," I thought out loud.

"Yes. It never caught on as a popular fruit—too many seeds, too gelatinous, people don't like to carry spoons with them. No one's found a way to machine-pollinate so it's highly labor-intensive. Nevertheless, it's a delicacy with a loyal following and demand exceeds supply. But for the Fates, Garland would have been wealthy."

My hands were sticky from handling fruit. I washed them in the kitchen sink. When I returned to the table the dog was curled at Maimon's feet, eyes closed, crooning low-pitched canine satisfaction as the grower stroked its fur.

A peaceful scene but it made me restless. I'd lingered too long in Maimon's Eden when there were things that needed to be done.

"I want to take a look at the Swopes' place. Is it one of those farms we passed on the way up?"

"No. They live—lived further up the road. Those weren't really farms, just old home tracts too small to be commercially viable. Some of the people who work in town like to live up here. They get a little more space and the chance to earn spare change growing seasonal cash crops—pumpkins for Halloween, winter melons for the Asian trade."

I remembered Houten's sudden anger when he talked of farming and asked if the sheriff had ever worked the land.

"Not recently," he said hesitantly. "Ray used to

have a plot nearby. Grew conifers that he sold to Christmas tree brokers."

"Used to?"

"He sold the place to a young couple after he lost his daughter. Moved into a rooming house a block from city hall."

The possibility that the sheriff had lied to discourage me from snooping around hadn't left my mind. I found myself wanting to know more about the man who was the law in La Vista.

"He told me about his wife dying of cancer. What happened to the daughter?"

Maimon raised his eyebrows and stopped stroking the Lab. The dog stirred and growled until the stimulation resumed.

"Suicide. Four or five years ago. She hung herself from an old oak on the property."

He recalled it matter of factly, as if the girl's death hadn't been surprising. I commented on it.

"It was a tragedy," he said, "but not one of those cases where one's initial reaction is stunned disbelief. Marla'd always seemed a troubled child to me. Plain, overweight, excessively timid, no friends. Always had her nose buried in a book. Fairy tales, the times I noticed. I never saw her smile."

"How old was she when she died?"

"Around fifteen."

Had she lived she'd be the same age as Nona Swope. The two girls had lived nearby. I asked Maimon if there'd been any contact between them.

"I doubt it. As little girls they sometimes played together. But not after they got older. Marla kept to herself and Nona ran with the wild crowd. You couldn't find two girls more dissimilar."

Maimon stopped stroking the dog. He rose, cleared the table, and began washing dishes.

"Losing Marla changed Ray," he said, turning off the water and picking up a dish towel. "And the town along with him. Before her death he'd been a hell-raiser. Liked to drink, arm-wrestle, tell off-color jokes. When they cut her body down from that tree he turned inward. Wouldn't accept solace from anyone. At first people thought it was grief, that he'd come out of it. But he never did." He wiped a bowl past the gleaming point. "Seems to me La Vista's been a little more somber since then. Almost as if everyone's waiting for Ray to give them permission to smile."

He'd just described mass anhedonia—the rejection of pleasure. I wondered if therein lay the key to Houten's tolerance of the ostensibly self-denying Touch.

Maimon finished drying and wiped his hands.

I got up.

"Thank you," I said, "for your time, the tour, and the fruit. You've created great beauty here." I held out my hand.

He took it and smiled.

"Someone else created it. I've simply displayed it. It's been a pleasure talking to you, Doctor. You're a good listener. Will you be going to Garland's place now?"

"Yes. Just to look around. Can you direct me?"

"Proceed along the road the way we came. You'll pass half a mile of avocado. Owned by a consortium of La Jolla doctors as a tax shelter. Then a covered bridge over a dry bed. Once off the bridge drive another quarter mile. The Swope place is to the left."

I thanked him again. He walked me to the door.

"I passed by the place a couple of days ago," he said. "There was a padlock on the gate."

"I'm a pretty good climber."

"I don't doubt it. But remember what I told you

about Garland's being antisocial. There are coils of barbed wire on top of the fence."

"Any suggestions?"

He pretended to look at the dog, and said with forced nonchalance: "There's a toolshed next to my back porch. Odds and ends. Rummage around, see if you find anything helpful."

He walked away from me and I exited the house.

The "odds and ends" were a collection of high quality hand tools, oiled and wrapped. I selected a heavy-duty bolt cutter and a crowbar and carried them to the Seville. I put them on the floor of the car along with a flashlight retrieved from the glove compartment, started up the engine, and rolled forward.

I looked back at the brightly lit nursery. The taste of the cherimoya lingered on my tongue. As I drove off the property the lights went out.

21

I'd received impressions of the Swopes from multiple sources but had yet to form a coherent image of the shattered family.

Everyone had thought Garland unusual—emotionally inappropriate, secretive, hostile to outsiders. But for a hermit he'd been surprisingly outgoing—Beverly and Raoul had both described him as opinionated and talkative to the point of boorishness, anything but socially reticent.

Emma had emerged as her husband's cringing subordinate, almost a nonentity, except in Augie Valcroix's view. The Canadian doctor had described her as a strong woman and hadn't rejected the possibility that she'd instigated the disappearance.

On the subject of Nona there seemed to be the most agreement. She was wild, hypersexual, and angry. And had been that way for a long time.

And then there was Woody, a sweet little boy. Any way you looked at it, an innocent victim. Was I deluding myself into believing he might still be alive? Engaging in the same kind of denial that had turned a brilliant physician into a public nuisance?

I had an intuitive distrust of Matthias and the

Touch but no evidence to back it up. Valcroix had visited them and I wondered if it had been only a single visit as claimed. Several times I'd watched him space out in a manner reminiscent of the meditation practiced by the Touch. Now he was dead. What was the connection, if any?

Something else stuck in my mind. Matthias had said the cult purchased seeds from Garland Swope once or twice. But according to Ezra Maimon, Garland had nothing to sell. All there was behind his gates was an old house and acres of dust. A minor point? Perhaps. But why the need to fabricate?

Lots of questions, none of them leading anywhere.

It was like a jigsaw puzzle whose pieces had been improperly tooled. No matter how hard I worked, the end product was maddeningly off-kilter.

I passed through the covered bridge and slowed down. The entrance to the Swope property was fronted by a sunken dirt driveway leading to rusty iron gates. The gates weren't high—seven feet at most—but they wore a coiffure of barbed wire that stretched another yard, and were bound, as Maimon had said, by padlock and chain.

I drove a hundred feet before finding space to pull over. Nosing the Seville as close as possible to a stand of eucalyptus, I parked, took the tools and flashlight, and backtracked on foot.

The lock was brand new. Probably affixed by Houten. The chain was plastic-coated steel. It resisted the bolt cutters for a moment then split like overcooked sausage. I opened the gate, slipped through, closed it, and rearranged the severed links to conceal the surgery.

The driveway was gravel and responded to my footsteps with breakfast cereal sounds. The flashlight revealed a two-story frame house, at first glance not unlike Maimon's. But this structure seemed to sag on its foundation, the wood splintered and peeling. The roof was tar paper and bald in several places, the windows framed by warped casements. I placed my foot on the first porch step and felt the wood give under my weight. Dry rot.

An owl hooted. I heard the rasping friction of wings, raised my beam to catch the big bird in flight. Then a broad swoop, the scurrying panic of prey, a thin squeak, and silence once again.

The front door was locked. I considered various means of snapping the lock and stopped midthought, feeling furtive and vaguely criminal. Looking up at the ravaged mass of the decrepit house, I remembered the fate of its inhabitants. Inflicting further damage seemed a heedless act of vandalism. I decided to try the back door.

I stumbled on a loose board, caught my balance, and walked around the side of the house. I hadn't taken a dozen steps when I heard the sound. An incessant dripping, rhythmic and oddly melodic.

There was a junction box in the same place as the one at Maimon's. It was rusted shut and I had to use the crowbar to pry it open. I tried several switches and got no response. The fourth brought on the lights.

There was a single greenhouse. I entered it.

Long heavy wooden tables ran the length of the glass building. The bulbs I'd switched on were dim and bluish, casting a milky glaze over the creations that rested on the heavy planks. At the peak of the ceiling were winches and pulleys designed to open the roof.

The source of the dripping sound became evident: a reptilian system of overhead irrigation operated by old-fashioned dialed timers and suspended from the crossbeam.

Maimon had been wrong about there being nothing but dust behind the Swopes' gates. The greenhouse contained a plethora of growing things. Not flowers. Not trees. *Things*.

I'd thought of the Sephardic grower's nursery as an Eden. What I saw now was a vision from Hell.

Exquisite care had been taken to create a jungle of botanic monstrosities.

There were hundreds of roses that would never fill a bouquet. Their blossoms were shriveled, stunted, colored a deathly gray. Each flower was ragged-edged, irregular, and covered with a layer of what looked like moist fur. Others boasted three inch thorns that turned stem and stalk into deadly weapons. I didn't stoop to smell the flowers but the stench reached me anyway, pungently warm, aggressively rancid.

Next to the roses was a collection of carnivorous plants. Venus's-flytraps, pitcher plants, others I couldn't identify. All were larger and more robust than any I'd seen. Green maws hung open. Sap oozed from tendrils. On the table was a rusty kitchen knife and a slab of beef cut into tiny pieces. Each cube teemed with maggots, many of them dead. One of the flesh-craving plants had managed to lower its mouth to the table and snare some of the white worms with its deadly-sweet exudate. Nearby were more goodies for the carnivores—a coffee can heaped to the brim with dried beetles and flies. The heap shuddered. Out crawled a live insect, a wasp-like creature with a pincer mouth and swollen abdomen. It stared at me and buzzed off. I followed its trajectory. When it had flown out the door, I ran over and slammed it shut. The glass panes vibrated.

And all the while the steady drip-drip from the pipes overhead, keeping everything nice and healthy . . .

Weak-kneed with nausea I walked on. There was a collection of bonsai oleanders, leaves ground to powder and stored in canisters. The granulate had apparently been tested on field mice for poison content. All that remained of the rodents were teeth and bones enshrouded in flesh tanned by rigor mortis. They'd been left to their terminal agonies, paws begging stiffly. The droppings had been used to fertilize trays of toadstools. Each tray was labeled: *Amanita muscaria. Boletus miniato-olivaceus. Helvella esculenta.*

The plants in the next section were fresh and pretty but equally deadly: Hemlock. Foxglove. Black henbane. Deadly nightshade. An ivylike beauty identified quaintly as poisonwood.

There were fruit trees as well. Acrid smelling oranges and lemons, pruned and twisted to nothingness. An apple tree laden with grotesquely misshapen tumors masquerading as fruit. A pomegranate bush slimy with mucoid jelly. Flesh-colored plums harboring colonies of gyrating worms. Mounds of fruit rotted on the ground.

On and on it went, a stinking, repulsive nightmare factory. Then suddenly, something different:

Against the far wall of the greenhouse was a single tree in a hand-painted clay pot. Well-shaped, healthy, and obtrusively normal. A hill had been formed from the dirt that floored the greenhouse and the potted tree rested on it, elevated, as if an object of worship.

A lovely looking tree, with drooping elliptical leaves and fruit resembling leathery green pine cones.

Once outside I gulped fresh air greedily. Behind the greenhouse was a stretch of barren land ending at a black wall of forest. A good place for hiding. Using the flashlight beam for guidance I made my way between the massive trunks of redwood and fir. The forest floor was a spongy mattress of humus. Small animals scampered in the wake of my intrusion. Twenty minutes of searching and prodding revealed no trace of human habitation.

I walked back to the house and switched off the greenhouse lights. The padlock on the back door was fastened to a cheap hasp that yielded to a single twist of the crowbar.

I entered the dark house through a service porch that connected to a large cold kitchen. Electricity and water had been shut off. The greenhouse must have run off a separate generator. I used the flashlight to guide me.

The rooms downstairs were musty and stingily furnished, the walls devoid of paintings or photographs. An oval hooked rug covered the living room floor. Bordering it were a thrift shop sofa and two aluminum folding chairs. The dining room was storage space for cardboard cartons full of old newspapers and bound cords of firewood. Bedsheets had been used for curtains.

Upstairs were three bedrooms, each containing crude, rickety furniture and cast-iron beds. The one that had been Woody's bore a semblance of cheer—a toybox next to the bed, superhero posters on the walls, a Padres banner over the headboard.

Nona's dresser was blanketed with cut-glass perfume atomizers and bottles of lotion. The clothes in her closet were mostly jeans and skimpy tops. The exceptions were a short rabbit jacket of the type Hollywood streetwalkers used to favor and two frilly party dresses, one red, one white. Her drawers were crammed with nylons and lingerie and scented with a homemade sachet. But like the rooms below, her private space was emotionally blank, unmarked by personal touches. No yearbooks, diaries, love letters, or souvenirs. I found a crumpled scrap of lined notebook paper in the bottom drawer of the dresser. It was brown with age and covered, like some classroom punishment, with hundreds of repetitions of the same single sentence: FUCK MADRONAS.

Garland and Emma's bedroom had a view of the greenhouse. I wondered if they'd woken in the morning, peered down at the chamber of mutations and been warmed by a self-congratulatory glow. There were two single beds with a nightstand between them. All available floorspace was given over to cardboard boxes. Some were filled with shoes, others with towels and linens. Still others held nothing but other cardboard boxes. I opened the closet. The parents' wardrobes were meager, shapeless, decades out of style and biased toward grays and browns.

There was a small hinged trapdoor cut into the ceiling of the closet. I found a stepstool hidden behind a mildewed winter coat, pulled it out, and stretched high enough to give the door a strong push. It opened with a slow pneumatic hiss, and a ship's ladder slid down automatically through the aperture. I tested it, found it steady, and ascended.

The attic covered the full area of the house, easily two thousand square feet. It had been transformed into a library, though not an elegant one.

Plywood bookcases were propped against all four walls. A desk had been constructed of the same cheap wood. A metal folding chair sat before it. The floor was speckled with sawdust. I looked for another entry to the room and found none. The windows were small and slatted. Only one mode of construction was possible: planks had been slipped through the trapdoor and nailed together up here.

I ran the flashlight over the volumes that lined the shelves. With the exception of thirty years' worth of *Reader's Digest* condensed books, and a case full of

National Geographics, all were on biology, horticulture, and related topics. There were hundreds of pamphlets from the U.C. Riverside Agricultural Station and the Federal Government Printing Office. Stacks of mail-order seed catalogues. A set of oversized leatherbound *Encyclopaedia of Fruit* printed in England, dated 1879, and illustrated with hand-tipped color lithographs. Scores of college texts on plant pathology, soil biology, forestry management, genetic engineering. A hiker's guide to the trees of California. Complete collection of *Horticulture* and *Audubon*. Copies of patents awarded to inventors of farm equipment.

Four shelves of the case closest to the desk were crowded with blue-cloth looseleaf binders labeled with Roman numerals. I pulled out Volume I.

The cover was dated 1965. Inside were eighty-three pages of handwritten text. The writer's penmanship was hard to decipher—cramped, backslanted, and of uneven darkness. I held the flashlight with one hand, turned pages with the other, and finally got a perceptual fix on it.

Chapter One was a summary of Garland Swope's plan to be the Cherimoya King. He actually used that term, even doodling miniature crowns in the margins of the book. There was an outline of the fruit's attributes and a reminder to check out its nutritional value. The section ended with a list of adjectives to be used when describing it to prospective buyers. Succulent. Juicy. Mouthwatering. Refreshing. Heavenly. Otherworldly.

The rest of the first volume and the nine that followed continued in this vein. Swope had authored eight hundred and twenty-seven pages of text lauding the cherimoya over a ten-year-period, recording the progress of each tree in his young grove and plotting his control of the market. ("Riches? Fame? Which is paramount? No matter, there will be both.")

Stapled in one of the books was an invoice from a printer and a sample brochure brimming with gushing prose and illustrated with color photographs. One picture showed Swope holding a bushel of the exotic fruit. As a young man he'd resembled Clark Gable, tall, husky, with dark wavy hair and a pencil mustache. The caption identified him as a world-renowned horticulturist and botanical researcher specializing in the propagation of rare food crops and dedicated to ending world hunger.

I read on. There were detailed descriptions of crossbreeding experiments between the cherimoya and other members of *annonaceae*. Swope was a compulsive reporter, painstakingly listing every possible climactic and biochemical variable. In the end that line of research had been abandoned with the notation that "No hybrid approaches the perfection that is *a. cherimoya.*"

The optimism came to an abrupt halt in Volume X: I opened to newspaper clippings reporting the freak frost that had decimated the cherimoya grove. There were descriptions of the agricultural damage wrought by the cold winds and projections of rises in food prices clipped from San Diego papers. A mournful feature on the Swopes specifically had been printed in the La Vista *Clarion*. The next twenty pages were filled with jagged, obscene scribbles, the paper deeply indented often to the point of tearing; the pen had been used to stab and slash.

Then new experimental data.

As I turned the pages, Garland Swope's fascination with the grotesque, the stillborn, and the deadly evolved before my eyes. It started as theoretical notations about mutations, and rambling hypotheses about their ecological value. Midway through the eleventh volume was the chilling answer Swope found to those questions: "The sublimely repugnant mutations of otherwise mundane species must be evidence of the Creator's essential hatefulness."

The notes grew progressively less coherent even as they increased in complexity. At times Swope's handwriting was so cramped as to be illegible, but I was able to make out most of it—tests of poison content on mice, pigeons, and sparrows; careful selection of deformed fruit for genetic culture; culling of the normal, nurturance of the defective. All part of a patient, methodical search for the ultimate horticultural horror.

Then there was yet another turn in the convoluted journey through Swope's mind: in the first chapter of Volume XII it appeared he'd dropped his morbid obsessions and gone back to working with *annonaceae*, concentrating on a species Maimon hadn't mentioned: *a. zingiber*. He'd conducted a series of pollinization experiments, carefully listing the date and time of each. Soon, however, the new studies were interrupted by accounts of work with deadly toadstools, foxglove, and dieffenbachia. There was a gleeful emphasis upon the neurotoxic qualities of the last exemplified by a footnote attributing the plant's common name, dumb cane, to its ability to paralyze the vocal chords.

This pattern of shifting between his pet mutations and the new *annonaceae* became established by the middle of the thirteenth volume and continued through the fifteenth.

In Volume XVI, the notes took on an optimistic tone as Swope exulted in the creation of "a new cultivar." Then, as suddenly as it had appeared, *a. zingiber* was discarded and dismissed as "showing robust breeder potential but lacking any further utility." I put my strained eyes through another hundred pages of madness and set the binders aside.

The library contained several books on rare fruit, many of them exquisite editions published in Asia. I looked through all of them but could find no reference to *annonaceae zingiber.* Puzzled, I searched the shelves for suitable reference material and pulled out a thick dog-eared volume titled *Botanical Taxonomy.*

The answer was at the end of the book. It took a while to comprehend the full meaning of what I'd just read. An unspeakable conclusion but agonizingly logical.

As the insights hit I was seized with acute claustrophobia and grew rigid with tension. Sweat ran down my back. My heart pounded and my breathing quickened. The room was an evil place and I had to get out.

Frantically I gathered up several of the blue cloth binders and placed them in a cardboard box. I carried it and my tools down the ladder, bolted the bedroom, and rushed to the landing. Teetering with vertigo, I ran recklessly down the stairs and crossed the frigid living room with four long strides.

After fumbling with the latch I managed to throw open the front door. I stood on the rotting porch until I caught my breath.

Silence greeted me. I'd never felt so alone.

Without looking back I made my escape.

22

Along with everyone else, I'd dismissed Raoul's conviction that Woody Swope had been abducted by the Touch. Now I wasn't so sure.

I'd seen no aberrant crops growing in the gardens of the Retreat, which meant Matthias had lied about buying seeds from the Swopes. On the surface it seemed a petty falsehood, serving no purpose. But habitual liars often lace their stories with demitruths for the sake of realism. Had the guru fabricated a casual connection between his group and the Swopes in order to obscure a deeper relationship?

The lie stuck in my craw. Along with the memory of my first visit to the Retreat, which, in retrospect, seemed suspiciously well orchestrated. Matthias had been too gracious about my intrusion, too pliant and cooperative. For a group that had been described as reclusive, the Touch had been strangely willing to endure scrutiny by a total stranger.

Had the generous welcome meant they had nothing to hide? Or that they had hidden their secret so well that discovery was out of the question.

I thought of Woody and allowed myself the luxury of hope: the boy might still be alive. But for how long?

His body was a biochemical minefield ready to explode at any moment.

If Matthias and his cultists had stashed the boy somewhere on their grounds, a more spontaneous inspection was in order.

Houten had gotten to the Retreat by driving through La Vista and turning right at a fork just outside the town limits. I wanted to avoid being seen and if my recollection of the county map was correct, the road I now traveled intersected the one from town, forming the right prong of the fork. I sped along, headlights off, and soon found myself nearing the gates of the former monastery.

Once again I hid the Seville under tall trees and walked to the entrance on foot. The bolt cutter was in my waistband, the flashlight in my jacket pocket, and the crowbar up one sleeve. I wouldn't stand a chance in an electrical storm.

My hopes for surreptitious entry were dashed by the sight of a male cultist patrolling inside the gates. His white uniform stood out in the darkness, the loose-fitting garments billowing, as he walked back and forth. A leather stash bag swung from the sash around his waist.

I'd come too far to turn back. A plan presented itself. I moved forward cautiously. Closer inspection revealed the guard to be Brother Baron, né Barry Graffius. This cheered me greatly. I'm not a violent person by inclination and had begun to feel more than a little guilty about what I was about to do. But if anyone deserved it, Graffius did. The rationalization didn't remove the guilt, but it did serve to lower it to a tolerable level.

I timed my footsteps to coincide with his and drew

closer. Unloading my tools, I waited, concealed behind high shrubbery, but able to see him through the branches. He continued his walk for a few minutes, then obliged me by stopping to scratch his rear. I gave a low hiss and he snapped to attention, straining to locate the source of the sound. Edging closer to the gate he peered out, sniffing like a rabbit.

I held my breath until he resumed pacing. Another pause, this one deliberate, inquisitive. *Hiss.* He reached under his blouse and drew out a little pistol. Stepped forward, pointing the gun in the direction of the sound.

I waited until he'd stopped and listened three more times before hissing again. This time he let out a curse and pressed his belly up against the iron bars of the gate, eyes wide with suspicion and anxiety. He raised the weapon, moved it in an arc like a turret gunner.

When the barrel was pointing away from me I rushed him, grabbed the gun arm and yanked it forward through the bars. A sharp perpendicular twist against the metal made him cry out in pain and drop the weapon. I put my fist in his solar plexus and as he gasped, employed a little trick I'd learned from Jaroslav. Grabbing his neck, I felt for the right places, found them, squeezed and shut down his carotid arteries.

The choke-held worked quickly. He went limp and passed out. As consciousness departed, his body grew heavy in my grasp. I struggled to keep my hold on him and lowered him carefully to the ground. It was tricky working through the bars but I managed to roll him over and loosen the drawstrings of the stash bag. The yield: a roll of breath mints, a small sack of sunflower seeds, and a ring of keys.

I left him the snacks, took the keys and unlocked

the gates. After retrieving the tools and the pistol, I walked through, closed and relocked the gates.

Stripping Graffius was harder than it looked. I used his clothes to bind his arms and legs. By the time I'd finished I was breathing hard. After ensuring that his nasal passages were clear I gagged him with one of his socks.

He'd be coming around soon and I didn't want him discovered, so I lifted him over my shoulder and carried him off the path, stepping into the bed of succulents. The plants squished underfoot, moist and cold against my trouser legs. I took him through to where the wooded area began, continued several yards, and deposited him between two redwoods.

Gathering my tools I began the walk to the Retreat.

A pale amber light shone above the door of the cathedral. The crucifix seemed to float above the belfry. A pair of male cultists patrolled the entrance at ten minute intervals.

I took my time crossing the viaduct, crouching to avoid detection, concealing myself behind the columns of the arbor. An arched gate was set into the wall to the right of the main building. When the time was right I made a run for it, found it unlocked, and walked through.

I was in one of the many courtyards I'd noticed during my first visit, a grassy rectangle rimmed on three sides by a hedge of eugenia. The church wall formed the fourth. At the far end of the lawn was a brass-topped sundial.

Draperies had been drawn over the clerestory windows, but a crescent of light escaped from one and whitened the grass. I bounded over to look but the windows were too high to see through, the stucco walls free of toeholds.

I searched for something to stand on, saw only the sundial. It was solid stone, far too heavy to carry. Roots had wrapped themselves around the base. By rocking it back and forth I was able to free it from its earthly mooring. Laboriously I rolled it to the window, hoisted myself up, and peeked in through folds of brocade.

The huge domed room was brightly lit, the biblical murals vivid to the point of vulgarity. Matthias sat in its center, cross-legged and naked, on a padded mat. His long body was as thin as a fakir's, soft and pale. Other mats ringed the periphery of the cathedral. Cultists squatted on them, fully garbed, men to the left, women to the right.

The pine table that had been at the center of the room during my first visit was pushed back behind the guru. One of the men—the black-bearded giant from the vineyard—stood by it. Several red porcelain bowls sat on the table. I wondered what was in them.

Matthias meditated.

The flock waited silently and patiently as their shepherd retreated into an internal world, eyes closed, palms pressed together. He swayed and hummed and his penis began to harden, tilting upward. The others gazed at the tumescing organ as if it were sacred. When he was fully erect he opened his eyes and stood.

Stroking himself, he regarded his followers with authoritarian smugness.

"Let the Touch begin!" he thundered in a deep metallic voice.

A woman rose, fortyish, pudgy, and fair. She walked daintily to the table. Blackbeard inserted a golden straw into one of the bowls. The woman stooped and put her nose to it, sniffed hard and inhaled the powder up into her sinuses.

The cocaine must have been high-quality. It took effect quickly. She swooned and grinned, broke into a giggle and did a little dancelike shuffle.

"Magdalene," called Matthias.

She walked to him, undid her clothes and stood naked before her master. Her body was pink and plump, the buttocks marbled and stippled. She knelt and took him in her mouth, licking, nibbling, breasts bobbling with each movement. Matthias rocked on his heels, gritting his teeth with pleasure. She serviced him as the others watched until he pushed her head away and gestured for her to go.

She rose, walked to the left side of the cathedral and stood in front of the men, arms at her sides, completely at ease.

Matthias spoke the name "Luther."

A short man, bald and stooped, with a fully gray beard, stood and disrobed. Upon command he went to the table, received a giant snootful of coke from the giant. Another stage direction from Matthias led him and the chubby woman to the center of the room. She dropped to her knees, teased him hard and lay down on her back. The bald man mounted her and they copulated frantically.

The next woman to dip into the snow and kneel before the guru was tall, bony, and Spanish-looking. She was paired with a heavily built, bespectacled, florid man who looked like he'd been an accountant in a former life. He had an unusually small penis and the angular woman seemed to swallow it whole as she worked energetically to arouse him. Soon the two of them joined the first couple in the horizontal dance on the cathedral floor.

The third woman was Delilah. Her body was

freakishly youthful, lithe, and firm. Matthias kept her with him longer than the first two and had four other women join in. They ministered to him like drones servicing a queen bee. Finally he released them and assigned them partners.

In the course of twenty minutes a fortune in coke had been consumed, with no letup in sight. I saw people go back for seconds and thirds, all in response to commands from Matthias. When one bowl was depleted the giant simply shoved his straw into another.

The padded mats held a writhing mass of wriggling bodies. The scene was sexual without being sensual, depressingly lacking in spontaneity, a mindless ritual, codified, choreographed, and based on the whims of one megalomaniac. A nod from Matthias and the cultists tumbled and thrust. The crook of an eyebrow and they heaved and moaned. I couldn't help being reminded of the maggots blindly burrowing through the meat in Garland Swope's greenhouse.

A roar rose from the cultists. Matthias had spurted. Women scurried to lick him clean. He lay back, sated, but their attentions made him hard again and the action resumed.

I'd seen enough. Climbing down from the sundial, I walked quietly to the gate. The two sentries were approaching from the right, brown-bearded, grim-faced, and goose-stepping in rhythm. I stepped back into the shadows until they had passed. When they'd turned the corners I sprinted out of the courtyard and raced to the iron-banded front door. Pulling it open a crack I peeked through and found the entrance unguarded. From behind the doors of the sanctuary came sounds of muffled bleating and the rhythmic slap of flesh on flesh.

To the left was the dead end punctuated by Matthias's office. I ran to the right, nearly tripping over a potted palm in my haste. The corridor was empty and white. I felt as conspicuous as a roach on a refrigerator. If discovered, I was a dead man: I'd seen the coke cache. I had no idea how long the orgy down the hall would last, or if the sentries' circuit took them indoors. Speed was of the essence.

I searched the laundry room, the kitchen, the members' library, looked for hidden tunnels, false walls, secret stairways. Found nothing.

Using a master key I discovered on the ring I'd taken from Graffius, I conducted a fruitless search of each room. Halfway through there was one false alarm: sudden movement under the bedcovers of one of the beds. For one heart-stopping moment I thought my search was over. But the body under the blanket was adult, male, hirsute, and thick, the face above it red-nosed, openmouthed, and mottled: a cultist sleeping off a cold. The man stirred under the beam of my flashlight, passed wind, and rolled over, dead to the world. I left quietly.

The next room was Delilah's. She'd kept some of her old reviews and press clippings in the bottom of a drawer filled with plain cotton underwear. Other than that her sleeping quarters were as barren as those of the others.

I went from room to room, checking another dozen cells before coming to the one I remembered was Matthias's. The door wouldn't respond to any of the keys on the ring.

I used the crowbar. The bolt was a long one and wouldn't surrender until the door was nearly shattered. Anyone passing by would notice the damage. I slipped inside, taut with pressure.

It was as before. Identical to the others except for the small bookcase. Low ceilinged. Cool. Walled and floored with stone. Dominated by a hard narrow bed covered with a coarse gray blanket.

The humble domicile of a man who'd forsaken the pleasures of the flesh for those of the spirit.

Ascetic. And false to the core.

For the man was anything but spiritual. Minutes ago I'd watched him defile a church, drunk with power, cold as Lucifer. Suddenly the books on his shelves seemed to stare out at me. *Mockingly.* Righteous tomes on religion, philosophy, ethics, morality.

Books had revealed secrets once already this evening. Perhaps they would again.

Furiously, I emptied the shelves, examining each volume, opening, shaking, searching for false spines, hollowed out pages, clues scrawled in margins.

Nothing. The books were pristine, bindings stiff, pages crisp and unfoxed.

Not a single one had been read.

The empty bookcase teetered, shifted on its base. I caught it before it fell. And noticed something.

The portion of the floor that had been under the bookcase was a clearly demarcated rectangle, a shade lighter than the rest. I knelt, pointed the flashlight, ran my fingers over the edges. Seams. Cut into the stone. I pushed. Faint movement.

It took some experimenting to find the proper fulcrum. Stepping on one corner of the rectangle lifted the block sufficiently to lodge the crowbar in the opening. I exerted pressure. The slab rose and I pushed it aside.

The hole was about eighteen inches by a foot, four feet deep and lined with concrete. Too small for a body. But more than ample for other booty:

I found double plastic bags tightly packed with powder in shades of chocolate and vanilla: snowy cocaine and a brownish substance that I recognized as Mexican heroin. A metal strongbox full of sticky dark resin—raw opium. Several pounds of hashish in foilwrapped chunks the size of soap bars.

And at the bottom of the hole, a single manila folder.

I opened it, read it, and slipped it into my shirt. By now I was carrying more cargo than the Southern Pacific. I turned off the flashlight, looked both ways down the hall. Heard the sounds of human voices. At the end of the corridor was a door leading outside. I sprinted as fast as I could and hurled myself through it, lungs aching.

Cultists were streaming out of the sanctuary, most of them still naked. I made it to the base of the fountain without being seen and hid under the oak trees. Matthias came out surrounded by women. One wiped his brow. Another—Maria, the blandfaced, grandmotherly woman who'd sat at the entrance the day of my first visit—gave him a neck rub and fondled his penis. Apparently oblivious to these ministrations, he led the group to the lawn and bade them sit. Five dozen people obeyed, the crowd collapsing like deflated bellows. They were no more than thirty feet away.

Matthias looked up at the stars. Mumbled something. Closed his eyes and began chanting wordlessly. The others joined in. The sound was raw and atonal, a primal wail, passionately pagan. When they reached a crescendo, I sprinted to the viaduct and ran straight for the front gates.

Graffius was lying a few feet from where I'd placed him, twisting like a worm on a griddle, struggling to get free. He seemed to be breathing well. I left him there.

23

I hadn't found what I was looking for. But between Swope's journals and the file I'd taken from Matthias's room I had plenty for show and tell. No doubt my pilferage violated all the rules of evidence, but what I'd found would be enough to get things going.

It was just past two A.M. I got behind the wheel of the Seville, adrenalized and hyperalert. Starting up the engine, I organized my thoughts: I'd drive to Oceanside, find a phone and call Milo or, if he was still in Washington, Del Hardy. It shouldn't take long to notify the proper authorities, and with luck the investigation could commence before dawn.

It was more important than ever to avoid La Vista. I turned the car around in the direction of the utility road and rolled into the dark. I passed the Swope place, Maimon's nursery, the homesteads and the citrus groves, and had reached the plateau of the foothills when the other car materialized from the west.

I heard it before seeing it—its headlights, like mine, were off. There was just enough moonlight to identify the make as it sped past. A late model Cor-

vette, dark, possibly black, its snout nosing the asphalt.
The rumble of an oversized engine. A rear spoiler.
Shiny mag wheels.

But it wasn't until I saw the big fat tires that I
changed my plans.

The Corvette turned left. I shot the intersection,
turned right and followed, lagging far enough behind
to stay out of earshot and struggling to keep the low
dark chassis in view from that distance. Whoever was
behind the wheel knew the road well and drove like a
teenage joyrider, popping the clutch, downshifting
around curves without breaking, accelerating with a
roar that signaled impending redline.

The road turned to dirt. The Corvette chewed it
up like a fourwheeler. The Seville's suspension shim-
mied but I held on. The other car slowed at the sealed
entrance to the oilfields, turned sharply and drove
along the perimeter of the mesa. It accelerated and
sped on, hugging the fence, casting an incision-thin
shadow against the chain link.

The abandoned fields stretched for miles, as deso-
late as a moonscape. Moist craters pocked the terrain.
The fossils of tractors and trucks rose from the sump.
Row after row of dormant wells encased in grid-sided
towers erupted from the tortured earth, creating the illusion of a skyline.

The Corvette was there one moment, gone the
next. I braked quickly but quietly, and coasted forward. There was a car-sized gap in the fence. The
chain link was ragged and curly-edged around the
opening, as if it had unraveled under the force of giant
shears. Tire tracks etched the dirt.

I drove through, parked behind a rusted derrick,
got out, and inspected the ground.

The Corvette's tires had created dual caterpillars
that wove a corridor through convex metal walls: oil

drums were stacked three-high, forming a hundred yards of barricade. The night air stank of tar and burnt rubber.

The corridor terminated in a clearing. In the open space sat an old mobile home on blocks. A smudge of light filtered through a single curtained window. The door was unadorned plywood. A few feet away was the sleek black car.

The driver's door opened. I pressed back, flat against the oil drums. A man got out, arms full, keys dangling from his fingertips. He carried four shopping bags as if they were weightless. Walking to the door of the mobile home, he knocked once, three times, then once again, and let himself in.

He stayed in there for half an hour, emerged carrying an axe, laid it on the Corvette's passenger seat, and got behind the wheel.

I waited ten minutes after he'd driven away before walking to the door and imitating his knock. When there was no response, I repeated it. The door opened. I looked into wide-set eyes the color of midnight.

"Back so soo—" The straight wide mouth froze in surprise. She tried to slam the door shut. I put my foot in and pressed. She pushed back. I got in and she edged away from me.

"You!" The girl was wild-eyed and beautiful. Her flaming hair had been tied up and pinned. A few fine strands had come loose, haloing the long supple neck. Two thin hoops pierced each ear. She wore cut-offs and a white midriff blouse. Her belly was tan and flat, her legs smooth and miles-long, tapering to bare feet. She'd painted her fingernails and toenails hunter green.

The trailer was partitioned into rooms. We were in a cramped yellow kitchen that smelled of mildew. One of the shopping bags had already been emptied. The other three sat on the counter. She fumbled in the dish drainer, came up with a plastic-handled bread knife.

"Get out of here or I'll cut you. I swear it!"

"Put it down, Nona," I said softly. "I'm not here to hurt you."

"Bullshit! Just like the others." She held the knife with both hands. The serrated blade made a wobbly arc. "Get out!"

"I know what was done to you. Hear me out."

She went slack and looked puzzled. For a moment I thought I'd calmed her. I took a step closer. Her young face contorted with hurt and rage.

She took a deep breath and lunged at me, knife held high.

I stepped away from the thrust. She plunged the blade where my thorax had been, stabbed air, and pitched forward awkwardly. I caught her wrist, squeezed and shook.

The knife fell, clicking against grubby linoleum. She went for my eyes with long green nails, but I got hold of both of her arms. She was delicately built, the bones fragile under smooth soft skin, but strengthened by anger. She kicked and coiled and spat, managed to gouge my cheek. On my bad side. I felt a warm trail flow ticklishly down the side of my face, then a sharp sting. Burgundy splotches dotted the floor.

I pinioned her arms to her sides. She went stiff, staring at me with the terror of a wounded animal. Suddenly she darted her face forward. I jerked back to avoid being bitten. Her tongue snaked out and caught a droplet of blood on its tip. She ran it over her lips, rouging them wetly. Forced a smile.

"I'll drink you," she said huskily. "Do anything you want. If you leave afterwards."

"That's not what I'm after."

"It would be if you knew. I can make you feel

things you've never imagined." It was a line from a low-budget skinflick, but she took it seriously, grinding her pelvis against mine. She licked me once more and made a show of swallowing the blood.

"Stop it," I said, arching away.

"Aw, c'mon." She wriggled. "You're a hunk. Those nice blue eyes and all of those thick dark curls. I bet your cock is just as pretty, huh?"

"Enough, Nona."

She pouted and kept rubbing against me. Her skin was saturated with musky dimestore cologne.

"Don't be angry, Blue Eyes. There's nothing wrong with being a big healthy guy with a big gnarly cock. I can feel it now. Right *there*. Oh yeah, it's *big*. I'd *love* to play with it. Put it in my mouth. *Swallow* you. *Drink* you." She batted her lashes. "I'll take off my clothes and let you play with me while I do you."

She tried to lick me again. I freed one hand and slapped her hard across the face.

She reeled backward, stunned, and looked at me with little-girl surprise.

"You're a human being," I said. "Not a piece of meat."

"*I'm a cunt!*" she screamed and tore at her hair, ripping loose the long ginger tendrils.

"Nona—"

She shuddered with self-loathing, sculpted her hands into quivering hooks. But this time they were aimed at her own flesh, inches from ripping open that exquisite face.

I grabbed her and held her tight. She fought me, cursing, then exploded into sobs. She seemed to curl up and diminish in size, crying on my shoulder. When the tears wouldn't come anymore, she collapsed against my chest, mute and limp.

I carried her to a chair, sat her down, wiped her

face with a tissue and pressed another against my cheek. Most of the bleeding had stopped. I retrieved the knife and tossed it in the sink.

She was staring at the table. I cupped her chin in my hand. The inky eyes were glazed and unfocused.

"Where's Woody?"

"Back there," she said dully. "Sleeping."

"Show me."

She rose unsteadily. A shredded plastic shower curtain divided the trailer. I guided her through it.

The back room was stuffy and dim and furnished with thrift shop remnants. The walls were paneled with fake birch, scarred white. A filling station calendar hung lopsided from a roofing nail. Digital time beamed forth from a plastic clock radio atop a plastic Parsons table. On the floor was a pile of teen magazines. A blue velveteen sleeper sofa had been opened to a queen-size bed.

Woody slept under faded paisley covers, coppery curls spreading on the pillow. On the adjacent nightstand were comic books, a toy truck, an uneaten apple, a bottle of pills. Vitamins.

His breathing was regular but labored, his lips swollen and dry. I touched his cheek.

"He's very hot," I told her.

"It'll break," she said defensively. "I've been giving him vitamin C for it."

"Has it helped yet?"

She looked away and shook her head.

"He needs to be in a hospital, Nona."

"No!" She bent down, took his small head in her arms. Pressed her cheek to his and kissed his eyelids. He smiled in his sleep.

"I'm going to call an ambulance."

"There's no phone," she proclaimed with childish

triumph. "Go leave to find one. We'll be gone when you get back."

"He's very sick," I said patiently. "Every hour we delay puts him in greater danger. We'll go together, in my car. Get your things ready."

"They'll *hurt* him!" she screamed. "Just like before. Sticking needles in his bones! Putting him in that plastic jail!"

"Listen to me, Nona. He has *cancer*. He could die from it."

She turned away.

"I don't believe it."

I held her shoulders.

"You'd better. It's true."

"Why? Cause that beaner doctor said so? He's just like all the others. Can't be trusted." She cocked her hip the way she'd done in the hospital corridor. "Why should it be cancer? He never smoked or polluted himself! He's just a little kid."

"Kids get cancer, too. Thousands of them each year. No one knows why but they do. Almost all of them can be treated and some can be cured. Woody's one of them. Give him a chance."

She frowned stubbornly.

"They were poisoning him in that place."

"You need strong drugs to kill the disease. I'm not saying it'll be painless but medical treatment's the only thing that can save his life."

"S'that what the beaner told you to tell me?"

"No. It's what I'm telling you myself. You don't have to go back to Dr. Melendez-Lynch. We'll find another specialist. In San Diego."

The boy cried out in his sleep. She ran to him, sang a low, wordless lullaby, and stroked his hair. He quieted.

She rocked him in her arms. A child cradling a

child. The flawless features trembled on the brink of collapse. The tears started again, in a torrent that streamed down her face.

"If we go to a hospital they'll take him away from me. I can take care of him best right here."

"Nona," I said, summoning all my compassion, "there are things even a mother can't do."

The rocking ceased for a moment, then resumed.

"I was at your parents' house tonight. I saw the greenhouse and read your father's notebooks." She gave a start. It was the first she'd heard of the journals. But she suppressed the surprise and pretended to ignore me.

I continued to talk softly. "I know what you've been through. It started after the death of the cherimoyas. He was probably unbalanced all along, but failure and helplessness drove him over the edge. He tried to get back in control by playing God. By creating his own world."

She stiffened, withdrew from the boy, put his head down on the pillow tenderly, and walked out of the room. I followed her into the kitchen, keeping an eye on the knife in the sink. Stretching, she took a bottle of Southern Comfort from a high cupboard shelf, poured a coffee cup half full, and, leaning rangily against the counter, swallowed. Unaccustomed to hard drinking, she grimaced and went into a paroxysm of coughing as it hit bottom.

I patted her back and eased her to a chair. She took the bottle with her. I sat opposite her, waited until she'd stopped hacking to continue.

"It started out as a series of experiments. Weird stuff using inbreeding and complex grafts. And that's all it was for a while—weird. Nothing criminal happened until he noticed you'd grown up."

She filled the cup again, threw her head back, and

tossed the liquor down her throat, a caricature of toughness.

Once upon a time she'd been anything but tough. A pretty little red-haired girl, Maimon had recalled, smiling and friendly. The problems hadn't started until she was twelve years old or so. He hadn't known why.

But I did.

She'd completed puberty three months before her twelfth birthday. Swope had recorded the day he'd discovered it: ("Eureka! Annona has blossomed. She lacks intellectual depth, but what physical perfection! First rate stock . . .").

He'd been fascinated with the transformation of her body, describing it in botanic terms. And as he observed her development, a hideous plan had taken shape in the wreckage of his mind.

One part of him was still organized, disciplined. As analytical as Mengele. The seduction was undertaken with the precision of a scientific experiment.

The first step was dehumanization of the victim. In order to justify the violation, he reclassified her: the girl was no longer his daughter, or even a person. Merely a specimen of a new exotic species. *Annona zingiber.* The ginger annona. A pistil to be pollinated.

Next came semantic distortion of the outrage itself: the daily excursions into the forest behind the greenhouse weren't incest, simply a new, intriguing project. The ultimate investigation of inbreeding.

He'd wait eagerly each day for her return from school to take her by the hand, and lead her into darkness. Then the spreading of the blanket on ground softened by pine needles, casual dismissal of her protests. There had been a full half year of rehearsal—an intensive seminar in fellatio—then finally, entry into the young body, the spilling of seed on the ground.

Evenings were devoted to the recording of data:

climbing into the attic, he'd log each union in his notebook, sparing no details. Just like any other research.

According to the journals, he'd kept his wife informed about the progress of the experiments. Initially, she'd offered faint protest, then stood by, passively acquiescent. *Following orders.*

Impregnating the girl hadn't been an accident. On the contrary, it had been Swope's ultimate goal, calibrated and calculated. He'd been patient and methodical, waiting until she was a bit older—fourteen—to fertilize her so that the health of the fetus would be optimized. Charting her menstrual cycle to pinpoint ovulation. Refraining from intercourse for several days to increase the sperm count.

It had taken on the first try. He'd rejoiced at the cessation of her menses, the swelling of her belly. A *new cultivar* had been created.

I told her what I knew, wording it gently and hoping the empathy came through. She listened with a blank look on her face, drank Southern Comfort until her eyelids drooped.

"He victimized you, Nona. Used you and discarded you when it was over."

Her head gave an almost imperceptible nod.

"You must have been so frightened, carrying a child at that age. And being sent away to have it in secret."

"Bunch of dykes," she muttered, slurring her words.

"At Madronas?"

She took another drink.

"Fuck yeah. Las Fucking Madronas Home for Bad Little Fucking Girls. In Mexi-fucking-O." Her head lolled. She reached for the bottle. "Big fat fucking beaner dykes running the place. Screaming in beaner. Pinching and poking. Telling us we were trash. Sluts."

Maimon had remembered vividly the morning she'd left town. Had described her waiting with her suitcase in the middle of the road. A scared little girl with all the mischief knocked out of her. About to be banished for the sins of another.

She'd come back different, he'd noted. Quieter, more subdued. Angry.

She was talking now, softly, drunkenly.

"It hurt so bad to push that baby boy out. I screamed and they covered my mouth. I thought I was coming apart. When it was over, they wouldn't let me hold him. Took him away from me. *My* baby, and they took him away! I forced myself to sit up and get a look at him. It near killed me. He had red hair, just like me."

She shook her head, baffled.

"I thought I could keep him after I got home. But *he* said no way. Told me I was nothing. Just a vessel. Just a fucking vessel. Fancy word for cunt. Good for nothing but fucking. Told me I wasn't really the momma. *She'd* already started being his momma. I was the cunt. All used up and tossed in the trash. Time to let the grownups take over."

She dropped her head on the table and whimpered.

I rubbed the back of her neck, said comforting things. Even in that state she reacted reflexively to the touch of a male, lifting her face and flashing me an intoxicated, come-hither smile, leaning forward to expose the tops of her breasts.

I shook my head and she turned away shame-faced.

I had so much sympathy for her it ached. There were therapeutic things I could have said. But now was the time to manipulate her. The boy in the back room needed help. I was prepared to take him out of there against her will but preferred to avoid another abduction. For both their sakes.

"It wasn't you who took him out of the hospital, was it? You loved him too much to endanger him like that."

"It's true," she said, wet-eyed. "They did it. To stop me from being his momma. All these years I'd let them treat me like garbage. Stayed out of the way while *they* raised him. Not saying anything to him about it cause I was afraid it would freak him out. Too much for a little kid to handle. Dying inside all the time." She raised one slender hand to her heart, reached down with the other and drained her glass.

"But when he got sick something tugged on me. Like a hook in my guts with someone reeling in the line. I had to reclaim my rights. I stewed about it, sitting with him in that plastic room, watching him sleep. My baby. Finally I decided to do it. Sat them down in the motel one night, told them the lies had gone on too long. That my time had come. To take care of my baby.

"They—*he* laughed at me. Put me down, told me I was unfit, a piece of shit. A fucking *vessel*. I should get the hell out and make it better for everyone. But this time I didn't take it. The pain in my guts was too strong. I gave it all back to them, told them they were evil. Sinners. That the ca—the sickness was God's punishment for what they'd done. *They* were the ones who were unfit. And I was gonna tell everyone about it. The doctors, the nurses. They'd kick them out and hand my baby over to his rightful momma when they found out."

Her hands trembled violently around her glass. I walked behind her and steadied them with mine.

"It was my right!" she cried out, whipping her head around and begging confirmation. I nodded and she slumped against my chest.

During Baron and Delilah's hospital visit, Emma Swope had complained the cancer treatment was dividing the family. The cultists had construed it as anxiety about the physical separation imposed by the Laminar Airflow room. But the woman had been worrying out loud about a far more serious rupture, one that threatened to rend the family as irreparably as a guillotine on neck-flesh.

Perhaps she'd known, then, that the wound was too deep to heal. But she and her husband had attempted to patch it anyway. To prevent the leakage of the ugly secret by taking the child and running ...

"They snuck him out behind my back," Nona was saying, squeezing my hand, digging in with the green nails. The anger was percolating within her once again. A thin film of sweat mustached the rich, wide mouth. "Like fucking thieves. *She* dressed up as an x-ray technician. In a mask and gown they swiped from the laundry bin. Took him down to the basement on a service elevator and out a side exit. *Thieves.*

"I came back to the motel and all three of them were there. My baby was lying on the bed, so small and helpless. *They* were packing and joking about getting away with it so easy. How nobody had recognized her behind the mask because none of them had ever looked her in the eye. Putting down the hospital. Him going on about smog and shit. Trying to justify what they'd done."

She'd given me an opening. It was time to renew my pitch. To convince her to come with me peaceably as I carried her son out of there.

But before I could say anything the door burst open.

24

Doug Carmichael crouched in the doorway like a commando in a martial arts movies. The arm that extended into the room held a rifle. The other hefted a doubled-edged axe as if it were balsa. He wore a black mesh tank top that exposed lots of hypertrophied muscle. His legs were thick and corded, carpeted with curly blond hair and encased in tight white swim trunks. His knees were misshapen and lumpy—surfer's knots. Rubber beach sandals cushioned large rough feet. The reddish-blond beard was neatly cropped, the thick layered hair precisely blow-dried.

Only the eyes had changed from the day I'd met him. That afternoon in Venice they'd been the color of a cloudless sky. Now I looked into a pair of bottomless black holes: dilated pupils surrounded by thin rings of ice. Mad eyes that scanned the trailer, shifting from the Southern Comfort bottle to the drowsy girl to me.

"I ought to kill you right now for giving her that poison."

"I didn't. She took it herself."

"Shut up!"

Nona tried to straighten up. She swayed groggily. Carmichael pointed the rifle at me.

"Sit down on the floor. Up against the wall, with your hands under you. Good. Now stay put or I'll have to hurt you."

To Nona: "C'mere, Sis."

She went to his side and leaned against his bulk. One massive arm went around her protectively. The one with the axe.

"Did he hurt you, babe?"

She looked at me, knew she was my jury, considered her answer, and shook her head woozily.

"Naw, he's been okay. Just talking. Wants to take Woody to the hospital."

"I'll bet he does," sneered Carmichael. "That's the party line. Pour more poison in and rake in the bucks."

She looked up at him.

"I dunno, Doug, the fever's no better."

"Did you give him the C?"

"Yeah, just like you said."

"What about the apple?"

"He wouldn't eat it. Been too sleepy."

"Try again. If he doesn't like the apple there are pears and plums, too. And oranges." He tilted his head at the shopping bags on the counter. "That stuff is super fresh. Just picked, totally organic. Get some fruit and fluid down him along with more C and he'll cool off."

"The boy's in danger," I said. "He needs more than vitamins."

"I said shut up! You want me to finish you off right here?"

"I don't think he means any harm," said the girl, meekly.

Carmichael smiled at her with genuine warmth and just a touch of condescension.

"You go back in there with the little guy, Sis. Work on nutrition."

She started to say something but Carmichael silenced her with a flash of white teeth and a reassuring nod. Obediently she disappeared behind the shower curtain.

When we were alone he kicked the trailer door shut and moved opposite me, his back to the counter. I stared up into the twin barrels of the rifle—a deadly figure eight.

"I'm going to have to kill you," he said calmly, then shrugged apologetically. "Nothing personal, you know? But we're a family and you're a threat."

The last thing I'd wanted to display was skepticism and I was sure I hadn't. But his psychic radar was hot-wired to go off unpredictably, the scrambled apparatus of the truly paranoiac. He squinted angrily and lowered the rifle, aiming at the tender concavity between my eyes. Hunching his massive shoulders he stared down menacingly.

"We *are* a family. And we don't need a blood test to prove it."

"Of course not," I agreed with a mouth full of cotton. "It's the emotional bond that's important."

He looked at me hard to make sure I wasn't patronizing him. I molded my face into a mask of sincerity. Froze it that way.

The axe swung loosely, whetted blade abrading the floor.

"Exactly. It's feelings that count. Our feelings have been *forged in pain*. We're three against the world. Our family is what it should be—a sanctuary against all the craziness out there. A safe zone. It's beautiful and precious. And I've got to protect it."

I had no plan for escape. For the time being there was no hope but to buy time by keeping him talking.

"I understand. You're the head of the family."

The blue eyes heated like gas flames.

"The only one there ever was. The other two were evil, parents in name only. They abused their rights. Tried to destroy the family from within."

"I know, Doug. I was over at the house this evening. Saw that greenhouse. Read some diaries that Swope kept."

A terrible look oozed onto his face. He lifted his arm and swung the axe in a blinding parabola, letting it smash into the counter. The trailer shook as the plastic shattered. The movement had been effortless, not even budging his rifle arm. There was stirring behind the curtain but no sign of the girl.

"I was going to destroy that shithole tonight," he whispered, jerking the blade free. "With this. Shatter every fucking pane. Take the house apart board by board. Then burn it to the ground. But when I got there the lock had been tampered with so I came back. Lucky I did."

He sucked in his breath, let it out with a hiss. Iron-pumper's breathing. He was sweating heavily, sizzling with agitation. I fought back the fear, forced myself to think clearly: I had to steer his attention to the crimes of the Swopes. And away from me.

"It's an evil place," I said. "Hard to believe people could be like that."

"Not hard for me, man. I lived it. Just like Sis did. My old man diddled me and beat me and told me I was shit for years. And the bitch who called herself mom just stood by and watched. Different theaters but the same movie. When I said forged in pain I meant it."

As he talked about the abuse he'd suffered, lots of things fell into place: the arrested development, the exhibitionism, the hatred and panic when he'd talked about his father.

"It's destiny, Nona and me," he said, with a satisfied smile. "Neither of us could have made it alone. But some kind of miracle brought us together. Made us a family."

"How long have you been a family?" I asked.

"Years. I used to come up summers, worked this field, roughnecking, sinking wells. The old bastard had big plans for this place. Carmichael Oil was gonna rape the land, carve it up, and squeeze every greasy drop out of it. Unfortunately, it was dry as a dead woman's tit." He laughed, banged the axe head against the floor.

"I hated the work. It was dirty and demeaning and boring but he forced me to do it. Every summer, like a jail sentence. I snuck away any chance I got, went hiking through the back roads, breathing clean air. Thinking of ways to get back at him.

"One day I met her while I was walking through the forest. She was sixteen and the most beautiful thing I'd ever seen, sitting on a stump and crying. She saw me and got scared but I told her it was okay. Instead of running, or talking, she started to—" The handsome face darkened and distorted with anger. "Put it out of your filthy mind, man. I never touched her. And that story I told you and the cop about the freeway blow job was bullshit. I was just trying to throw you off."

I nodded. Another explanation for the fantasy suggested itself: wishful thinking. But for now his sexual impulses toward the girl he called his sister were safely repressed and I hoped they'd stay that way.

"It was because I treated her differently from the other men that something special grew between us. Instead of jumping her bones I listened to her. To her pain. Shared my own. All summer we met and talked.

And the summer after that. I started looking forward to working the wells. We got to know each other bit by bit, discovered we'd been through the same thing, realized we were alike—two halves of one person. Male and female components. Brother and sister, but more. Know what I mean?"

I strained to look sympathetic, wanting him to keep on talking. "You formed a common identity. Like some twins do."

"Yeah. It was beautiful. But then the old bastard closed down the wells. Locked everything up. I drove up anyway. On weekends. During holidays for a week at a time. Crashed right here—used to be the night watchman's place. I cooked for her. Taught her how to cook. Helped her with her homework. Showed her how to drive. Took long walks at night. Always talking. About how we wanted to kill our parents, erase our roots. Start fresh, with a new family. We had picnics in the forest. I wanted the little guy to come along, so he could be part of the family, too. But they wouldn't let him out of their sight. She talked a lot about him, how she wanted to claim her rights. I told her she should, taught her about liberation. We made plans for next summer. The three of us were gonna run away to some island. Australia, maybe. I'd started collecting brochures to find the best place, then he got sick.

"She called me as soon as she got to L.A. Wanted me to help her get a job as a prize girl on one of the game shows, but I told her you needed heavy connections for that. Besides, I'd already lined up the gig with Adam and Eve. Got Rambo to let us work as partners. The skits went smooth as silk. We didn't need any rehearsal because each of us knew what the other was thinking. It was like working with yourself. We got big tips and I gave them to her to keep.

"Then one night she phoned me in a panic. Said she'd confronted them and they'd snatched the little guy out. I'd never liked the idea of him being in that hospital in the first place but I was afraid they were gonna disappear south of the border, take him where she'd never see him again.

"I rushed over and got there just as they were leaving. Swope was coming out the door when I opened it. I'd never met him, but I knew damn well what kind of shit he was. He started mouthing off and I hit him in the face. Knocked him out. The woman came at me then, screaming, and I hit her, too, along the side of the head.

"Both of them were lying there, grokked. The little guy was kind of dazed, mumbling in his sleep. Nona got pissed all of a sudden and started to tear up the room. I calmed her down, told her to wait right there, and managed to load both of them in the 'Vette. Stuffed her in the back, put him in the front seat. Drove 'em to the beach at Playa Del Rey and when one of the planes passed overhead, finished 'em off. Then I hauled them to a place I knew in Benedict and dumped them. They deserved to die."

He twirled the axe handle like a baton, chewed on a strawlike mustache hair.

"The police found the remains of another body up there," I said. "A woman." I let the question hang in the air.

He grinned.

"I know what you're thinking, but no. I would have liked to put mom there but she had the bad manners to have a stroke and die in bed a couple of years ago. It pissed me off, because I'd been planning it for years—there's a plot reserved for the old man that I'll fill one day. But she escaped. Then I got lucky. I was doing a late gig at Lancelot's and this old broad in the front row was really coming on to me. Stuffing ten dollar bills down my jock, licking my ankles. Turns out she was a doctor. Radiologist. Divorced a couple of months and out for a wild night. She came to my dressing room, sloshed to the gills, started pawing me, sending out real strong signals. It turned me off and I was gonna kick her out. But when I turned on the lights I saw it: she could have been the old bitch's twin sister. Same dried-up face, upturned nose, rich bitch manner.

"I smiled, said *Come on in, honey.* Let her do me, right there in the dressing room. The door was un-locked, anyone could have come in. She didn't care, just hiked up her skirt and got on top. Later we went to her place, condo penthouse in the Marina. Made it again and then I strangled her in her sleep." His eyes widened innocently. "The burial plot had been chosen. Someone had to fill it."

He leaned the axe against the oven, reached into one of the shopping bags with his free hand and brought out a large peach.

"Want one?"

"No thanks."

"They're good. Good for you, too. Calcium, po-tassium. Lots of A and C. Make a great last meal."

I shook my head.

"Suit yourself." He took a large bite out of the fruit, licked the juice from the ends of his mustache.

"I'm no threat to you," I said, choosing my words carefully, "I just want to help your little brother."

"How? By pumping him full of poisons? I read all about that stuff they wanted to use on him. That shit *causes* cancer."

"I'm not going to lie and tell you the drugs they use are harmless. They're strong—poisons just like you said. But that's what it takes to kill the tumors."

"Sounds like a load of shit to me." His jaw tightened and the beard bristled. "She told me all about the doctors there. Who's to say you're any different?"

He finished the peach and threw the pit in the sink. Took out a plum and dispatched it, too.

"Come on," he said, picking up the axe. "Stand up. Let's get it over with. I wish for your sake that I'd gotten you the first time, with the shotgun. You wouldn't even have known what hit you. Now you're gonna have to suffer a bit, waiting for it to happen."

25

I walked to the door, the tip of the rifle nudging the small of my back.

"Open it slowly and carefully," instructed Carmichael. "Keep your hands on your head and look straight ahead."

I obeyed him shakily and heard the rustling of the shower curtain, the sound of Nona's voice.

"You don't need to hurt him, Doug."

"Go back in. Let me handle this."

"But what if he's right? Woody's burning up—"

"I said I'll handle it!" the blond man snapped, with sudden loss of patience.

Her unseen response caused him to soften his voice.

"I'm sorry, Sis. It's been heavy and we're all stressed out. When I finish with him, we'll settle down, drop some B-twelve. I'll show you how to cool the little guy down. Couple weeks he'll be fine and we'll split. This time next month I'll be teaching him how to shoot the waves."

"Doug, I—" she began. I hoped she'd continue to plead my case, providing diversion for a sudden run.

But she stopped midsentence. Padded footsteps were followed by the whisper of the curtain closing.

"Move," said Carmichael, angered by the hint of rebellion and expressing it by jamming cold steel into my kidney.

I pushed the door open and stepped into darkness. The chemical stench in the air seemed stronger, the bleakness of the mesa more pronounced. The husks of the unused machines were giant, rusting carcasses, sprawled passive and silent across the ravaged terrain. It was far too ugly a place in which to die.

Carmichael prodded me through the corridor created by the stacked oil drums. My eyes darted from side to side, searching for escape, but the black cylinders formed high metal barricades, mercilessly seamless.

Several yards before the end of the passageway he started talking, offering me options.

"I can do it while you're standing, kneeling, or lying on the ground the way I did the Swopes. Or, if being still freaks you out, you can make a run for it, get a little exercise to take your mind off what's coming. I won't tell you how many steps I'll give you, so you can pretend it's like a regular run. Make believe you're in some kind of marathon. When I run I get high. Maybe you will, too. I'm using a heavy load so you won't feel a thing. Kinda like one big rush."

My knees buckled.

"Come on, man," he said, "don't fall apart. Go out with style."

"Killing me won't do you any good. The police know I'm here. If I don't return they'll be swarming over this place."

"No sweat. As soon as you're out of the way, we're splitting."

"The boy can't travel in his condition. You'll kill him."

The rifle jabbed painfully.

"I don't need your advice. I can take care of my own."

We walked in silence until we reached the mouth of the metal hallway.

"So how do you want it," he demanded, "standing still or running?"

A hundred yards of flat, empty land lay before me. The darkness would provide some cover for a run but I'd still be easy to pick off. Just beyond the void were hills of scrap metal—strips of sheet-iron, coils of wire, the derrick behind which I'd hidden the Seville. Meager sanctuary, but finding cover among the detritus would gain me time to plan . . .

"Take your time," Carmichael said magnanimously, savoring the starring role.

He'd played this scene before, was working hard at coming across cool and in control. But I knew he was as unstable as nitro and just might start blowing his lines if provoked. The trick was to get him sufficiently distracted to lower his guard, then flee. Or attack. It was a deadly gamble—a sudden burst of rage could just as easily yank his trigger finger. But there wasn't much to lose at this point and the idea of submitting passively to slaughter was damned distasteful.

"Make up your mind?"

"It's a bullshit choice, Doug, and you know it."

"What?"

"I said you're full of shit."

Growling, he spun me around, tossed the rifle away, and grabbed the front of my shirt, pulling it tight. He raised the axe and held it poised in the air.

"Move and I'll slice you like cheese." He panted

with anger, face glistening with sweat. A feral smell emanated from the mass of his body.

I kneed him hard in the groin. He yelped in pain and relinquished his grip reflexively. I pulled away, landed on the ground, scurried backward like a crab, scraping my knees and palms. While fighting to push myself upright I pressed my foot against something round. A large metal spring. It rolled, I was upended, and fell flat on my back.

Carmichael charged forward, hyperventilating like a child coming out of a tantrum. The edge of the axe caught a glint of moonlight. Shadowed against the blackness of the sky he seemed immense, fictional.

I yanked myself up and crawled away from him.

"You've got a big mouth," he gasped. "No class, no style. I gave you the opportunity to end it peacefully. I tried to be fair but you didn't appreciate it. Now it's gonna hurt. I'm gonna use this on you." He hefted the axe for emphasis. "Slowly. Turn you into garbage piece by piece and make it last. In the end you'll beg for a bullet."

A figure stepped out from behind the oil drums.

"Put it down, Doug."

Sheriff Houten stepped into the clearing, trim and sure-footed. The Colt .45 extended like a nickel-plated handshake.

"Put it down," he repeated, leveling the firearm at Carmichael's chest.

"Leave it alone, Ray," said the blond man. "Got to finish what we started."

"Not this way."

"It's the only way," insisted Carmichael.

The lawman shook his head.

"I just got off the phone with a fellow named Sturgis at L.A. Homicide. He was making inquiries about the doctor here. Seems somebody took a shot at him last night and gunned down the wrong man. Next day the doctor disappeared. They're looking for him in earnest. I figured he might have ended up here."

"He's trying to break up my family, Ray. You warned me about him yourself."

"You're confused, boy. I told you he'd asked about the back road so you'd find yourself another hiding place. Not to put you up to killing the man. Now drop that axe and we'll talk about it calmly."

He held his gun steady and looked down at me.

"Damn stupid of you to go snooping around, Doctor."

"It seemed better than being a stationary target. And there's a little boy in that trailer who needs medical attention."

He shook his head fiercely.

"Boy's gonna die."

"Not true, Sheriff. He can be treated."

"That's what they told me about my wife. I let them cut her up and fill her with poisons and the cancer ate her up just the same." He returned his attention to Carmichael:

"I backed you up to a point, Doug, but it's gone too far. Lay down the axe."

The two of them locked eyes. I seized the opportunity to roll out of hacking range.

Carmichael saw me and swung his weapon.

The .45 blazed. Carmichael jumped back, screaming in pain. He clamped one hand to his side, blood seeping out around his fingers. Incredibly, the other continued to grip the axe.

"You—you hurt me," he muttered, incredulous.

"Just a flesh crease," said Houten evenly. "You'll survive. Now let go of the damned axe, boy."

I stood and inched toward the discarded rifle, staying out of the blond man's swinging range.

The door to the trailer opened, spilling cold white light down the pathway. Nona ran out calling Carmichael's name.

"Get the rifle, Sis!" he yelled. The command emerged from between pain-clenched jaws. The hand holding the axe was shaking. The one at his side was glossy red from wrist to fingertips. Blood rolled viscously over his knuckles and dripped to the ground.

The girl came to a stop, watching wide-eyed as the dirt at Carmichael's feet sprouted a spreading crimson flower.

"You killed him!" she shrieked and ran toward Houten, striking out blindly. He straight-armed her while keeping a bead on the wounded man. She flailed away at him without doing any damage. Finally he shoved her aside and she staggered off-balance before falling.

I edged closer to the rifle.

Nona picked herself up.

"You filthy old fuck!" she screamed at the Sheriff. "You were supposed to help us and now you've killed him!" Houten looked past her woodenly. Suddenly she flung herself at Carmichael's feet. "Don't die, Doug. Please. I need you so bad."

"Get the rifle!" he screamed.

She looked up at him blankly, nodded, and marched toward the weapon. She was closer to it than I and it was time to move. As she stooped to retrieve it I dove.

Carmichael saw me out of the corner of his eye, pivoted and slashed down at my arm with the axe. I jerked back. He grunted in agony, his wound leaking copiously, and slashed again, missing me by inches.

Houten crouched, two-handed the .45, and shot Carmichael in the back of the head. The exit trajectory tore open his throat. He clutched at his neck, sucked in air, gurgled, and dropped.

The girl snatched up the rifle and cradled it knowingly. She stared at the body on the ground. Carmichael's limbs twitched autonomically and she watched, transfixed, until they were still. Her hair was loose and blowing in the night breeze, her eyes frightened and moist.

Carmichael's bowels opened with a burst of flatulence. The beautiful face hardened. She looked up, pointed the weapon at me, shook her head and arced around, aiming at the sheriff.

"You're just like the rest," she spat at him.

Before he could reply she shifted her attention back to the corpse, began talking to it in a singsong voice.

"He's just like the rest, Doug. He didn't help us because he was good, because he was on our side like you thought. He did it because he was a fucking coward. Afraid I'd tell his dirty secrets."

"Quiet, girl," warned the sheriff.

She ignored him.

"He fucked me, Doug, just like all the other filthy, evil old men with their filthy cocks and their sagging balls. When I was just a little girl. After the monster broke me in. The righteous arm of the law." She sneered. "I flashed him a sample and he lapped it up. Couldn't get enough. Had to have it every day. In his house. In his truck. Picked me up while I walked home from school and drove me up to the hills to do it. What do you think of our old friend, Ray, now, Doug?"

Houten shouted for her to shut up. But his voice lacked conviction and he seemed to sag, looking shriveled and helpless despite the big gun in his hand.

She continued to address the body, sobbing.

"You were so good and trusting, Doug ... You thought he was being our friend, helping us hide out because he didn't like doctors any better than we did ... Because he understood. But that wasn't it at all. He would have given us up in a minute but I threatened to expose him if he did ... To tell everyone that he fucked me. And *knocked me up*."

Houten looked at the Colt. Harbored a terrible thought and dismissed it. "Nona, you don't wa—"

"He thinks he's Woody's daddy, cause that's what I've told him all these years." She stroked the rifle and giggled. "Course now, maybe I was telling the truth, maybe I wasn't. Maybe I don't even know. We never did do any blood tests to find out, did we, Ray?"

"You're crazy," he said. "You'll be locked up." To me: "She's crazy. You can see that, can't you?"

"Is that so?" She put her finger around the trigger and smiled. "I guess you know all about crazy. All about crazy little girls. Like little old fat crazy Marla, always sitting by herself, rocking and writing dumb crazy poems. Talking to herself, wetting her pants, and carrying on like a baby. *She* was crazy, wasn't she, Ray? Fat and ugly and a real head case."

"Shut your mouth—"

"You shut yours, you old bastard!" she screamed. "Who the hell are you telling me what to do? You fucked me every day, taking sloppy seconds without complaining. Shot your scum into me and knocked me up." She smiled eerily. "Maybe. Least that's what I told Crazy Marla. You shoulda seen the look in those piggy little eyes. I gave her *all* the details. About how you lapped it up and begged for more. *Sheriff*. I must have upset the poor thing, 'cause the next day she took a rope and—"

Houten bellowed and came at her.

She laughed and shot him in the face.

He collapsed like wet tissue paper. She stood over him and pulled the trigger again. Braced herself against the recoil and put yet another slug into him.

I peeled her fingers off the weapon and let it fall between the two corpses. She offered no resistance. Put her head on my shoulder and gave me a lovely smile.

I took her with me and went looking for the El Camino. It wasn't hard to find. Houten had parked it just outside the gap in the fence. Watching her closely, I used the radio to make my calls.

26

Late on a quiet Sunday afternoon, I stood on the lawn across from the entrance to the Retreat and waited for Matthias. Furnace-blast winds had strafed the southern half of the state without letup for thirty-six hours and though sunset was drawing near the heat refused to dissipate. Sticky, itchy, and overdressed in jeans, chambray shirt, and a calfskin jacket, I sought the shade of the old oaks circling the fountain.

He emerged from the main building encircled by a cocoon of followers, glanced in my direction and bade them disperse. They moved to a hilly spot, sat and began to meditate. He approached slowly and deliberately, staring downward, as if searching for something in the grass.

We came face to face. Instead of greeting me, he dropped to the ground, folded himself into a lotus position, and stroked his beard.

"I don't see pockets in the outfit you're wearing," I said. "No place to hold a substantial wad of cash. I hope that doesn't mean you didn't take me seriously."

He ignored me and stared off into space. I tolerated it for a few minutes then made a show of losing my patience.

"Cut the holy-man crap, Matthews. It's time to talk business."

A fly settled on his forehead, walked nimbly along the edge of the crater-scar. It didn't seem to bother him.

"State your business," he said softly.

"I thought I was pretty clear over the phone."

He picked a stalk of clover and twirled it in his long fingers.

"About certain things, yes. You confessed to trespassing, assault on Brother Baron, and burglary. What remains unclear is why there should be any—business for you and me to conduct."

"And yet you're here. Listening."

He smiled.

"I pride myself on maintaining an open mind."

"Listen," I said, turning to go. "I've had a rough couple of days and my tolerance for bullshit is at an all time low. What I've got will keep. You want to think about it, go ahead. Just add a thousand a day in late fees."

"Sit down," he said.

I settled opposite him, crossing my legs and tucking them under me. The ground was as hot as a waffle iron. The itch in my chest and belly had intensified. Off in the distance the cultists bowed and scraped.

His hand left his beard and stroked the grass idly.

"You mentioned a substantial sum of money over the phone," he said.

"A hundred and fifty thousand dollars. Three installments of fifty thousand each. The first today, the following two at six-month intervals."

He worked hard at looking amused.

"Why in the world would I pay you that kind of money?"

"For you it's petty cash. If the party I saw a couple of nights ago is typical, you and your zombies shovel that much up your noses in a week."

"Are you implying that we use illicit drugs?" he asked, mockingly.

"Perish the thought. No doubt you've removed the stash, stowed it somewhere else, and would welcome a police search with open arms. Just like you did the first time I was here. But I've got Polaroids from the party that would make great porno for the geriatric set. All those worn-out bodies grinding away. Bowls of snow and straws up noses. Not to mention a couple of clear shots of the cache under your bookcase."

"Photographs of consenting adults having sex," he recited, sounding suddenly like an attorney, "bowls on a table containing an unknown substance. Plastic bags. It doesn't add up to much. Certainly not a hundred and fifty thousand."

"How much is avoiding a murder rap worth?"

His eyes narrowed and his face changed into something lupine and predatory. He tried to stare me down but it was no contest. The itch had grown nearly unbearable and gazing back at the brutal mask was a welcome distraction.

"Go on," he said.

"I made three copies of the file, added a page of interpretation to each one, and put them in separate safe places. Along with the pictures and instructions to several attorneys in the event of my untimely demise. Before I copied I read through it several times. Fascinating."

He looked composed but his right hand gave him away. The bony white fingers had clawed the ground and ripped out a handful of grass.

"Generalities are worthless," he whispered harshly. "If you have something to say, say it."

"All right," I said. "Let's flash back a little over

twenty years ago. Long before you discovered the guru scam. You're sitting in your office on Camden Drive. A mousy little woman named Emma is on the other side of the desk. She's travelled all the way from a hick town called La Vista to Beverly Hills and has paid you a hundred dollars for a confidential legal consultation. A lot of money in those days.

"Emma's story is a sad one, though no doubt you think of it as third-rate melodrama. Finding herself trapped in a loveless marriage she'd sought comfort in the arms of another man. A man who made her feel things she'd never imagined possible. The affair had been heavenly, true refuge. Until she became pregnant by her lover. Panicked, she hid the fact for as long as possible and when she started showing, told her husband the child was his. The cuckold had been ecstatic, ready to celebrate, and when he uncorked the champagne she nearly died of guilt.

"She's considered an abortion but had been too scared to go through with it. She prayed for a miscarriage but none came. You ask her if she's told her lover about the problem and she says no, horrified at the thought. He's a pillar of the community, a deputy sheriff charged with upholding the law. On top of that, he's married, with a pregnant wife of his own. Why destroy two families? Besides he hasn't called in a long time, confirming her suspicions that for him the relationship had been primarily carnal all along. Does she feel abandoned? No. She's sinned and now she's paying for it.

"As the fetus grows in her womb so does the burden of her secret. She lives the lie for eight and a half months until she can't take it any longer. On a day when her husband is out of town she gets on the bus and heads north, to Beverly Hills.

"Now she sits in your big glossy office, so out of

her element, just weeks from delivery, confused and terrified. She's considered her options for plenty of sleepless nights and has finally come to a decision. She wants out. A divorce, quick and easy, with no explanation. She'll leave town, have the baby in solitude, maybe in Mexico, put it up for adoption, and start a new life far away from the site of her transgression. She's read about you in the pages of a Hollywood fan magazine and is sure you're the man for the job.

"As you listen to her, it's clear that quick and easy is out of the question. The case would be a messy one. That by itself wouldn't have stopped you from taking it on, because the messy cases bring in the fattest fees. But Emma Swope wasn't your type of client. Drab and unglamorous and strictly small town. Most important, she didn't smell of money.

"You took her hundred, and discouraged her from engaging your services. Gave her a line about doing better with a local attorney. She left red-eyed and heavy-bellied and you filed it away and forgot about it.

"Years later you get shot in the head and decide to make a career switch. You've built up lots of connections with the big money people, which in L.A. includes the dope trade. I don't know who suggested it first, you or one of them, but you decide to go for megabucks as a coke and smack middleman. The fact that it's illegal adds to the appeal because you see yourself as a victim, as having been failed by the system you'd served faithfully. Dealing dope is your way of saying fuck the system. The money and power aren't too shabby, either.

"For the enterprise to be successful you'll need a place close to the Mexican border and a good cover. Your new partners suggest one of the small agricultural towns south of San Diego. La Vista. They know of an old monastery for sale just outside the town limits. Secluded and quiet. They've been considering it for a while but need a way of keeping the locals from prying. You look at a map and something flashes. The bullet didn't destroy the old memory. Back into the files. How am I doing so far?"

"Keep talking." His palm was wet and green from compressing the torn grass into a ball.

"You do a little research and find out that Emma Swope never did get another lawyer. Her visit to you had been a single burst of initiative in an otherwise timid existence. She reverted to type, swallowed the secret and lived with it. Gave birth to a beautiful little red-headed daughter who's now grown up into a wild young teenager. Lover Boy's still around, too, busy enforcing the law. But he's no longer a deputy. He's the head honcho. The man everyone looks up to. So powerful he sets the emotional tone of the town. With him in your pocket you'll have a free ride."

All traces of serenity had passed from the long bearded face. He touched his beard and stained it green, tasted grass and spat.

"Sleazy little people with their stinking little intrigues," he snarled. "Laboring under the delusion that there's some meaning to their lives."

"You sent him a copy of the file, invited him to Beverly Hills for a chat, half-expecting him to ignore you or tell you to go to hell. What's the worst that would have happened? A minor scandal? Early pension? But he was there the next day, wasn't he?"

Matthias laughed out loud. It wasn't a pleasant sound.

"Bright and early," he said, nodding, "in that ridiculous cowboy costume. Trying to look macho but quaking in his boots—the fool."

He reveled cruelly in the memory.

"You knew, right away," I continued, "that you'd

touched on something vital. Of course, it wasn't until the following summer, when the girl worked for you, that you figured it out, but you didn't have to understand the fear to capitalize on it."

"He was a yokel," said Matthias. "A sucker for a bluff."

"That summer," I said, "must have been an interesting one. Your brand-new social structure threatened by a sixteen-year-old girl."

"She was a little nympho," he said contemptuously. "Had a thing for older men. Went after them like a vacuum cleaner. I heard rumors from the time she got here. One day I discovered her blowing a sixty year old in the pantry. Pulled her off and called Houten. The way they looked at each other tipped me off as to why the file had turned him to jelly. He'd been screwing his own daughter without knowing it. I knew then that his balls were in my pocket. Forever. From that point on I pressed him into service."

"Must have come in handy."

"Exceedingly," he grinned. "Before elections, when the Border Patrol came down hard, he'd go into Mexico and pick up the cargo for us. Nothing like a personal police escort."

"It's a hell of a nice setup," I said. "Well worth preserving. If I were you I'd view the hundred and fifty as a bargain."

He shifted his weight. I took the opportunity to recross my legs. One foot had fallen asleep and I shook it gently to restore circulation.

"All I've heard up to this point is pure supposition," he said coolly. "Nothing worth trading for."

"There's more. Let's talk about Dr. August Valcroix. A refugee from the sixties and a devotee of situational ethics. I'm not sure how the two of you got together but he'd probably been dealing up in Canada and knew some of your partners. He became one of your salesmen, handling the hospital trade. What better cover for it than a bona fide M.D.?

"The way I see it, he could have gotten hold of the stuff in two ways. Sometimes he came down here to collect, under the guise of attending a seminar. When that was inconvenient, you sent it up to him. Which is what Graffius and Delilah were doing in L.A. the day they visited the Swopes. A courtesy call after a dope transfer. They had nothing to do with the Swopes' reluctance to treat Woody or the abduction, despite Melendez-Lynch's suspicions.

"Valcroix wasn't much of a human being but he knew how to listen to patients and get them to open up. He used that talent to seduce and—sometimes—to heal. He developed a good rapport with Emma Swope—he's the only one who described her as other than a nonentity, as being strong. Because he knew something about her no one else did.

"The diagnosis of cancer in a child can throw a family off-kilter, disrupt old patterns of behavior. I've seen it happen plenty of times. For the Swopes, the stress was crushing; it turned Garland into a pompous jester and caused Emma to sit and brood about the past. No doubt Valcroix caught her at a particularly vulnerable moment. She got in touch with her guilt and spilled out her confession because he seemed like such a compassionate fellow.

"Anyone else would have considered it just another sad story and kept it confidential. But for Valcroix the information had larger implications. He'd probably observed Houten and wondered why he was so willing to take orders from you. Now he knew. And he was unethical—confidentiality meant nothing to him. When his future as a doctor began to look shaky, he drove down here and confronted you with his knowledge, demanding a bigger piece of the pie. You feigned concession, doped him up until he fell asleep, had one of your faithful drive him halfway back to L.A., to the Wilmington docks. Another followed in a second car. They set up a fatal accident, watched it happen, and drove off. The technique is simple enough—wedge a board between the seat and the accelerator . . ."

"Close." Matthias smiled. "We used a tree branch. Apple tree. Organic. He hit the wall at fifty. Barry said he looked like a tomato omelet afterward." Licking his mustache, he gave me a hard meaningful look. "He was a grasping, greedy pig."

"If that's supposed to scare me off, forget it. A hundred and fifty. Firm."

The guru sighed.

"By itself the hundred and fifty is a nuisance," he said. "And a palatable one. But who's to say it'll stop there? I've looked you up, Delaware. You were a top man in your field but now work only irregularly. Despite your apparent indolence, you like to live well. That worries me. Nothing feeds greed more quickly than a sizable gap between want and have. A new car, couple of fancy vacations, down payment on a condo in Mammoth, and it's all gone. Next think I know, you're back with an outstretched palm."

"I'm not greedy, Matthews, just resourceful. If your research was thorough you'd know I made a bunch of good investments that are still paying off. I'm thirty-five and stable, have lived comfortably without your money and could do so indefinitely. But I like the idea of ripping off a master rip-off artist. As a one-shot deal. When the one fifty's safely in my hands you'll never see or hear from me again."

He grew thoughtful.

"Would you consider two hundred in coke?"

"Not a chance. Never touch the stuff. Hard cash."
He pursed his lips and frowned.

"You're a tough bastard, Doctor. You've got the killer instinct—which I admire in the abstract. Barry was wrong about you. He said you were a straight arrow, sickeningly self-righteous. In actuality you're a jackal."

"He was a lousy psychologist. Never did understand people."

"Neither do you, apparently." He stood suddenly and gestured to the cultists on the hill. They rose in unison and marched forward, a battalion in white.

I bounded up quickly.

"You're making a mistake, Matthews. I've taken precautions for exactly this contingency. If I'm not back in L.A. by eight the files get opened. One by one."

"You're an ass," he snapped. "When I was an attorney I chewed up people like you and spat them out. Shrinks were the easiest to terrorize. I made one wet his pants up on the stand. A full professor, no less. Your bush-league attempt at arm twisting is pathetic. In a matter of minutes I'll know the location of every single one of those files. Barry wants to handle the interrogation personally. I think it's an excellent idea—his desire for revenge is quite robust. He's a nasty little slime, very well suited to the job. It will be excruciating, Delaware. And when the information is in my hands you'll be dispatched. Another unfortunate accident."

The cultists marched closer, robotlike and grim.

"Call them off, Matthews. Don't dig yourself deeper."

"Excruciating," he repeated and beckoned them closer.

They formed a circle around us. Blank, middle-aged faces. Tight little mouths. Empty eyes. Empty minds . . .

Matthias turned his back on me.

"What if there are other copies? Ones I didn't tell you about?"

"Good-bye, Doctor," he said, scornfully, and began to exit the circle.

The others stepped aside to let him through and closed ranks immediately after he'd passed. I spotted Graffius. His puny frame quivered with anticipation. An ellipse of drool dotted his lower lip. When our eyes met the lip drew back hatefully.

"Take him," he ordered.

The black-bearded giant stepped forward and grabbed one of my arms. Another large man, heavy-set and gap-toothed, grasped the other. Graffius gave the signal and they dragged me toward the main building, followed by two dozen others chanting a wordless dirge.

Graffius ran alongside and slapped my face teasingly. Cackling with glee, he told me about the party he'd planned in my honor.

"We've got a new designer hallucinogen that makes acid seem like baby aspirin, Alex. I'll shoot it right into your veins with a Methedrine chaser. It'll be like being dipped in and out of hell."

He had lots more to say but his oration was cut short by a sudden, brief stutter of gunfire, punctuating the silence like a symphony of giant bullfrogs. The second burst was longer, the unmistakable belch of heavy-duty firearms.

"What the fuck!" exclaimed Graffius, chin whiskers trembling like charged filaments.

The procession stopped.

From that point on everything seemed to happen in fast-forward.

The sky filled with thunder. Whirring blades and blinking lights assaulted the gathering dusk. A pair of helicopters circled overhead. From one of them boomed an amplified voice:

"This is Agent Siegel of the Federal Drug Enforcement Agency. The shots were a warning. You are surrounded. Release Dr. Delaware and lie face down on the ground."

The message was repeated. Over and over.

Graffius started screaming unintelligibly. The rest of the cultists stood rooted in place, looking up to the heavens, as baffled as primitives discovering a new god.

The helicopters swooped low, rustling the trees.

Agent Siegel continued to reiterate his command. The cultists didn't comply—out of shock, not defiance.

One of the helicopters aimed a high-intensity beacon on the group. The light was blinding. As the cultists shielded their eyes, the invasion began.

Scores of men, flak-jacketed and wielding automatic weapons, converged on the grounds with the silent efficiency of soldier ants.

One group of raiders materialized from beneath the viaduct. Seconds later another emerged from behind the main building transporting a downcast herd of shackled cultists. A third swept in from the fields and stormed the cathedral.

I tried to break loose but Blackbeard and Snaggletooth held catatonically firm. Graffius pointed at me and jibbered like a monkey on speed. He ran over and raised his fist. I kicked out with my right foot and caught him hard in the center of his kneecap. He yelped and did a one-legged rain dance. The big men looked at each other idiotically, unsure of how to react. Within seconds the decision had been taken out of their hands.

We were surrounded. The raiders from the viaduct had formed a concentric ring around the circle of cultists. They were a mixed group—D.E.A. agents, state police, county sheriffs, and at least one L.A. detective whom I recognized—but functioned with the smoothness of a seasoned unit.

A Hispanic officer with a Zapata mustache barked the order to lie down. This time compliance was immediate. The big men released my arms as if they were electrified. I stepped away and observed the action.

The raiders made the cultists spread their legs and frisked them, two officers for every captive. Once searched, they were handcuffed, removed from the group one by one like beads pulled off a string, read their rights, and taken into custody at gunpoint.

With the exception of Graffius, who was dragged away kicking and screaming, the men and women of the Touch offered no resistance. Numb with fear and disorientation, they submitted passively to police procedure and shambled off to captivity in a forlorn procession periodically spotlit by the circling helicopters.

The heavy door to the main building swung open and disgorged another parade of captors and captives. The last to exit was Matthias, guarded by a phalanx of agents. He walked woodenly and his mouth worked frantically. From a distance it looked like one hell of a closing statement but the din from the copters blotted out the sound. Not that anyone was listening.

I watched his departure and, when the grounds were still, became once more aware of the heat. I removed my jacket and tossed it to the side, and was unbuttoning my shirt when Milo came over in the company of a hatchet-faced man with a five o'clock shadow. The man wore a gray suit, white shirt, and dark tie under his flak jacket and walked with a military stride. This morning, I'd found him humorless but reassuringly thorough. The boss D.E.A. agent, Severin Fleming.

"Great performance, Alex." My friend patted my back.

"Let me help you with that, Doctor," said Fleming, untaping the Nagra body recorder from my chest. "I hope it wasn't too uncomfortable."

"As a matter of fact it itched like crazy."

"Sorry about that. You must have sensitive skin."

"He's a very sensitive guy, Sev."

Fleming conceded a smile and concentrated on checking the Nagra.

"Everything looks in order," he announced, returning the machine to its case. "Reception in the van was excellent—we got a first-rate copy. An attorney from Justice was sitting in and she's of the opinion there's plenty to work with. Once again, Doctor, thanks. Be seeing you, Milo."

He shook our hands, gave a small salute, and walked away, cradling the Nagra like a newborn.

"Well," said Milo, "You keep revealing new talents. Hollywood's bound to be knocking on your door."

"Right," I said, rubbing my chest. "Call my agent. We'll take a meeting at the Polo Lounge."

He laughed and undid his flak jacket.

"Feel like the Michelin tire man in this thing."

"You should be so cute."

We walked together toward the viaduct. The sky had darkened and quieted. Beyond the gates engines rumbled to a start. We stepped onto the bridge, treading on cool stone. Milo reached up, plucked a grape from the arbor, split it with his teeth, and swallowed.

"You made a big difference, Alex," he said. "Eventually they'd have gotten him on the drug thing. But it's the murder rap that'll put him away. Combine that with lowering the boom on Stinky Pants and I'd say it's been a fine week for the good guys."

"Great," I said wearily.

Several yards later:

"You okay, pal?"

"I'll be all right."

"Thinking about the kid?"

I stopped and looked at him.

"Do you need to head back to L.A. right away?" I asked.

He put a heavy arm around my shoulder, smiled and shook his head.

"Getting back means diving into a mess of paperwork. It can wait."

27

I stood at a distance and looked through the wall of plastic.

The boy lay on the bed, still but awake. His mother sat by his side, rendered nearly anonymous by spacesuit, gloves, and mask. Her dark eyes wandered around the room, settling momentarily on his face, then upon the pages of the story book in her hands. He struggled upright, said something to her and she nodded and held a cup to his lips. Drinking exhausted him quickly; he fell back against the pillow.

"Cute kid," said Milo. "What did that doc say his chances are?"

"He's severely infected. But the I.V. is pumping in high-dose antibiotics and they feel it will eventually clear up. The original tumor has enlarged—it's begun to press against the diaphragm, which isn't good—but there's no evidence of any new lesions. Chemotherapy will start tomorrow. Overall, the prognosis is still good."

He nodded and went into the nurses' office.

The boy was asleep, now. His mother kissed his forehead, drew the blankets around him, and looked at the book again. She flipped a few pages, put it down and began straightening the room. That done, she returned to sitting bedside, folded her hands in her lap, and remained motionless. Waiting.

The two marshals emerged from the nurses' office. The man was thick-waisted and middle-aged, the woman petite and dyed-blond. He looked at his watch and said "It's time" to his partner. She walked over to the module and tapped on the plastic.

Nona looked up.

The woman said, "It's time."

The girl hesitated, bent over the sleeping child and kissed him with sudden intensity. He called out and rolled over. The movement caused the I.V. pole to vibrate, the bottle to sway. She steadied it, stroked his hair.

"Come on, honey," said the female marshal.

The girl stiffened, stumbled out of the module. She took off the mask and gloves and let the sterile suit fall around her ankles, revealing a jumpsuit underneath. On the back was stenciled PROPERTY SAN DIEGO COUNTY JAIL and a serial number. Her copper hair was drawn back in a ponytail. The golden hoops had been removed from her ears. Her face looked thinner and older, the cheekbones more pronounced, the eyes buried deeper. Jailhouse pallor had begun to dull the luster of her skin. She was beautiful, but damaged, like a day-old rose.

They handcuffed her—gently, it seemed—and led her to the door. She passed by me and our eyes locked. The ebony irises seemed to moisten and melt. Then she hardened them, held her head high, and was gone.

28

I found Raoul in his lab, staring at a computer screen on which were displayed columns of polynomials atop a multicolored bar graph. He'd mutter in Spanish, examine a page of printout, then turn to the keyboard and rapidly type a new set of numbers. With each additional bit of datum the height of the bars in the graph changed. The lab was airless and filled with acrid fumes. High-tech doodads clicked and buzzed in the background.

I pulled up a stool next to him, sat and said hello.

He acknowledged me with a downward twist of his mustache and continued to work with the computer. The bruises on his face had turned to purplish-green smudges.

"You know," he said.

"Yes. She told me."

He typed, hitting the keyboard hard. The graph convulsed.

"My ethics were no better than Valcroix's. She came wiggling in here in a skintight dress and proved that."

I'd come to the lab with the intention of comforting him. There were things I could have said. That

Nona had been turned into a weapon, an instrument of vengeance, abused and twisted until sex and rage were inexorably intertwined, then launched and aimed at a world of weak men like some kind of heat-seeking missile. That he'd made an error in judgment but it didn't negate all the good he'd done. That there was more good work to be done. That time would heal.

But the words would have rung hollow. He was a proud man who'd shed his pride before my eyes. I'd witnessed him ragged and half-crazed in a stinking cell, obsessively intent on finding his patient. His quest had been ignited by guilt, by the mistaken belief that his sin—ten lust-blinded minutes of Nona kneeling before him, ravenous—had caused the removal of the boy from treatment.

Coming to see him had been a mistake. Whatever friendship we'd had was gone, and with it, any power I might have had to reassure.

If salvation existed, he'd have to find it for himself.

I placed my hand on his shoulder and wished him well. He shrugged and stared at the screen.

I left him with his nose buried in a pile of data, cursing out loud at some arcane numerical discrepancy.

I drove east on Sunset slowly, and thought about families. Milo had once told me that family disputes were a cop's most dreaded calls, for they were the most likely to erupt in violence that was murderously sudden, stunningly intense. A good chunk of my life had been spent sorting out the scrambled communications, festering hostilities, and frozen affections that characterized families in turmoil.

It was easy to believe that nothing worked. That blood ties strangled the soul.

But I knew that a cop's reality was skewed by the daily struggle against evil, that of the psychotherapist distorted by too many encounters with madness.

There were families that worked, that nurtured and loved. Places in the heart where a soul could find refuge.

Soon a beautiful woman would meet me on a tropical island. We'd talk about it.

RAGE

AN ALEX DELAWARE NOVEL
BY JONATHAN KELLERMAN

AVAILABLE IN BOOKSTORES EVERYWHERE MAY 24, 2005

Troy Turner and Rand Duchay were barely teenagers when they kidnapped and murdered a younger child. Troy, a remorseless sociopath, died violently behind bars, while the hulking, slow-witted Rand managed to survive his stretch. Now, at age twenty-one, Rand Duchay has emerged a haunted, rootless young man with a pressing need: to talk—once again—with psychologist Alex Delaware. But the young killer comes to a mysteriously brutal end before that conversation ever takes place.

Now that suspicion has been raised about the old case, Alex Delaware and Detective Milo Sturgis must retrace their steps through a grisly murder that devastated a community and left a chilling legacy of madness, suicide, and even uglier truths waiting to be unearthed.

Rage finds Jonathan Kellerman in phenomenal form—orchestrating a relentlessly suspenseful, devilishly unpredictable plot to a finale as stunning and thought-provoking as it is satisfying.

 A Ballantine Books Hardcover · www.ballantinebooks.com